CRUISING THE DANUBE

JENNIFER SKULLY

Redwood
Valley
Publishing

GET A FREE STORY!

CRUISING THE DANUBE
A ONCE AGAIN NOVEL

Book 9

The romantic Danube, the cruise of a lifetime, and two sisters who aren't looking for love...

But love just might be looking for them. Especially when they each meet irresistible silver foxes.

Cathe Girard is still struggling to come to terms with the loss of her husband, but all her beliefs are challenged when she meets the charming and magnetic Jack Kelly. Despite her attraction to him, Cathe is convinced her heart will always belong to her late husband. And she can never love again.

Still reeling from a bitter divorce, Celia Winters is on the lookout for a good time, determined to prove to herself that she still has what it takes to attract a man. When she meets the sophisticated and intriguing Gray Ellison, she finds herself irresistibly drawn to him. But even as they embark on a delicious fling, she remains convinced she can never trust another man with her heart after her ex-husband's betrayal.

Amid the picturesque backdrop of the Danube from breathtaking historic Budapest to stunningly beautiful Vienna, the two sisters find themselves torn between their fears and the undeniable pull of love.

Can they let go of the past and open their hearts to a second chance at love?

Let yourself be swept away on a journey of love, healing, and self-discovery in this later in life, second chance, holiday romance.

ACKNOWLEDGMENTS

A special thanks to Bella Andre for this fabulous idea and to both Bella and Nancy Warren for all the brainstorming on our 10-mile walks. Thank you also to my special network of friends who support and encourage me: Laurel Jacobson, Kathy Coatney, Shelley Adina, Jenny Andersen, Jackie Yau, and Linda McGinnis. As always, a huge hug of appreciation for my husband who helps my writing career flourish. And to Wriggles, that crazy little cat who never fails to make me laugh, especially when she's chasing her tail! She never quite seems to catch it. Go figure!

To our fabulous cruise mates, Cathe and Jack, and Kathy and Greg. Thanks for the inspiration!

"Oh my God," Celia said with an awe Cathe hadn't heard in months. Not since Celia's divorce a year ago. And probably not for a couple of years before that.

It was hard to drum up enthusiasm after the long flight. "What?" Cathe grumbled. They'd upgraded seats for extra legroom and better food, but it wasn't first class, and she hadn't slept. Since the plane had left San Francisco late in the day and they didn't arrive in Budapest until late afternoon, she'd been up twenty-four hours.

"You have to see this view." Celia waved her hand.

Cathe pushed herself off the bed, joined her sister at the window, and gasped at the breathtaking view that lay before them. All right, it was worth getting up.

Their corner room offered a magnificent view of the Hungarian Parliament Building across the Danube, its domes a deep burgundy against the evening sky. Matthias Church, gleaming in the setting September sun, was right next door to the hotel.

"Quick." Cathe grabbed her phone. "We need pictures."

Camera phones in hand, they snapped their first photos of Budapest, from the Parliament Building across the river, to Fisherman's Bastion with its Romanesque lookout towers below their window, to the spire of Matthias Church and its unique mosaic roof tiles in mostly geometric patterns.

Celia grabbed her, hugged her. "I can't believe we're in Budapest and ready for our river cruise."

They'd been planning the trip for months. "I thought it would never happen."

Their hotel was on Buda Hill. Everyone called the Hungarian capital Budapest, but it was actually two cities, the Pest side and the Buda side, famous for its medieval castle. To the east on the Pest side stood the iconic Parliament Building she'd seen in so many photos, along with St. Stephen's Cathedral.

"Too bad about the Chain Bridge." Celia groaned. "We can't even see the lions it's so famous for."

Below them, the oldest bridge—and the most well-known —connecting the east and west sides lay covered in scaffolding, closed for renovations. They'd wanted to walk across it, probably with a million other tourists. Instead, they'd have to cross the Danube over either the Elizabeth Bridge to the south or the Margaret Bridge to the north.

Entranced by the views, Cathe sighed out her pleasure. "It's so amazing to see it for real. I never thought we'd make it."

The last couple of years have been tough for them both.

Her husband Denny had died of a heart attack two years ago. Two whole years. It didn't seem possible.

But she couldn't think about that now. They were here to enjoy themselves, and she wouldn't go down the rabbit hole of grief. Not here, not now.

"I'll be right back." Celia headed to the bathroom, leaving Cathe with the view.

Celia, being the amazing sister she was, had planned this sisters-only cruise, sailing the Danube from Budapest to Vienna to Germany, and a lot of small towns in between. She'd insisted Cathe needed to get away. They would have gone last September, a year ago, if Celia's marriage hadn't imploded.

Celia and her husband Bart had problems long before Denny died. They didn't fight, but there was a lot of passive-aggressiveness between them. The issue came down to the biggie: sex. Bart didn't want it anymore, Celia did. It was supposed to be the other way round, right? The woman hits menopause and loses her interest. But not for Celia. And quite frankly, it hadn't been that way for Cathe either.

In her opinion, Bart and Celia should have divorced years ago, but they'd stayed together for the kids. Now all three of her nephews were well-adjusted adults. And hopefully they'd learned a thing or two about marriage and what they didn't want. Cathe could only hope.

The marriage had ended when Celia discovered Bart was having an affair with his former girlfriend from college. They'd reconnected and had been carrying on hot and heavy for six months. While he was claiming he wasn't interested in sex anymore, he'd been diddling his first love, his *only* love, Celia had decided.

She'd been livid, devastated, broken. And humiliated. When Celia got angry, she went for the jugular, and she'd taken Bart for everything he was worth, which was a lot since he was a partner in a firm of over one hundred lawyers.

They'd postponed the trip while Celia took Bart to the cleaners.

But they were here to forget. Not that Cathe would ever forget Denny. He was the love of her life. She almost lost herself when she lost him.

But he wouldn't have wanted her to shut herself away in

their house for the rest of her life. And she was doing her best by coming on this cruise with her sister.

Putting her phone down, Cathe stood at the window really *seeing* the amazing view in front of her eyes. The Fisherman's Bastion—built as a fortification that was never actually used—lay below, with its splendid statues and steps leading up to a promenade that ran atop its colonnade.

She made out the form of a man seated on a step beside the fountain, another man leaning on a walker two stairs above him. Though she could see nothing of the seated man's face, she imagined the two were close, maybe father and son.

The sight reminded her of Denny. He'd taken such good care of his father, who'd eventually succumbed to Alzheimer's. He'd been a good son, a good father, a good husband.

She blinked away tears as Celia strolled out of the bathroom after fixing her makeup. "Let's get something to eat. I need—" Celia groaned, fisting her hand in her blouse. "—a champagne cocktail. Now."

"How can you be hungry after everything we ate on the plane?" Cathe still faced the window and the tableau below.

Celia huffed out a breath. "We had half a sandwich and a cup of coffee on the last leg. There was all the time we waited in London for the next flight too. And now I'm starving."

As if reminded, Cathe's stomach rumbled. "All right. Let's see what we can find." Though she was tired, it was too early for bed yet.

Downstairs, Celia pointed to the bar. "I feel like bar food." The lobby was relatively empty, only a couple of people milling around the reception desk, and they headed into the lounge. It, too, was empty.

Cathe glanced at her watch. "Seven o'clock," she said. "Maybe we're too early for cocktails. Don't they do everything later in Europe?"

The bartender directed them to a corner by the window with a view of the old stone walls that flowed into concrete. "You think they built this hotel on top of some ancient structure?" She propped her hand on her chin. "Or maybe they just made it all look old."

The hotel was in a U shape, with this courtyard overlooking the river. Gazing out the window, she saw a slice of the Parliament Building and a statue on Fisherman's Bastion.

The menu was both in Hungarian and English, but the prices were Hungarian forints.

"I'm having soup," Celia declared.

"I thought you were starving."

"Soup and a champagne cocktail will fill me up."

Cathe studied the menu for a moment. "I want goulash. If I'm in Hungary, I want to eat Hungarian."

A champagne cocktail was on the menu too. "Thank God." Celia breathed a sigh of relief.

But the Hungarian forints were almost four times as much for a champagne cocktail as for the goulash. Pulling out her phone, Cathe looked up the exchange rate and did the calculation. "Oh my God," she gasped. "A champagne cocktail is sixteen dollars." Mouth agape, she looked at Celia.

Her sister narrowed her eyes. "Please don't nitpick every dollar we spend here. We're on vacation. And I'm ordering a champagne cocktail."

Cathe had always been conscious of the cost. Their father had been a penny pincher, and she took after him, while Celia had gone the opposite way. Of course, Celia had that very generous divorce settlement.

"I'll have a champagne cocktail too. But I still want to know how much I'm paying for it." She pointed at the menu. "Especially when the goulash is only six dollars." She raised a brow.

"These are hotel prices. It'll be a lot cheaper in town."

Celia signaled the waiter, and they ordered goulash, chicken noodle soup, and champagne cocktails.

Then they relaxed back into their seats, and Cathe felt exhaustion taking over again.

"It's pronounced *gouyash*," Celia said phonetically, swapping out the *L* for a *Y*. "Our driver would be horrified at your pronunciation."

Their airport shuttle driver had indeed been horrified when she told him she wanted to sample real Hungarian goulash. "This is how we say it," he'd said in his heavily accented English. "*Gouyash*."

Cathe laughed at the reminder. "And we can't forget that all Hungarian drivers are idiotas," she quoted their middle-aged driver.

Celia chuckled. "I have to use that at home every time another driver pisses me off on the freeway. I'll shake my fist and yell, 'You idiota!'"

They gossiped about the man who'd entertained them with his antics on the ride from the airport. "I never knew Kentucky Fried Chicken and McDonald's were conceived in Hungary."

When they'd both remarked on the American icons, the driver had looked at them in the rearview mirror, and, with a straight face, told them, "You know they were both started here in Hungary."

The sisters had looked at each other and giggled as he took a wide turn onto a broad street, shouting at the other idiota drivers who got in his way.

"He was highly amusing." Cathe snorted a laugh just as the waiter brought their champagne cocktails.

Out of one split, he poured the champagne into two glasses with bitters-soaked sugar cubes already at the bottom.

"What a rip-off," Celia said with disgust once he was

gone. "Two champagne cocktails but we only get one bottle?" Although the bottle had filled both glasses.

"Why don't you say something?"

While Cathe would merely grumble, Celia was the one who would call anyone out if she was upset.

But Celia drawled, "I'm not ruining my vacation by engaging in warfare the very first night."

After their chicken noodle soup and goulash arrived, Cathe stared at her bowl. "I thought goulash—"

"*Gouyash*," her sister corrected.

"I thought *gouyash* was a stew." Spoon in the bowl, she stirred the broth filled with vegetables. "This is like soup."

"Probably because it's hotel *gouyash*."

Cathe tasted the first spoonful, then fanned herself. "Oh my God, that's spicy. It's good, but I wasn't expecting so much spice." But with each spoonful, she grew more used to the fiery taste. "And the bread is absolutely delicious." She bit into a slice of the soft, flavorful bread.

Just as they'd finished their soup, the bartender brought the bill. Before they charged to their room, Cathe had to look. Smiling, she pointed. "He only charged us for one champagne."

Celia threw up her hands in triumph. "I didn't even have to go into battle mode."

"I'm not super tired yet." The goulash had given Cathe a second wind. "Let's try to stay up until nine thirty, and hopefully we'll be on Hungarian time by tomorrow. Why don't we walk around the Fisherman's Bastion and the church?"

"Just don't drag me on a two-hour tour."

Cathe smiled. "I promise, not more than an hour."

Outside, even though the sun had set, they were bathed in warm evening air. Early September in Hungary seemed much the same as the San Francisco Bay Area. Cathe didn't even need the jacket she'd put on.

She snapped pictures of the church spire silhouetted against the night and photographed the wide esplanade that led down to the Fisherman's Bastion. Few people were about, and she got a good picture of King Saint Stephen's statue, the martyr seated on his noble steed.

Celia wasn't into the picture-taking as much as Cathe, who took photos everywhere, even on a trail she'd hiked a hundred times. There was always something new to see. They had a full day in Budapest before they boarded the cruise ship the following day. They hadn't booked any tours for tomorrow, so they were free to roam at will. Cathe planned on taking lots of pictures.

Atop the colonnade, a semicircular promenade bordered the bastion, but the turnstiles to get up there were closed. Instead, they walked along the lower level filled with narrow cafés overlooking the river.

Celia pointed at a menu outside one of the closed bistros. "See, I told you the champagne was expensive at the hotel." The small café also offered open-face sandwiches, bowls of goulash, and carrot soup. The champagne was a quarter of the price.

From the bastion, wide stone steps flanked by marble frescoes led down to the waterfront. They stood beneath the stone colonnade, once again entranced by the vista over the river, the iconic Parliament Building lit up like a Christmas tree, its lights reflected in the gently lapping waters of the Danube.

While Cathe snapped picture after picture, one was enough for Celia. "You don't need more than one."

"I just pick out the best and delete the rest," Cathe explained. "Let's get a selfie."

"We suck at selfies." They'd done a Vegas spa week last February, and every selfie they'd taken had been horrible. Their necks were too wrinkled or the lines on their faces were too prominent or the angle of their heads gave them double chins.

"Come on," Cathe begged. "I've been practicing at home."

As she positioned them, a deep voice resonated in the quiet night. "Would you like me to take the picture?"

With salt-and-pepper hair, the man was absolutely gorgeous. Muscles filled out his trim body, his biceps bulging beneath his O'Neill T-shirt. O'Neill was a Santa Cruz company, only an hour over the mountains from her home in Belmont. Of course, he could have purchased the shirt online, and though his accent was American, that didn't mean he lived near them.

She handed over her phone happily. "Thank you so much."

Celia's slack jaw showed how dazzled she was by the man's extraordinary good looks.

"Move a bit that way." He waved his fingers. "Now I've got the whole Parliament Building in there."

"We can take pictures of you," Cathe offered.

"Thanks," he said, "but I don't have anyone to show them to."

His ring finger was bare, and he probably didn't have kids if there was no one to see his vacation photos.

He began walking away in the wake of Cathe's thank-you when Celia came out of her daze, shifting as if she might sprint after him.

"That man is perfect." Celia fully intended to have a fling on this trip, making her intentions clear long before they'd made their final booking.

"Don't tell me you want to start tonight," Cathe whispered. "We aren't even over jet lag."

As he disappeared around the corner of the church, Cathe pulled Celia in the other direction, heading for the fountain she'd seen from their room.

"Did you not see that man?" Celia darn near dug in her heels.

"You mean that he was drop dead gorgeous? Yeah, I noticed." She grinned. "Let's not fight over him." And she flapped her fingers in the direction he'd taken. "Why don't you run after him?"

Celia snorted. "It's pathetic to run after a man. Besides, a shipboard romance is so much better. I'll have seven days to work on whoever I chose."

"I knew you'd have it all figured out." Cathe headed toward the fountain on the other end of the Fisherman's Bastion, the steps leading down to a row of shops. Stopping, she laughed and shook her head. "They actually have a Starbucks." Taking a picture, she added, "I have to show this to my barista back home." A white chocolate mocha was one of her few luxuries.

She turned to the fountain, stopping a long moment just to look.

"What?" Celia asked.

"Nothing. I took some pictures from our room." She pointed above. "I wondered if I'd see the same thing down here."

"What did you expect to see?"

Cathe shook her head. "Nothing." The man was gone. Maybe he'd been a figment of her imagination, a reminder of Denny. "Nothing at all."

Cathe managed to stay up until ten o'clock, hoping that would put her on Budapest time. But she woke up at four in the morning.

Celia, still asleep, snored so softly that if it hadn't been quiet, Cathe would never have heard her. She turned on her bedside lamp, hoping the light wouldn't wake Celia through her sleep mask.

She texted her daughter, saying they'd arrived safely. It was early evening back home, and knowing Sarah, she was probably still hard at work. At twenty-seven, her daughter was on an upward trajectory and moving fast.

Then she opened the journal she'd left by the bedside. Denny had loved making a trip diary of all their vacations, whether it was Disney World with Sarah or the Rome holiday for their twentieth wedding anniversary. Except for the Vegas spa weekend Celia had begged her to go on, she hadn't left home in the two years since he died. When she'd agreed to this trip, she'd promised herself she'd keep a journal the way he had. And now, in the quiet night, she wrote down all the details, including the man by the fountain, and how, together with the elderly gentleman on the walker, he'd reminded her of Denny with his father.

And finally, she slept for another two hours.

Celia was already in the shower, and after her shower fifteen minutes later, Cathe felt refreshed. Maybe staying up until ten had beaten back jet lag.

The tour package included breakfast, and they entered the dining room only ten minutes after it opened. Celia ordered poached eggs, but Cathe chose euro-style from the buffet, meats, cheeses, and fresh crusty bread, eating the sandwich open-face like the Europeans.

As they drank their coffee, the man she'd seen by the fountain entered with his father—at least she assumed they were father and son—and the hostess seated them on the far side of the dining room where the tables were well spaced and the elderly man slid his walker right up to the table.

"What do you want to see today?" Celia failed to notice that Cathe's gaze had wandered.

She dragged her attention back to her sister. "Buda Castle. Then we should walk up to that statue we saw on the hill." Visible as they drove across the Elizabeth Bridge to Buda Hill, it had reminded her of the Winged Victory in the Louvre.

"I wonder what it's all about." Celia pulled out her phone to search.

And Cathe switched back to the man. He retrieved their food, scrambled eggs, potatoes, baked beans, and toast, and returning to the table, he set one plate in front of the old man.

He reminded her of Denny, not only his attentiveness, but his looks. Tall and fit, with dark hair like Denny's, silver threaded through it, which, most likely, put him somewhere in his fifties.

Celia interrupted her thoughts. "The Liberty Statue is on Gellért Hill. Originally built by the Soviets, after the Wall came down, the Hungarians changed the inscription and made it their own. There's a path from that waterfall we saw above the Elizabeth Bridge."

With Celia returning to her browsing, Cathe took another chance to watch the Denny look-alike. Was he as handsome as Denny? Yes, he was. And he smiled a lot, the way Denny had. He seemed... kind.

Celia then began synopsizing what she'd found. "It looks like most of Buda Castle is a museum and an art gallery." She wrinkled her nose. "I don't like wandering around galleries when we can be outside."

"I'm more interested in the architecture," Cathe said. "We'll stroll through the complex and take pictures."

"Deal." Celia set down her phone to sip her coffee. Then her gaze shifted, held.

And Cathe asked, "What?"

"It's that guy from last night, the one who took our picture," Celia said in a hushed voice, as if the man was right behind them.

"Is his wife with him?" Though he wore no ring, that didn't mean he wasn't married.

Celia shook her head, just a barely there movement. "He's alone."

"Does he look like he's saving a place for anyone?"

Again, Celia shook her head. "It doesn't matter. There's no way I feel like working my magic for just one night."

Celia didn't actually believe she had any magic. Bart, her horrible ex, had leached that out of her simply by ignoring her. He hadn't touched Celia in the final five years of their marriage.

At first Celia had only talked about the problem with him, then she'd tried seducing him, moved on to begging, then threatening, and finally, screaming at him. Nothing had worked. Finally, she'd hired a private detective and learned Bart had been having an affair for the past six months. But what about the years before that when he'd refused to touch Celia? She'd thought it would help if she could feel it was all about another woman, but Cathe knew it hadn't. Bart's lack of desire for her had left Celia sexually empty. He'd left her believing she was unwanted, undesirable, and, worst of all, unworthy.

Cathe hated Bart for that. He could have explained it was a lack of libido. He could have taken drugs. But he'd turned his back on her, slept with another woman, and Cathe couldn't forgive him for that.

Since the divorce, Celia had gone through several men, trying to prove she was both worthy and desirable. Even now Celia didn't believe in herself, though she'd never admitted that aloud. But Cathe knew.

After breakfast, they set out on foot to explore Buda Hill. Nothing was very far away. The hill itself could only be accessed through a toll gate, keeping the number of tour buses to a minimum on the narrow streets. A building across the street from the hotel was covered in scaffolding, as were several of the old structures they passed on the way to the castle. Reading signs posted on fences around the construction areas, they quickly learned that Buda Hill was undergoing a historic renovation after the damage done by extensive bombing in World War II and neglect during the Soviet reign. Cranes filled the skyline, moving concrete blocks while workmen wearing hardhats climbed over newly erected girders.

"The nerve," Celia grumbled. "Having all this construction during our vacation. We don't get to see anything."

The day was already warm as they made their way to a

lower pathway around Buda Castle, following the old stone walls and coming upon a set of wooden stairs that led up to the castle walkway.

Looking at Celia, Cathe crossed her eyes when she couldn't get a decent picture of the nymphs cavorting around a beautiful fountain. A workman was cleaning it, the water drained and calcified coins embedded in the bottom.

She opted instead for a monument of a horse guard surveying the Danube. Standing by the statue, she got some amazing pictures of the Parliament Building on the other bank with the Chain Bridge covered in scaffolding in the foreground. Closer still was the Four Seasons Hotel, looking as if it had been there for centuries, the dome of St. Stephen's Cathedral beyond it.

A wide marble staircase led up to another courtyard with a majestic eagle, a sword clutched in its talons. She zoomed in, capturing a man leaning on a wooden balustrade beneath the statue.

"Don't look now," she advised. "But I think your hot guy is up by the eagle." As Celia shaded her eyes, Cathe nudged her. "You don't need to be so obvious."

But Celia smiled, waved. And the gorgeous man waved back.

"He's alone again," Cathe mused. "I don't think he's traveling with anyone."

"Or the wife and kids were too tired to get out of bed." Celia turned and headed down the castle promenade. "Anyway, we're getting on the ship tomorrow. I'll never see him again."

How would she feel if her sister found a man? And ditched her? Before, it had been theoretical. But they'd board tomorrow, and then anything could happen. Would it make her miss Denny even more?

She couldn't let it matter. This voyage was supposed to be a coming out for her sister. It was supposed to be Cathe's coming out, too, according to Celia.

But there was still too much of Denny in her heart. There always would be.

The castle's exterior was stunning. She'd read it wasn't the original; much of that had been destroyed back in the sixteenth century. Royal palaces had been built over the ruins but were heavily damaged in the Second World War. When renovation began, parts of the medieval castle were unearthed and restored.

At the end, they strolled out a causeway which might have once been a guard lookout over the Danube. From there they could see the Liberty Statue on Gellért Hill.

"It's not that far." Cathe craned over the parapet, excited by everything she saw. "Let's head over."

She'd noted a flight of stairs that would take them to river level, and from there, they could make it to the bridge. But on the way down, they found an ornate tower with an intricate glass dome above and a staircase spiraling down.

Peering over the railing, she said, "Let's see where this goes."

Celia didn't even groan and down they went. The stairs were wide, with little depth. Cathe stopped to take a picture up into the colored glass dome with griffins painted around its base. At the bottom, she pushed through the door that took them out onto the long riverside promenade fronting shops and restaurants.

Cathe spied a paper store filled floor-to-ceiling with notebooks. Tables in the center crowded were with all manner of journals, leather-bound, cloth-bound, event books, and daily calendars.

"We have to stop on the way back. I want to get a journal

for Sarah. She'd love something from Budapest." The sign said the store was open until six.

Celia smiled her agreement.

Cathe's daughter had inherited Denny's journaling bug. It wasn't so much a diary of her thoughts and feelings as a daily account of her classes, lessons, and homework when she was in university. And later, the notebooks were all about her work, with her schedule, the people she met, impressions of contacts she made. Sarah was in marketing, and one day, she'd be vice president of sales. She could be CEO, but she said that would take her too far away from the marketing she loved.

The walk to the bridge was a lot longer than it had looked from atop Buda Hill, but finally they made it to the Elizabeth Bridge and the waterfall above it. After a couple of selfies to prove they'd done at least that much, they started up the switchback. Cathe took pictures at vista points over the Danube. But it was getting hotter and the stairs steeper, trees and shrubs on one side of the path and stone cliffs on the other.

Then Celia, ahead of her, called out, "Oh my God, here it is."

But a fence blocked their way, and the most they could do was peer through the chain-link at the cracked, weed-choked courtyard. Yet the gold Liberty Statue glinted in the light, still magnificent, still the embodiment of Hungarian freedom. Even if the Soviets originally built it.

Celia sighed. "Why did they have to be renovating everything while we're here?"

"I can still get a good picture." Cathe focused her camera phone between the fence links, and captured an amazing image—if she did say so herself—of the statue against a foreground of weed-infested concrete, as if it had been there for centuries.

Denny would have loved the adventure, never knowing what they'd find, surprised around every corner.

God, how she missed him.

﷽ 3 ﷽

"**I**'m dying for a coffee and a muffin or something, anything." Celia wheezed after the long climb back down the hill.

"Sounds fabulous," Cathe agreed. "But I want to get a journal for Sarah at that paper store we saw. Is that okay?"

Celia clucked her tongue. "Yes, but you don't get more than fifteen minutes."

Cathe had been known to spend hours in stationery stores. But this one was just journals. She could manage only fifteen minutes.

After zigzagging back through the streets to the river walk, she found the store again and breathed in the scent of paper and leather and ink the moment she entered.

Denny had loved wandering through stacks of journals. He could spend hours in bookstores too. And now, she felt immersed in a world she'd shared with him. There were leather-bound journals, paperback ones, ones with a velvety feel, colorful ones, lined ones, blank ones. Journals filled the floor-to-ceiling shelves, daily diaries, planners, calendars, even ones tracking nautical signs or celestial bodies or the tides.

Denny would have adored this place, and Celia's fifteen minutes could easily stretch into half an hour as Cathe pawed through the shelves and the crammed tables. Then she found it, leather-bound, lined pages, a drawing of the Queen Mary on the front, and when she turned it over, the ship was steaming away.

Denny would love it.

The pressure of tears prickled in her eyes. Denny would never love anything again.

She wanted to break down and weep right there. But she couldn't. After the first few months of grief, Celia began trying to snap her out of it. After a while, Cathe stopped crying in front of her. She tried to be cheerful. Or at least not to look maudlin. She grieved in private, crying at the oddest times, like watching the final season of *The Walking Dead* and knowing Denny would never get to see how it all turned out.

He'd wanted to take a cruise on the Queen Mary from New York to Southampton, enthusing over the planetarium on the ship and all the fascinating guest speakers and the high tea they served every afternoon. He was even excited about bingo because he'd always played with his father at the memory care home, completing both cards when his dad was no longer capable of doing his own.

She would not cry. Not in front of Celia. And certainly not in front of the saleslady.

Celia's rational voice saved her from meltdown. "Here's a real cute one with lots of cats on it." Celia held it up. As hard as she worked, Sarah still lived with a cat, and she was always sending funny cat memes.

It was only when Cathe compared the journal to the one in her hand that she realized she'd been shopping not for her daughter but for her dead husband, running her fingers over journals he would have liked, forgetting completely about Sarah.

She took the cat journal. "You're right. This one's perfect."

"Then we're ready for coffee and a muffin now?" Celia smiled hopefully.

"Absolutely." And Cathe turned to pay for the journals, hoping her sister didn't notice she'd bought the Queen Mary notebook as well. She would use it herself.

Once outside, they made their way back up to the hilltop and along to the main shopping area with several cafés where they chose the first shop that lured them inside with the scent of coffee. Miraculously the café had decaf for Cathe while Celia ordered regular. "I need a good shot of caffeine to wake me up."

"Let's share one of those big strudels. Do you want to try poppyseed?"

Celia made a face. "That sounds gross."

But they bought a poppyseed-and-apple strudel and found a table in the shade out on the patio where they could people-watch. The strudel tasted amazing, tart poppyseeds combined with sweet apples. And the coffee was a delicious brew despite being decaf.

They measured each other's steps recorded on their phones, Cathe having an incredible twenty-five thousand and Celia two thousand less. "How the hell does that happen?" she scoffed. "We walked exactly the same route."

Cathe had to smile. "It was always like that with Denny too. He had bigger strides, so I set mine up to be smaller."

She felt the pain, ignored it, and concentrated instead on Celia's aghast expression. "So you cheat."

Cathe laughed.

They chattered about the tour the next morning before they boarded the ship and about what they wanted for dinner. Then jet lag suddenly caught up with Cathe, her eyes drooping as Celia's voice faded in and out. Maybe she should have had the regular coffee.

Before her head actually dropped on her arm, she muttered, "Not that you're boring, but I can't focus on a single word you're saying."

Celia snorted. "You mean I'm so boring I'm putting you to sleep."

She smiled away her sister's indignation. "I need a nap," and Celia leaned in to whisper, "Me too."

As they walked through to the café's front door, she saw him. And she was suddenly as wide awake as she'd been at four o'clock in the morning.

He carried the tray of coffee and cake while the old man wheeled his walker. Definitely father and son, they had the same jawline, the same nose, the same blue eyes, though the elderly gentleman's had faded with age.

And the son was beautiful. She didn't want to think he was beautiful to her only in his resemblance to Denny, for his height or his eyes or his dark hair shot through with silver, or for the laugh lines at the corners of his eyes and mouth that were so like Denny's. He smiled at her as he passed, the tray balanced on one hand, his other on his father's back guiding him, caring for him. Just like Denny and his dad.

She wondered if he smiled because he'd seen her at the hotel that morning.

Yet her heart wanted to say he'd smiled because he'd seen a pretty woman at a café.

She chanced a quick look at Celia, but her sister had missed the exchange, thank God. Listening to Celia's spiel about how she needed to get out, meeting men or at least meet other people would have ruined the moment. She wasn't ready. She'd never be ready. She missed Denny more than her last breath.

Of course, she wasn't looking at that beautiful man

because she wanted him. It was just that she'd been thinking so much about Denny, especially in the shop surrounded by all those journals. She'd looked only because he reminded her of Denny.

Back in their hotel room, the bed felt luxurious. Her last thought before she fell asleep was that she should have taken that Queen Mary cruise with her husband.

"GOSH, I FEEL GOOD," CELIA SAID AS THEY STEPPED outside the hotel. They'd slept a solid two hours, and she felt completely rested. "It's not even five o'clock yet, so let's see what's down that way." She pointed in the opposite direction of the castle. "Then work our way back to the restaurants." They'd noticed several lovely sidewalk restaurants with traditional Hungarian menus. "And I'll be ready for my champagne."

Cathe grinned at her. "It's five o'clock somewhere in the world."

The cobblestone streets were narrow with a few cars parked along them, but mostly they were empty of traffic. They headed down past yet another church, its spire like something out of a Russian fairytale. Cathe filled her phone with photos of everything, and Celia admitted she'd end up begging for Cathe's photo album. Why not, since her sister loved photography?

They reached the gates to Buda Hill, the long arm of the barrier rising and falling for the few cars that entered. Cathe made her stand in front of the National Archives with colorful mosaic roof tiles similar to Matthias Church.

They passed old two-story houses with connecting walls which were probably apartments now, and headed to a bell tower that rose above the buildings. The church that had

23

once been central to the small square was long gone, only its bell tower still standing amid the old foundations.

Cathe brimmed with excitement. "Let's climb the bell tower. It'll have some amazing views."

They paid in euros and pushed through the turnstile to the narrow spiral staircase. Each step was tall, and without a railing, Celia kept her hand on the wall to pull herself up. It had been much warmer outside, but inside the stone walls were cold beneath her fingers. On the second and third levels, interpretive signs explained the history of the Church of Mary Magdalene. It had been bombed during the Second World War, then demolished after a failed restoration, leaving only the bell tower intact.

On the top floor, the windows had been opened over wrought iron railings, and just as Cathe had predicted, the views were spectacular, from the mosaic rooftop of the National Archives to the city gate, and across the Danube to the Pest side. In the far distance, a helium balloon with a basket floated in the sky.

They moved from window to window. "No wonder we can't see any of the buildings," Celia said as she counted. "There are no less than eight cranes out there." They filled the skyline and beyond them was Gellért Hill and the Liberty Statue.

The boys would love Budapest. Not that she could have gotten any of her sons to come on an "old folks" cruise. Besides, this was a sisters' trip. She'd pushed for it originally to help Cathe. It broke her heart to watch her sister fading away with grief and loss. She'd tried to bring Cathe out of her melancholy by suggesting she start dating. But it had been far too early. But Celia had to do something. Finally, Cathe had agreed to the cruise. And when they'd had to postpone because of the divorce, Celia felt even worse, as if she was letting her sister down.

But she wouldn't let her down now. They were going to have fun. After all the years of having her sexuality ignored, she would break loose of those bonds. And she wanted to help Cathe do the same. Of course, it was completely different for Cathe. Losing Denny had broken her spirit. But for Celia, divorce was like snapping the chains that bound her. She tested out a few men along the way, but preferred brief trysts, wanting only to explore her sexuality. She wanted the freedom to do whatever she wanted whenever she wanted without worrying that in a few weeks or months whoever she was with would tire of her.

She wished Cathe could see sex the same way. It didn't have to be about love. Sex could be good just for itself. Maybe she'd learned that only because Bart had ignored her for so long. It had almost destroyed her. The worst wasn't even that he'd cheated on her. It was all the years before, when he hadn't wanted her, when he'd made her feel worthless. The affair was final proof that she wasn't good enough. So she'd divorced him and picked herself up again, moved on. She'd shown Bart. She'd proven she was desirable over and over again.

Now she was enjoying some of the best sex of her life, and along the way, she'd learned exactly what worked for her. And if the particular man she was with didn't like it, she was out of there. *My way or the highway.*

But for Cathe, sex was tangled up with love. It was *making love.*

She looked at her sister now. Cathe still took care of herself. Like Celia, she dyed most of the gray out of her blond hair, leaving behind only lovely wisps of silver. She was an attractive woman, wearing just enough makeup to accentuate her features, a little blue eye shadow to match her blue eyes as well as lip liner and a pretty plum lipstick.

Yet with Denny's loss, she'd lost her vibrancy.

Celia swore she would help her get it back on this trip.

Putting her arm around her sister's shoulder, she pulled her toward the spiral stairs. "Let's go find our champagne."

They chose a restaurant on a street corner with a view of the Matthias Church spire and ordered champagne before the hostess even handed them menus. The first sip was perfect.

Still wanting to try everything Hungarian, Cathe decided on the chicken paprikash, while Celia ordered salmon in pesto lime sauce. And Celia dove into the conversation that had to happen during this trip. "My darling sister, you know how much I love you."

Cathe groaned. "Please, don't start."

"I'll just say my piece and then I won't talk about it anymore."

Cathe huffed out an annoyed breath. "That's what you say every time."

All right, so this wasn't the first time they'd had this conversation. But they were finally on their trip, and it needed to be said again. "Let me rephrase. I won't mention it anymore while we're on the boat."

Tipping her head back, Cathe pinched the bridge of her nose. "All right. Say it. Then promise you won't bring it up again, not just during this trip, but ever."

She couldn't make a promise she knew she'd break. "I promise I won't bring it up again," she agreed, then quickly added, "on this trip."

"And don't expect me to do anything about what you say either."

"Where you're concerned, I have no expectations," she said dryly.

The food arrived, and Cathe groaned with relief. "Saved by the bell."

Celia stretched a smile. "I can talk and eat at the same time."

Cathe dug into her paprikash, the sauce red and redolent with Hungary's sweet paprika.

Leaning close, Celia grimaced. "What's the white stuff with it?"

Cathe swirled her fork through the mixture. "It's pasta in sour cream. It's very rich. But the chicken is so moist and delicious. Here, try." She cut off a piece, spearing some pasta too.

"Ooh, yum." And it was good, though the pasta was a little too chewy for Celia's taste. Before returning to the conversation, she cut off a forkful of salmon. "This is so tender." Then she tasted the pesto sauce. And almost wanted to spit it out. "Way too salty." She held out a bit of salmon in sauce for her sister to try.

Cathe made a face that mirrored how Celia felt. "Oh, yeah. And you like a lot of salt."

That didn't stop Celia from enjoying the melt-in-your-mouth salmon while Cathe mooned over her chicken paprikash.

"Okay, so here's what I have to say."

Groaning around a mouthful of chicken, Cathe admitted, "I thought the food would make you forget."

Celia smiled. "I never forget anything."

Her sister's shoulders slumped. "Might as well get it over with."

"I want you to consider having a fling with a man onboard."

"I'm not interested in a fling."

"Then how about a little flirtation? Pick some attractive guy and just flirt. You don't have to sleep with him. Just flirt a little."

She thought something flickered in Cathe's eyes. Something that might have been interest. But interest in what? "Have you met someone at home that you want to tell me about?"

Cathe snorted. "No," she said emphatically. "Where would I even meet someone?"

Since Denny died, Cathe's life had closed down. Other than her volunteering—where she would never meet eligible men—she barely saw anyone except Sarah.

"Honestly, Cathe, I understand how you feel. But you can't spend the rest of your life alone." Celia feared that's exactly what Cathe would do.

"I'm not ready for another man in my life."

Celia knew how much Cathe adored Denny. And he was a great guy. But he was gone, and Cathe was still young. She wasn't even sixty yet. Celia was the one who would turn the big six-oh in a few short months. "Denny wouldn't have wanted you to bury yourself away."

Cathe snorted, setting down her fork and knife as if she was done with the paprikash. And done with the conversation. "I don't know what Denny would've wanted. All I know is that I don't want another man in my life. I'm fine."

"What about trips like this?" Celia spread her hands. "Don't you want a companion to go on holiday with? It doesn't have to be a sexual relationship. You can just be friends."

"I'm fifty-seven years old. I have a full life without adding a man to it, even if you want to call him a companion. I don't want to deal with any expectations."

"Then you just tell them that up front. That it's just for fun." Celia wanted that for her sister so badly. It had been agony witnessing Cathe's pain over the last two years. "Haven't you heard that sixty is the new forty? This is when people start living their lives again. With the kids out of the house, they can do whatever they want. And you have so much life ahead of you."

"If you will recall, longevity isn't in our family." Both their parents had died in their sixties, Mom from cancer, and Dad went only a short time later. The doctors called it a heart attack, but Celia knew it had been an attack on his heart, and the enemy had been a grief so huge it broke him.

"It doesn't have to be like that for us if we're active. What about our weekly hikes? And you walk every day. You're healthy and vital." And she had to say it. "You can still have a healthy, vital sex life too. You don't have to fall in love." She emphasized that with a shake of her head. "I'm not falling in love. I'm enjoying myself. I want you to enjoy yourself too."

Cathe's jaw tensed as if she were grinding her teeth. "The circumstances are different."

She knew exactly what Cathe was thinking. Celia had a bad marriage. Her husband didn't want her anymore. He'd cheated on her. Of course everything was about sex for her.

But Denny and Cathe had a good sex life. Celia knew that secret smile on her sister's face after she had a really good night. And Celia had to admit she'd been jealous. She'd wanted that secret smile too.

But now she was divorced, and Cathe was a widow. And she wanted her sister to enjoy life again. God forbid she should mention marriage, but if Cathe could just find someone she could talk to, have fun with, hike with, or visit museums, even go to a movie. It could eventually lead to something bigger and better.

As if Cathe read her thoughts, she said, "I'm deep into menopause." She held up her hand in an explanatory gesture. "I don't even think about sex anymore. It would probably be painful anyway."

She wondered if her sister bothered taking care of her

own sexual needs. But there were some places even sisters couldn't go. At least not her and Cathe.

"Like I said, it doesn't have to be a sexual relationship. I just think you need a friend."

Cathe's mouth set in a stubborn line. "I have plenty of friends. And I have you to travel with."

But for how much longer? Celia didn't voice that aloud. She didn't want a relationship, but she did dream of a romantic cruise with a man. Or a European holiday. Touring during the day, hot sex at night. Sure, it was great cruising with her sister, but she didn't want them turning into old maids touring the world together.

Romance and good sex would be wonderful for Cathe. It didn't matter how good her sex life with Denny was; after you'd been with somebody for thirty years, everything got toned down. Which was fine, but Cathe needed romance.

"You know, there are hormones that can help with the physical side."

Cathe held up her hand as if the word *stop* was written on her palm. "Please. I don't want a relationship. I don't want sex. I don't want a male companion. I just want to live my life the way I want to live my life. Now—" Her hand was still in the air. "—you said your piece. And I'll hold you to that promise. We're not talking about it anymore on this holiday."

At least Cathe had specified *this* holiday. It gave Celia the chance to harp on it when they got back home.

But maybe she'd find a man on the ship who would be absolutely perfect for Cathe. She didn't have to tell her sister what she was doing. She could simply steer him in Cathe's direction.

That was the ticket. It was up to her to find a man for Cathe.

Because her sister would never do it on her own.

4

Their bags needed to be outside the room by eight in the morning, but they'd have time for breakfast before their tour started at ten. When they arrived at the ship in the afternoon, their bags would already be in their stateroom.

It was all so exciting.

True to her word, Celia didn't mention finding a man on this trip again.

Cathe sighed in relief. She'd known the conversation was coming, and she'd girded her loins, so to speak. But it still hurt, reminding her of all she'd lost. Denny and their life together hadn't been perfect, but no marriage was. They had their fights, their tense moments. But they'd long ago promised each other they'd talk things through and never go to sleep angry. There'd been a few times they hadn't lived up to that promise, but then there'd been the makeup sex. Which had pretty darn amazing. Of course, that wasn't always true. After all, they'd been married for thirty years. What did she expect? But when Sarah left for college, they'd gone wild with the freedom, having sex in every room, even stopping at a motel on the way home from visiting Sarah's university because Denny couldn't wait. It had been wonderful, but she wouldn't deny that stopped years ago. They'd still made love, and it had still been good, but Cathe had to prepare for it. She'd often signaled her desire by taking a sexy novel to bed. Denny loved her erotic novels, even though he hadn't read a single one.

But those days were over. She didn't read sexy novels anymore. She didn't think about sex. Not unless Celia brought it up. She didn't need a second marriage, she didn't need a lover, she didn't need romance. She didn't even need a companion to take her on a trip.

Truth be told, she didn't need a holiday at all. She'd come along on this cruise for Celia's sake.

Her sister had never wanted Cathe to grieve, as if grief was infectious. Every time Cathe started to cry, Celia gathered her in her arms and whispered, "Don't cry. You'll be okay. We'll get through this together. I'm here for you. You don't need to cry."

Celia had always been there. And Cathe was grateful for that.

But sometimes she wanted to howl out her grief *with* Celia. Sometimes she craved commiseration. Yet it was as if watching Cathe let go, Celia feared she'd start howling herself. She didn't want to let go of her anger. That's what all the men were about. Not payback, but a slap in the face, showing Bart, showing *herself*, that she was a beautiful, attractive woman.

Celia needed to learn that she was beautiful and attractive and desirable without having to sleep with men she didn't care about.

There were times she'd tried to go there, but Celia had shut her down.

Just like Cathe had shut Celia down last night.

And right now, she wanted nothing more than to enjoy a pleasant meal in the hotel's dining room.

And then *he* walked in.

Her heart did a weird thumpity-thump before she dragged her gaze away. God forbid Celia should see her looking at a man.

But he was dazzling. Steering his father's walker past her table, she noted again how much he resembled Denny. His short dark hair with dashes of silver had a bit of wave in it, and his face was clean-shaven. So many men these days liked that scruffy look. There were even shavers that groomed it that way. But not this man. His skin was smooth. Touchable.

Oh no. She was not going there. And she was absolutely not letting Celia see her interest. It was just... comparison.

Thank God Celia was concentrating on her eggs because when the man passed, he smiled.

Cathe felt it all the way to the pit of her stomach.

It was Denny's smile.

She quickly looked away, blinking, tears biting at her eyes. She would not cry. Not on this trip.

She absolutely couldn't in front of Celia.

DONE WITH BREAKFAST, THEY HEADED TO THE LOBBY TO catch the tour bus.

For the first organized tour of their trip, they had an hour's drive outside of Budapest to a small town called Szentendre, where they would have a goulash-making lesson, a tour of a Hungarian farm, then shopping time in town.

Celia had said from the very beginning, "We should do at least one tour every day. Some of them are freebies."

They couldn't sit on the ship the whole time, and with a tour, they'd get the lay of the land and could strike out on their own in the afternoons. With the exception of a day or two, most of the cruising was done at night, leaving plenty of time to tour the cities they visited.

In the hotel lobby, the tour guide gathered them round, and Cathe didn't know whether she was happy or terrified that Denny's look-alike and his father were on the same tour.

Which meant they were also on the same ship.

Her stomach felt jumpy contemplating eight days on the boat with him.

All she had to do was keep her eyes off him and Celia wouldn't have a clue. Right. Easy.

She judged him to be about her age, with laugh lines at his mouth and eyes. As he spoke animatedly to his father, she imagined he was a happy man.

But when her gaze dropped to his hand to look for a wedding band, she pulled herself back. It didn't matter if he was married. She wouldn't speak to him. She most certainly wouldn't flirt with him the way Celia suggested she do.

Celia rushed to the bus, and noticing Cathe wasn't right behind her, she mouthed, "I'll get us a good seat."

She didn't think she'd done it on purpose, but Cathe found herself getting on behind the lovely man as he helped his dad onto the bus and into a seat in a slow, laborious process.

The deep timbre of his voice shivered through her. "I'll just help the driver put your walker in the hold."

Just as he turned, the latch on the old man's fanny pack gave way, and it tumbled to the floor, almost at Cathe's feet.

Though the man swore under his breath, he smiled. "No worries, Dad, I'll get it."

Cathe beat him to it, retrieving the fanny pack. "Here you go."

Denny's look-alike smiled. "Thanks. You're a lifesaver."

He had such a beautiful smile, the smile of a man who was

happy with himself and his life. Though she could be making that up. People put on faces for strangers. But he didn't appear impatient or angry with the slow pace or the other difficulties of a physically challenged elderly man.

He was just like Denny, who'd never gotten angry with his father, never yelled, never scolded. But sometimes, late at night after he'd taken his father out for the day, tears filled his eyes. She wondered if this man had a wife at home who comforted him as he grieved for his father's decline.

Waiting a moment until the old man had settled, she exchanged another smile with the son, then squeezed past him to the seat Celia had saved.

She was gratified there were no grumbles or groans at the delay. Most of the passengers were older, some with their own infirmities, and they all seemed to understand the need for extra time.

Celia had secured a spot halfway back, and Cathe slipped in beside her.

"You're so sweet." Celia smiled, meaning it.

Cathe snorted. "What was I supposed to do, run them over?" But she felt like she'd done her random act of kindness for the day.

The hour bus ride passed quickly as their guide, a middle-aged Hungarian woman named Anna, pointed out sights along the way, speaking in excellent, melodic English. She regaled them with the history of the region, especially the Hapsburgs, to whom the Hungarians had turned to expel the invading Turks back in the 1500s. And who had then stayed for another three hundred years.

"We're a small country," Anna said. "Someone has always wanted to take us over. But since the liberation from the Soviets in 1989, we have ruled ourselves. And we will not give up our sovereign rule again."

The bus rolled by fields of crops and bales of hay

wrapped up like Easter eggs. Since Celia had the window seat, Cathe didn't get any decent pictures. And finally, they pulled into a long gravel drive leading to the farm. Buses packed the small parking lot while tourists crowded into the modest museum and gift shop. As she and Celia alighted from the back door, the driver retrieved the old man's walker. The bus emptied, and the old man was the last to step off, his son holding out his hands to steady his father as he climbed down.

Cathe didn't realize the sight had transfixed her until Celia said, "Isn't that the sweetest thing?" When Cathe looked at her, she jutted her chin at father and son. "It reminds me of how good Denny was with his dad."

Tears welled up in less than a breath, and Cathe struggled to push them away.

Celia touched her arm. "I'm sorry. Don't cry. I didn't mean to upset you. Please don't cry."

Celia hadn't been able to abide her crying since they were teenagers, when Cathe had cried at the drop of a hat, a lost boyfriend, a fight with a friend, a bad score on a test. Celia always wanted to talk her out of her tears while she herself never cried, not even when she'd discovered her husband's affair.

"I'm okay." Cathe gave one small sniff. "But you're right, they make me think of Denny and his dad."

"He was a total saint."

Celia rarely spoke like that. In her books, no man was a saint. But she'd always admired how Denny had cared for his father.

Anna directed them slowly around the farm, through the rooms set up to depict farm life in years long past and onto the barns where the animals were kept.

Cathe did her best not to watch the man or his father.

"Oh my God, look at the horns on those sheep." Celia

leaned on the fence while Cathe photographed the sheep being fed.

The males' spiral horns were like something on a unicorn. Magically, even as they crowded around to feed off a bale of hay secured in a round cage, they didn't poke each other's eyes or get their horns stuck in the bars.

A windmill turned lazily in the breeze while cows, goats, pigs, and horses filled the pens, and ducks wandered through the yard. A peacock lounged on a patch of grass. The cutest puppy, a black Portuguese Water Dog with a white forelock, white chest, and white paws, raced up to Cathe while she framed a photo of the peacock.

Adorable with all his silky ringlets, he sniffed her leg, then bumped her to make sure she patted his head. Then the dog bounded off again, throwing himself at a young girl seated by the stables. It was such an idyllic setting.

Finally, Anna gathered them round. "We will go to the main hall now where you will learn how to make goulash." She held up her hands. "And there will be a delicious goulash lunch afterward where we will sample the fruits of your efforts." Her lyrically accented speech was as fluent as a native English speaker.

The cooking demonstration was held beneath a patio canopy where tables had been set up with cutting boards, knives, and vegetables. A massive stew pot hung suspended from a tripod, a fire already glowing beneath it. They each received an apron, and by the time she'd tied it on, the tables were already filling up.

Celia had grabbed a table, but as Cathe headed to her, two white-haired women took the last vacant spots. Her sister gave a what-can-I-do shrug.

It didn't matter. They weren't joined at the hip. Cathe turned to an empty space at a table near the stew pot.

It was only when she looked at her neighbor to politely

ask if the spot was taken that she realized he was the Denny look-alike, his father across from him. Her heart tripped all over itself, though she didn't know why she should be nervous. And forgetting all about asking to join the table, or even to say hello, she picked up the knife and centered stalks of celery on her cutting board.

She would have remained ridiculously mute if he hadn't said, "Thanks so much for picking up Dad's pack."

This close, the blue of his eyes and the smile creasing his mouth mesmerized her. Silver-dusted dark hair curled just above his polo shirt's collar, and with the strong set of his chin, he stole her breath.

She managed to say, "No problem at all," but was afraid her voice came out as little more than a croak.

"I'm Jack Kelly. And that's my dad Rupert." He pointed across the table to his father seated on his walker, the cutting board on his lap while he made fast work of a tomato. The elderly man's smile transformed his face from ancient to delightful, and Cathe guessed him to be somewhere in his mid-eighties.

"I'd shake your hand," Jack said with a smile that set her heart racing. "But I'm holding a knife, and I wouldn't want to stab you."

They both laughed. He had a deep laugh she felt in the pit of her stomach. "My name's Cathe Girard. It's nice to meet you. Anything I can do to help, just let me know."

He grinned. "Thank you." Then he jutted his chin at Celia. "Your sister?"

"How'd you know?" They could have been partners or friends traveling together.

He motioned a hand over her hair and her face. "Same pretty blond hair, same blue eyes, same nose, same mouth."

Wow. He'd been observing her just the way she'd noticed

him. "We planned this trip over a year ago," she explained. "And after a postponement, we're finally here."

He nodded. "Yeah, you just have to do it, even when life gets in the way."

She wondered if something had gotten in the way for him. She didn't look specifically for a ring, but both his hands were on display as he chopped a carrot.

And his ring finger was bare.

Not that she was interested. She had no intention of flirting the way Celia wanted her to.

Yet her heart gave a little leap.

Across the table, Rupert Kelly centered a turnip on his cutting board. "So you two young ladies—" Cathe stifled a snicker at his use of the word *young*. "—have ditched your husbands to come on this trip, leaving them behind to do all the chores?"

Her heart plummeted. But she grabbed it, held it in her hands, and told herself to smile. "No husbands to leave behind," she said, trying to sound sweet and unaffected. She wasn't sure it worked. "My sister is divorced, and I'm a widow."

Rupert's mouth drooped. "I'm so sorry. Jack's always telling me I have foot-in-mouth disease."

Cathe shook her head. "Please, Rupert, don't worry about it."

Next to her, Jack said, "I'm sorry for your loss. Was it long ago?"

How long was long ago? "Two years."

Rupert put a finger to the corner of his eye as if wiping away a tear for her. "Loss is such a terrible thing to go through."

But she refused to let the day get morose. "Where are you two from?" That was usually the first question out of anyone's mouth on a trip like this, but she'd been so stunned by Jack that she hadn't thought to ask before.

Rupert's craggy face lit up with an enchanting smile. "California. The Oakland Hills, if you're at all familiar with the San Francisco Bay Area."

That made her grin for real. "Oh my gosh. I live on the Peninsula, in Belmont. It's right across the San Mateo Bridge." The Bay Area was a big place, and it was impossible to know exactly where all the small communities were.

"I know where that is," Jack said. "A nice area."

"Yes," she agreed. "We have so many good places to walk out there."

"Just like we do," Rupert said, the wrinkles on his face filling out with his smile. "I've lived in Oakland all my life. So has Jack." He waved his hand at his son.

Funny how places and dates could fling themselves at you. She remembered the Oakland Firestorm, the nineteenth of October, 1991. Her and Denny's anniversary. Two years before that, the Loma Prieta Earthquake. And there'd been Black Monday, when the stock market crashed on the same day in 1987 and people were jumping out windows.

She couldn't stop the lurch of her heart. Denny had always joked about the bad luck talisman of their anniversary. And he'd died close to their anniversary too. Maybe it had been waiting for them all along, when his heart attack struck like the earthquake.

But these nice people didn't need to know specifics about her tragedy, and as she chopped a potato, she asked politely, "You live in the Oakland Hills too?"

Jack nodded. "Right now, I'm living with Dad. He needs a little extra help."

Rupert waved a hand. "We're just too old bachelors." He shrugged a shoulder in Jack's direction. "Well, Jack's divorced so I guess he's not a bachelor. But he's a good boy, Jack is, taking care of his old dad."

So. Jack was divorced. And what were the odds they would actually live in the Bay Area as well?

She knew what Celia would say. That it was meant to be. But Cathe knew better.

There would never be another Denny, not even a divorced man who looked so much like her husband that her heart ached.

5

J ust as Cathe finished chopping a potato, their chef for
the day, an older man with a large belly, clapped his
hands, calling out in a strong, mellifluous accent, "I see
you have all finished your work. And now it is time to
make our *gouyash*."

He pointed to the big pot sitting over the fire. "From
your recipe—" Each cutting board had come with a recipe
card. "—first we add our meat to brown." He poured in a
big bowl of cubed beef, stirring it for a couple of minutes.
"And now for the aromatics. All of those with chopped
celery and onions, please step forward and drop them into
our pot."

Cathe, along with several other people, poured her celery
into the pot.

"Now we will need someone good at stirring." He pointed
at Rupert and winked. "Dear gentleman, you are perfect for
our task. Could you come over here?"

Jack rounded the table, helping his father stand.

The chef added graciously, "It is good if you wish to sit,
sir." Jack aided Rupert in swinging his walker around. Then

the chef handed him a big wooden spoon. "Now please stir our onions and other aromatics."

Rupert stirred, waving his hand at Jack. "Don't hover, boy. I can handle it."

Jack retreated to his position at the table beside Cathe, leaning close to say tongue-in-cheek, "And he says *I'm* bossy,"

"Now we will add our spice." The chef grabbed a prep bowl filled with spices. "The main staple is, of course, paprika." He waved the bowl under his nose. "Our Hungarian paprika is famous all over the world. We sprinkle it on everything, scrambled eggs, sour cream and noodles, even on our cottage cheese. You will be going to the little town of Szentendre, and there I suggest you purchase true Hungarian paprika. We have sweet, hot, and smoked, and they all have their different uses."

He sprinkled the spice mixture into the pot and said to Rupert, "Stir well, my dear man." Then he looked at his audience. "We use mostly sweet paprika in *gouyash*, with a bit of hot paprika. However, if you like yours spicier, add more." His English was flawless, and leaning over the pot, he wafted steam to his nose. "Aw, it is perfect. And now we add broth." Retrieving a large jug, he poured, careful not to splash Rupert as he stirred.

"Now we bring that to a good simmer," he told them. "We are fond of potatoes, carrots, turnips, and tomatoes. But first —" He held up another prep bowl. "I like to add a bit of tomato paste." He spooned the paste into the bubbling pot as Rupert stirred. "It is perfect timing for you to add your diced vegetables." And he waved everyone forward.

Jack whispered, "He's a good showman." His aftershave wafted over her. It wasn't strong, just a tempting aroma that titillated her senses.

They walked to the pot, scraping their diced vegetables into the simmering brew. And it smelled good.

Almost as good as Jack.

Looking up, she met Celia's gaze, turning quickly before her sister did something embarrassing like waggling her brows.

Back at the table, Jack smiled, picking up the knife. "We could've used something a little sharper."

She laughed, saying, "Maybe they're afraid we'd cut ourselves," and tried not to feel Celia's eyes on her. She would never hear the end of this.

Once again, their chef clapped. "We will take our pot inside and let it bubble and brew while we have lunch. You will be eating yesterday's *gouyash* because we like it to sit for hours over a low heat until the vegetables and the meat are tender." He kissed his fingertips, adding, "For vegetarians, we have a special pot with tofu instead of beef. Do we have any takers?"

Only two people raised their hands, a younger couple in their forties.

Then he turned to Rupert and had a handed him a small package. "We have a gift for doing such an amazing job with our *gouyash*."

Rupert grinned from ear to ear. "How exciting. I didn't know I get a prize." He opened it to find a small packet of paprika.

The chef chuckled. "The rest of you will receive a certificate saying you have completed your Hungarian *gouyash* lesson." He marched to the main hall, waving his hand for them to follow.

Before Jack collected Rupert, he asked, "I hope you and your sister will join our table."

"Of course. Thank you."

As he helped his father turn his walker, Celia rushed over. "Who was that hunk?" she hissed under her breath.

"Jack Kelly. And his father Rupert."

Celia eyed him. "He's totally yummy."

"Jack or his father?"

Celia chuckled. "I give you first dibs on the son."

"I don't have dibs on anyone." She barely restrained a huff of indignation.

"Here's my thought." Celia raised a brow. "There won't be a lot of single men on this trip. So you better put your dibs on him right now, or I might have to steal him out from under you."

For a moment, Cathe couldn't answer. She didn't want to flirt. Did she? But she'd noticed Jack the very first night from their hotel window. The thought of Celia flirting with him, even worse, the thought of him flirting back, well, it would be like watching Celia flirt with Denny. She couldn't handle it. Not that she begrudged her sister finding a man. But not Jack. And she said softly, "Dibs."

Celia squealed like a teenager and threw her arms around Cathe. "I'm so happy."

Over Celia's shoulder, Jack looked back at them as he and Rupert headed into the recreation hall.

Thank God Celia kept her voice low. "I'm not saying you have to sleep with him. Just flirt."

Cathe nodded, a flush heating her body. It was probably just a hot flash.

Then they followed the tail end of the group heading into the dining room.

Jack had already seated his father at a table by the window, and Celia dove right in. "Cathe tells me you've invited us to sit with you. Thank you so much." She stuck out her hand to shake Jack's. "Celia Winters. And you are?"

"Jack Kelly. And this is my dad, Rupert."

Celia smiled without an ounce of the guile she'd shown outside. "So nice to meet you both."

The tour group had a room to themselves, nicely set with

tables covered in blue-and-white-checked tablecloths. Celia sat next to Rupert and Cathe took his other side by Jack.

Immediately Celia asked questions. "Where are you two from? I'm sure Cathe already told you we're from San Francisco."

Rupert answered brightly, "Yes, and we live in the Oakland Hills."

Celia darn near squealed. Again. "I can't believe you two live so close to us. What an amazing coincidence." Cathe was terrified Celia would look at her and wink. "And I live in San Carlos." Her sister put her hand to her chest, drawing attention to the sexy tank top beneath a multicolored see-through vest. With anyone else, it would have been flirtatious, but Cathe had already her put dibs on Jack, and if anything, Celia was flirting with Rupert. Elderly men loved to flirt. "I'm sure Cathe mentioned she's in Belmont. Just across the San Mateo Bridge from you." Oh God. Was that a hint? Then Celia smiled at Rupert. "Now we've got that out of the way, what do you do with your day in the Oakland Hills?"

The old man beamed beneath the attention. "Why, I'm retired. I don't do anything."

Celia gave a musical laugh. "Please don't tell me you sit in front of the TV all day watching game shows and soap operas. You look like you've had an extremely interesting life. You should write your memoirs."

Jack gave a hearty laugh, while Rupert's was no less humorous, if a little weaker.

"I was a philosophy professor at Berkeley. But no one cares much about philosophy anymore, especially when you talk about Epictetus, Marcus Aurelius, and Aristotle, old white guys like me." He smiled that transformative smile again.

Then it was Jack's turn. Celia was always so much better

at making conversation than Cathe. "What you do, Jack. Are you retired too?"

He smiled with a slight shake of his head. "Not yet. I work for a manufacturing company."

Across from him, Rupert snorted. "He's downplaying himself. My son is the CEO of a manufacturing company he started."

Cathe liked Rupert's pride in his son. "That's wonderful. What do you manufacture?"

"Ultrasonic testing devices."

"Jack designed the first one himself. And he's got the patent to show for it."

This time, Jack laughed. "While my father says I downplay myself, he likes to make it appear that I'm more than I am. A friend and I designed the device together. We both have the patent."

Cathe had to say, "It's still impressive that you invented something and started your own company, even if you were working with a friend."

"What about you ladies?" Rupert asked. "What do you both do?"

Celia jumped immediately. "I donate my time as an event coordinator for nonprofits."

Cathe felt inadequate admitting she was *just* a home-maker. Although raising a child and keeping the house wasn't for sissies either. "I'm a homemaker." Except that she had no one to make a home for anymore.

"And now," Celia added, "Cathe volunteers at her local senior center as well as the hospital."

She wasn't sure if Celia was making fun of her. What she did was nothing as important as the fundraisers Celia organized that brought in thousands for the charities. But Jack said, "I find that pretty amazing too."

An unbidden blush crept into her cheeks. "I just wanted

to fill up my time after my daughter went off to college." Even more so after Denny died and the walls of the house closed in on her.

"A daughter. Hopefully she still lives nearby?" Jack asked.

Cathe beamed with pride and pleasure. "Sarah works in San Francisco. She's in marketing, and she loves it."

"But she's got a good accounting background, too, like her father," Celia explained for Cathe.

Once again, Cathe wasn't certain if Celia was poking fun. She'd been fond of saying that Denny was an accountant and too boring to be of interest, an old Monty Python line. Then again, Cathe was overly sensitive. Celia didn't mean anything by it, just kept the conversation going. But Cathe decided it was time to take the attention off herself.

Turning to Jack, she asked, "What about you? Any kids?" He was divorced, but that didn't mean he was childless.

Just like Cathe, Jack smiled with pride. "Two daughters. They're both in college."

Rupert grumbled, "Two *girls*. Not that I don't love them to pieces. But this line of the family will die out. I have only the one son, and he goes and has two girls." Rupert glowered at Jack. "What happened to those little XY swimmers of yours?"

Instead of being offended or embarrassed, Jack laughed. "You have two brothers to carry on the line, Dad. And I have several male cousins doing their duty in that regard."

Rupert threw up his hands in disgust. "Yes, but they're on the East Coast. You're letting down the West Coast side."

Jack shrugged, shaking his head, his mouth flirting with a smile. "There's not much I can do about it now."

Then Rupert turned his attention to Celia. "What about you? Kids?"

Celia fell in with his game. "There was no problem with XY swimmers in my house, thank you very much."

Cathe couldn't resist adding. "Celia has three beautiful sons."

"And they're always wishing Mom would back off and let them live their own lives." Everybody laughed at that. "I keep bugging them all to give me grandchildren, but Peter, my eldest, is the only one who even has a girlfriend." She threw her hands out in a can-you-believe-it gesture.

The waiter arrived at the table with a basket of warm bread, and right behind him came the wine steward. The man boomed out a hardy, "We have red wine for you, excellent with your *gouyash*."

They accepted. After all, they weren't driving the bus.

Celia tasted first. "Thank you. Quite delicious." She saluted the steward with her glass.

A third server arrived with an enormous pot, ladling goulash into their bowls, the rising steam fragrant with spices and tomatoes. "But it's really more of a soup," Cathe said. "I thought *gouyash* was stew." She pronounced it like the locals. Tasting it, she found it wasn't as burningly spicy as the hotel goulash. "It's very good. Just not what I expected."

"This is *Hungarian*," Rupert emphasized. "The Czech goulash is the stew. And they serve it with potato dumplings to sop up all the juices." Then he added, "If you're on the Prague extension after the cruise, you'll be able to try it there."

Celia pouted, though her eyes shone. "Unfortunately, we're missing that. But I've heard Prague is absolutely beautiful. What about you two?"

Jack answered, "We did the two days in Budapest beforehand and then three nights in Prague after the cruise."

Cathe didn't say a thing. Why did her stomach drop when she realized they would miss two extra days with Jack and Rupert?

"My wife and I," Rupert said, "planned the trip for our

49

sixtieth wedding anniversary. Unfortunately, she passed last year."

For the first time, Cathe saw strain on the old man's face. He'd been putting on a good show, just the way she hoped she did. "I'm so sorry to hear that, Rupert." She wrapped her fingers around his hand, his parchment-thin skin cool to the touch.

"Thank you, my dear."

But Jack kept things upbeat. "Dad and I decided we'd do the trip in Mom's honor."

"That's lovely," Celia agreed.

Both men were grieving, one for a wife, one for a mother.

When you lost a parent as a child, it was a terrible thing. But as an adult, you were supposed to deal with it as if it were a fact of life. That didn't make it any less devastating. Both she and Celia knew, having lost their parents so closely together. It had been twenty years, but she still missed them both.

"It's a wonderful tribute to your mother." Her words were heartfelt.

"Thank you." Jack smiled, but she recognized the hint of sadness. "This was the trip Mom wanted. The Danube."

"And she wanted to see Budapest," Rupert added. "And Prague."

"And try all the pastries and desserts everywhere," Jack added.

Rupert laughed. "She did love her sweets."

Cathe was glad he had happy memories and could still smile over them.

She struggled with that herself. And it had been two years. Was it different if you were older? When you knew there was only a finite time left together? She and Denny were planning their retirement, where they wanted to live, planning what they would do in their golden years together.

Jack added to his father's comments. "We booked several excursions. We wanted to make sure we saw everything. Not a single wasted moment."

She knew what he meant. When you lost someone, you suddenly realized how many moments you'd wasted.

"We've booked several excursions ourselves," Celia said. "Perhaps we'll be on some of the same ones."

She looked at Cathe. And thankfully didn't wink this time either.

"Which ones are you doing?" Rupert asked.

Celia waved her hand negligently. "I can't remember. We booked them all so long ago."

Jack laughed. "I'm with you. I've forgotten most of them."

Cathe tucked into her goulash before it went cold. The vegetables were soft but not mushy, the meat tender, and the crusty bread perfect for dipping.

"It's delicious." She savored another spoonful, then tipped her chin at Rupert. "I'll have to make Czech goulash at home."

"Then you'll need to buy paprika in Szentendre," Jack said.

"Cathe loves to cook." Celia popped a bite of bread in her mouth.

Cathe had to smile. Her sister had been singing her praises all along. And setting her up with Jack.

She had to be grateful to Celia, who'd found out everything they needed to know. Along with Rupert, who had no problem talking about his son's life.

They demolished their goulash, the bread basket and wineglasses all empty. Their server came by to collect everything, and just as he'd whisked their table clean, another waiter served dessert.

It looked like some sort of cake. But it tasted... weird.

Cathe couldn't even describe it. "I'm not sure what to make of this."

Jack wore the same expression, and Celia spoke for all of them. "It's definitely not worth the calories."

"It's made with cottage cheese." Jack put down his fork. "Good to try, but I don't need any more."

Rupert, because he was old and could do whatever he wanted, spat a mouthful onto his plate and screwed up his face. "That's just plain gross."

Cathe laughed. He sounded so like Sarah or one of her nephews.

The meal wound down quickly after that, people rising to use the bathroom, their guide Anna giving them ten minutes before the bus left.

"Ladies, thank you so much for joining us." Rupert's smile reached all the way to his white hair.

"It was a pleasure," Celia said, Cathe echoing her.

Back on the bus, after stowing the walker, Jack sat up front with Rupert, while Cathe and Celia headed back to their original seats. Cathe took the window, Celia sliding in beside her.

"He is certainly a hottie," she murmured in Cathe's ear.

"Rupert?" Cathe asked tongue in cheek, although the old man was a sweetie.

"Don't give me that crap." Celia elbowed her.

"You're so bad."

Her sister winked. "If you don't take him, I will."

Even if Cathe didn't intend to do anything herself, she was absolutely sure she couldn't sit back and watch her sister flirt with Jack Kelly.

6

From the farm, they headed out to the quaint village of Szentendre a short distance away. Celia compared it to Solvang, a touristy Nordic town just north of LA. The narrow cobblestone streets and charming shops had a storybook feel to them.

First on the list, they bought Hungarian paprika, sweet, hot, and smoked.

"You made it sound like you don't even cook," Cathe said dryly.

Celia laughed. "I wanted them to know you're a great cook. Mom always said the way to a man's heart is through his stomach."

Cathe bumped her shoulder. "I told you I'm not looking for another man," she said in that singsong of hers.

Her sister was just afraid. She'd been married so long, and she didn't know how to be with anyone else. Celia understood, though their situations were so different. She'd had a nasty divorce, while Cathe had lost the love of her life. But that didn't mean it had been easy for Celia to step out either. She'd had fears too. Fears that no man would find an almost sixty-year-old woman attractive. Fears that she couldn't perform sexually. Fears she'd meet someone who was only after her money. She'd found an amazing divorce attorney who'd gotten her a stupendous settlement from a man who'd ignored her for the last five years, then cheated on her. And they'd had sexual issues far longer than that. But she wouldn't remain bitter about it.

And she didn't want her sister to spend the rest of her life alone. Cathe was young. She was attractive. She needed to have a little fun, kick up her heels. Even if she didn't actually sleep with Jack, she could still have fun.

Wasn't it nice, too, that Cathe had found the perfect candidate on her own? Celia didn't have to search. All she had to do was push Cathe toward the deliciously hunky Jack.

Cathe carried their bags of paprika out of the shop. "You're singing my praises so much it's embarrassing."

Celia just laughed. "You're certainly not going to do it."

Stopping in the middle of the cobblestone road, Cathe narrowed her eyes. "If I get Jack, who's probably the only single man under eighty on the boat, what are you going to do?"

Waggling her eyebrows, Celia hoped it came off lasciviously. "Don't you worry, I'll find someone." She nudged Cathe. "Ooh. What if I went for the captain? I bet he has a fabulous stateroom."

Laughing, Celia looped her arm through her sister's and led them up the road.

They drifted through shops filled with leather goods and woolen clothes and wooden toys. Then they found the marzipan store.

"Oh my God." Celia wheezed out a breath. "Peter adores marzipan. Nolan and Leo do as well. I've been racking my brain about what to bring back. Even if they all said not to bring anything."

Not just a store, the shop was a factory. In the back rooms, ladies sat at tables making elaborate scenes out of an amazing array of colored marzipan.

One woman worked on a forest scene of trees with elaborate leaves, tiny blades of grass, a brook bubbling over rocks, a squirrel climbing a tree, a rabbit disappearing into its burrow, and a sneaky fox eyeing the rabbit. Another woman fashioned a hobbit house out of marzipan, a door in a tree partly open to reveal a hobbit leg just stepping out. There were flower gardens and cottage scenes, a castle on a marzipan hill.

"And look at that replica of the Parliament Building in Budapest. These are just amazing." Cathe harrumphed. "I can't get my gingerbread houses to look this good."

The woman rolled marzipan on her table until it was as thin as a blade of grass and fitted it into her forest scene.

"It must take weeks to do all this." Celia would never have the patience. She hadn't lied to Jack about Cathe. Since their mom passed, Cathe was the best cook in the family, saving all of their mother's recipes. If anyone could make a marzipan Parliament Building, it was Cathe.

Back in the main shop, they wandered through the aisles filled with candy in all shapes and sizes.

"I wish I had grandkids." Cathe sighed. "I'd buy all these little animals."

"Peter is just a big kid. I'll get him one of these marzipan pigs covered in chocolate."

Her sister smiled then. "I'm getting a rabbit, a squirrel, and a fox. And if Sarah doesn't want them, I'll eat them. Or maybe I'll put them on a shelf like ornaments."

They left the shop loaded down with marzipan in a dozen shapes and colors, big and small, chocolate-covered and plain.

"Oh my gosh." Cathe groaned, looking at her watch. "We'll have to rush to get to the bus on time."

They weren't the only ones. Celia saw several members of the tour group, even Anna, their guide. Jack and Rupert were also making leisurely progress back to the parking lot.

Rupert smiled giddily when he saw them. "You ladies look like you did some wonderful shopping."

Celia liked the old man. He was funny and didn't take himself too seriously. It was mean to say, and somebody would slap her for being politically incorrect, but some old people could be crotchety. Not Rupert. He was a doll.

Cathe held up their bags. "Paprika and marzipan."

Then there was Jack. What a handsome specimen. He was fit, as if he actually worked in his manufacturing plant rather than running it from an office. His dark hair was cut attractively short, and he was tall. She adored a tall man.

And Celia didn't miss the stars in his eyes when he looked at Cathe. He was perfect for her.

"I totally missed the marzipan store." Jack's lips curved in a boyish grin.

Cathe opened her bag to gloat. "There's a pig and a rabbit and a fox and a squirrel. And lots of chocolate-covered marzipan too." She smiled to match his grin. "I might see my way to letting you have one piece." She held up a finger. "But just one."

That might actually be a bit of flirting. It was hard to tell with Cathe.

Rupert pounded his fist on his walker. "What about me, young lady?"

"You like marzipan too?" Cathe winked at him.

The old man wrinkled his nose. "No. I just don't want to be left out." They all had a good laugh at that.

It had been a good day. They'd loaded up with goodies, had lunch with a yummy man, enjoyed his father's company, too, and Celia had skillfully uncovered all their details.

If she'd left it up to Cathe, her sister wouldn't have learned a thing.

Now Celia just had to find a man for herself. She hadn't been joking when she'd suggested the captain. It made perfect sense. On this cruise, most men would be part of a couple. Jack was probably the only unattached male in the right age group.

Yes, the captain. Or maybe the cruise director. Someone in charge who would hopefully have a very nice stateroom.

THE BUS DROPPED THEM OFF AROUND THREE IN FRONT OF their cruise ship, a long, low affair bobbing gently on the water. Check-in was easy, and soon they were in their cabin, which was below the waterline, one long window high up to give them light. They'd chosen the cheapest cabin to save money, especially since they wouldn't be spending a lot of time there.

The second and third decks had rooms with verandas and deck chairs, some with French balconies that had sliding glass doors but only a railing. You got air and light, but you couldn't step out.

"Wow," Celia exclaimed as she opened the door.

It couldn't be called a stateroom. To Cathe, a stateroom implied stately. And roomier than this.

Celia said it for them both. "This is pretty darn small. I mean, are we even able to unpack all our stuff?" She stopped short of growling. "The bathroom isn't even big enough for two of us to use it at the same time."

The view out the window at the top was of another boat docked next to theirs, cutting out most of their light. But the narrow twin beds were covered in thick, fluffy duvets. A mirror filled the wall above the long sideboard, with a set of drawers and a small refrigerator underneath.

Cathe pointed to the mirror. "One of us can put on makeup and blow-dry here while the other is showering." She added optimistically, "That won't be a big deal."

"You're right," Celia finally agreed. "At least the shower is big enough that we don't have to worry about banging our elbows on the walls."

"And look at this." Cathe flipped a switch. "It's got a heated bathroom floor." A wide, full-length closet lay opposite the bathroom, with shelves and room to hang clothing. "With the closet and the drawers, there's plenty of room for all our stuff."

Celia frowned, flaring her nostrils. "But where are we supposed to store our suitcases?"

Kicking under the bed, Cathe lifted the skirting. "Under here, no problem."

"You always were a look-on-the-bright-side kind of woman." And finally, Celia laughed.

Though Cathe had to snort. "You make that sound like a bad thing. Let's unpack, then explore the boat. I want to see what's for dinner."

All the reviews said the food was fabulous, and they'd purchased the drinks package so they could have champagne whenever they wanted. Altogether, it had been a wonderful day. Even if she hadn't exactly flirted, she'd enjoyed the conversation with Jack and Rupert over lunch. She wouldn't let the size of the cabin get her down.

Unpacking took twenty minutes, and they stood back to survey their efforts. "You were right," Celia admitted. "Everything fits. This'll be great. We'll just stagger our bathroom times. Which bed do you want, window or inside?"

"Window," Cathe ventured. "If you don't care."

With everything settled, they decided to explore the boat.

From the lowest deck, they came up the stairs onto the reception level, with the dining room at the front of the boat. Dinner was at seven, which was late for Cathe, but she'd survive. Though the dining room doors were closed, they examined the posted menu, the left side detailing the always-available items of salmon, chicken, steak.

"Ooh, dessert is crème brûlée." Cathe's favorite. "Along with a cheese plate, a fruit plate, or ice cream."

"I'm sold." Celia shivered with delight. Crème brûlée was her favorite too.

"But look here on the other side." Cathe took a picture so she could remember what they had each night, three courses, starter, main dish, and dessert. At the top were the regional items, tonight's being chicken paprikash. "Darn. I already had paprikash." There was also shrimp risotto and beef remoulade. "I'll have the salmon."

Celia put her hand to her stomach. "It all looks so good. I want the steak. In fact, I might eat steak every night since I don't get it at home."

They giggled like schoolgirls. "And I'm having a dessert every night," Celia added. "I'll start with crème brûlée."

"Look at us. It's only four o'clock and we're already picking out our meals."

They shared a smile, and Cathe asked, "Is it too early for a champagne cocktail?"

Celia was already taking the stairs to the lounge on the next deck. "It's never too early for a champagne cocktail, especially when we're on vacation."

The lounge took up the front half of the ship with a coffee bar by each of the two entrances. Both bars included an espresso machine for lattes, macchiatos, and mochas, along with regular and decaf coffee. A basket held a selection of cookies and pastries. But they were on a champagne cocktail mission.

With passengers still checking in, the lounge wasn't full. Since another boat had docked next to theirs, they chose the harborside and sat in a grouping of four chairs. With the bar on one end, tables ran down the middle to the front of the ship, and then the lounge opened onto a terrace overlooking the water. So far, only a few couples had taken seats along the windows.

Though it was a lovely, sunny day, after the bus ride, it was nice to sit on comfortable inside chairs. A waiter arrived promptly with a bowl of mixed nuts and took their orders.

"I didn't realize I'd been waiting all day for this," Celia said with a sigh as their cocktails arrived. They clinked glasses and cheered to their first day on the boat.

"What are we doing tomorrow?" Celia wanted to know.

Cathe opened the cruise app she'd put on her phone. "Let's see." She scrolled the screen. "A city bus tour in the morning. And the thermal baths in the afternoon."

"Fabulous. Thank God I remembered my swimsuit."

Then Celia's eyes widened, her lips parting, and her cheeks actually turned pink as if she was blushing. And Celia wasn't a woman who blushed.

Leaning forward, she whispered, "If I start to fan myself, you put a stop to it, do you hear me? And do not turn your head to look."

Was it Jack?

As Cathe involuntarily turned her head, Celia hissed again. "I said do not look."

She jerked back to front and center. "What?"

"It's him," Celia murmured, her eyes still wide. "The man."

As if Cathe was supposed to understand. "What man?"

"The silver fox. The one who took our pictures at the Fisherman's Bastion. The sexy man who made me almost faint with desire."

Cathe wanted to laugh at Celia's drama, but she knew exactly who it was. The sexy hunk. But not as sexy and hunky as Jack. "Is he with anyone? Like a wife?"

Celia said softly, minus the hiss this time, "He's alone."

"Should we invite him to sit with us?"

Celia looked at her with stifled indignation. "You're kidding, right? I'm playing hard to get." But she gave Cathe a blow-by-blow. "He's ordering a drink at the bar. Now he's looking around the lounge."

Then she gasped. "He's coming over here."

The silver fox stopped at their table. "Don't I know you from somewhere?" He chuckled unselfconsciously, obviously remembering all along. "Fisherman's Bastion. Two lovely ladies who needed their pictures taken."

With Celia strangely tongue-tied, Cathe answered for them both. "You took our pictures for us. And imagine that, we're on the same cruise." Not an ounce of sarcasm dripped from the words. Most of the people at the hotel the last two nights were on the cruise.

He was gorgeous, more pepper than salt in his hair, aquiline features like an Italian movie star. His accent, though, was all-American. "Let me introduce myself. My name is Gray Ellison. May I join you ladies?"

"Of course, have a seat. I'm Cathe Girard and this is my sister, Celia Winters," she said graciously.

Because Celia looked like she might actually faint.

7

"They were two very nice young ladies." Rupert sat in his walker while Jack unpacked.

They'd booked a veranda suite, with handicapped facilities in the bathroom and grab bars on the walls. A regular cabin would have been too small for Dad to maneuver around. The crew had made up the bedroom with two single beds, and they had a living room where they could sit if the veranda grew too cold.

"Who?" Jack played it nonchalantly.

His father harrumphed, a rumble rising from his belly. "Don't be coy with me, son. You know who I'm talking about."

"I wouldn't exactly call them *young* ladies. At least not at my age."

"I'm eighty-five. You all look young to me."

Jack had to laugh. His father had always been a character, something one would never suspect of a Berkeley philosophy professor. That description made him think of a crotchety old geezer. His father was anything but.

But he had to nip this in the bud. "Don't start match-making for me."

"Who says I'm matchmaking?" Dad shrugged as if he were entirely innocent.

Jack stared him down until his father finally added, "I'm not matchmaking. I'm just suggesting that you spend too much time with your old man, and you need friends your own age. You were your mother's part-time caretaker while she was ill, even though you were working at the same time. And that bitch left you five years ago, so I think it's time you got out and had some fun." His father always had a way of putting things succinctly.

"She wasn't a bitch, Dad."

He and Tina simply weren't compatible. He'd stayed for the girls, though he now knew that living with parents who no longer loved each other—who didn't even like each other —wasn't any better for kids than having to switch between two households every other week. He was never sure why Tina stayed as long as she did. Maybe she'd found nothing better, at least as far as the money went. He'd given her a decent settlement, and she'd latched onto a new man only a month later. Maybe he'd been waiting in the wings. Jack couldn't say and didn't care.

"You know what they say about horses. If you get thrown off, you have to get right back in the saddle."

Jack sagged onto the bed, chuckling. "I'm not a horse."

His father shook his finger at him. "But you've been thrown and you need to get back out there and start riding again." He grinned. "No pun intended."

Jack sobered. "I'm not interested in marriage. I'm not even interested in dating. I'm happy with my life now. I have no desire to get back in that particular saddle."

His father's expression softened, his eyes melting into a

light gray, but that might have been his cataracts. "Not every woman is like Tina."

"I know. But I'm not willing to try right now." And maybe never.

His marriage to Tina had been volatile almost from the beginning. If Fiona, their firstborn daughter, hadn't come a year after the wedding, and Hailey only a year later, the marriage probably wouldn't have lasted. He'd been so tired of the fights, the low-key arguments, the angry silences that went on for days, the times Tina would tell the children to ask their father to do something instead of speaking to him herself. It demoralized him, ate away at his psyche, even his soul. He never wanted to go back to that. Though he knew his father was right, that not all women were like Tina and not all marriages were like theirs, he wasn't ready to put himself out there.

"But what about sex?" his father asked in almost a wail.

Jack laughed again. "I'm not discussing my sex life with you." He held his hand up in the universal stop sign.

But that never stopped his father. "You're fifty-eight years old and I'm eighty-five. We're both old enough to talk about sex."

Jack leaned back on his hands and raised his eyes to the ceiling. "One is never old enough to talk about his sex life with his parent."

"A man has needs," Dad insisted. "Even I have needs."

Jack almost put his fingers in his ears. The thought made him smile. "Then let's find *you* a lovely lady."

His father waved his hand. "I haven't seen anyone old enough on this boat."

"Don't you want someone younger? So she can fulfill your needs?"

His father waggled his eyebrows lasciviously. It was the

scariest thing Jack had ever seen. "Oh, you'd be surprised what old ladies can do."

This time Jack put his fingers in his ears and sang, "Lalala," as he laughed inwardly at himself.

He could see his father laughing and saw him mouth, "I just want you to be happy."

Jack dropped his hands. "I'm happy the way I am for right now." When his father opened his mouth again, he held up his hand, effectively stopping Dad. "I'm not saying that'll last forever. I'm just saying that for right now, I'm satisfied with the life I have."

"But you're living with your old man like you're fresh out of college."

"I'm living with you, first, because Mom got sick, and now, because you need a little help."

Jack was his father's caregiver, just as he'd been his mother's carer when she'd fallen ill. He'd had helpers in, of course, while Mom was ill, and towards the end, hospice workers came daily. Mom didn't want to die in a hospital. And now he had a male caregiver come in every day to help his father bathe and dress and check on him. Knowing his father was being taken care of was the only way he could go to work. Dad could get around well enough on his own as long as he used his walker. He didn't have dementia, but his bones were brittle and weak from arthritis, and he'd had a couple of falls. But Jack was home religiously by six o'clock every night.

They both knew Dad would eventually need twenty-four-hour care, but that time hadn't come yet.

"I love you, son. But I'm afraid that when I'm gone, you'll be all alone. I can't abide that."

"Dad, if I ever meet the right woman, I promise I won't turn her away."

"What if you've met the right woman today?"

Jack wondered if he meant Celia, the talkative one. Or Cathe, the one with hidden depths.

HAVING SHIFTED TO GET A BETTER VIEW OF THE LOUNGE'S entry, Cathe saw Jack the moment he entered.

She felt his eyes on her, then shifting immediately to the man beside her.

Did she even know him well enough to say that was a slight tightening of his mouth?

Of course she didn't. And she was well aware that Gray Ellison had seated himself beside her so it was easier to look at Celia. The man seemed riveted by her conversation, at least after Celia finally found her voice.

Cathe listened politely as Gray talked of his day. "I struck out on my own, walking the Margaret Bridge." He pointed north along the river. "I went around Margaret Island. It's in the middle of the river, a pretty cool place with old medieval ruins, a monastery and a convent. The water tower had some fantastic views. And the gardens were awesome, a rose garden, even a Japanese garden. It was worth the walk."

Celia jumped in. "Hopefully we'll see that tomorrow on the bus tour." The ship didn't sail until tomorrow evening, and they had another full day in Budapest.

But Cathe had a hard time caring about Margaret Island. She raised her hand, waving at Jack and his father and motioning them over. "Please, sit with us," she said when Rupert headed straight to them.

So what if she was embarrassing herself with her eager-ness? She didn't even mind if Celia gave her a wild-eyed look. Maybe she'd be glad Cathe had taken the initiative.

"We'd be happy to." Rupert wheeled his walker around, plunking himself down onto its seat.

Jack took the chair next to Celia, throwing Cathe off balance. He seemed so far away, and they'd have to talk over Celia and Gray. But then she could look straight at him without having to turn.

Celia made the introductions. "This is Gray Ellison. He's just joined us." She pointed from Jack to his father. "And this is Jack and Rupert Kelly." The men shook hands. Then she turned back to Gray. "They were on the tour with us today. Did I tell you we made goulash?"

Gray gave her a cheeky smile. "Hungarian goulash or Czech goulash?"

That delighted Celia whose musical laugh floated over them all. "It was Hungarian, the soupy kind. But it was still good. And the crusty bread and the wine were delicious." She put her hands to her heart and made yummy sounds.

"It was all good," Jack said. "We enjoyed it, didn't we, Dad?"

Rupert had to add, "I stirred all the ingredients, the meat, the vegetables. So technically, even though these folks helped —" He waved a hand over them like they were peasants and he was royalty. "—I actually made the goulash."

Everyone laughed, even Jack, as if he didn't mind that Rupert wanted the limelight.

Cathe liked that about him. Younger people should let old people take the limelight. They deserved it for having lived through so much. Being old wasn't for sissies, as her mother used to say, even if she hadn't been much older than Cathe was now.

The waiter popped over to take their drink orders, Jack having a rum and coke and his father a beer.

Then Celia took over. "Gray was telling us that he didn't take any of the tours today."

Gray, with a swift look at Rupert's walker, said, "I did a lot of walking, but the buses are great. You get to see so much more. I just figured that since we were going to be on a boat for seven days, I'd get my walking in now."

Rupert was unoffended. "They have a walking loop up on the top deck. I plan to take my walker up there during downtimes and do several laps."

Jack smiled, maybe with pride. "Dad's a great walker. He's out there doing at least a mile a day."

As their drinks arrived, Rupert nodded his head, his jowls jiggling. "As long as it's flat. I'm not so good on hills. Which was why I didn't want to traipse down to the river when we were on Buda Hill."

"There are some pretty steep hills around here." Cathe didn't mention the elevator or the funicular that went down the hill. "Celia and I were exhausted yesterday after walking up to the Liberty Statue on Gellért Hill." She smiled wickedly at her sister. "I even fell asleep while Celia was talking to me over a coffee and strudel at a little café near Matthias Church."

Wagging his finger, Rupert said. "I thought I saw you there."

Cathe laughed. "I hope you didn't see me falling asleep."

Celia couldn't seem to resist adding, "I swear she was drooling."

They all laughed, and while sometimes she wasn't sure if Celia was making fun of her, she didn't take offense. Her sister was adept at making conversation.

Jack sat back in his chair. "So where did you walk today, Gray?"

She couldn't help admiring the way Jack's shirt stretched over his muscled chest. And even more, she didn't mind that he caught her looking.

It wasn't flirting. It didn't need to lead anywhere. It was just appreciation.

"As I was telling the ladies," Gray said. "I walked over to Margaret Island."

"Tomorrow," Rupert got in on the conversation, "we're on the panoramic bus tour in the morning so hopefully we'll see a lot. In the afternoon, we visit the thermal baths. I've heard they're relaxing. And good for my arthritis too."

Celia clapped her hands. "That's our afternoon tour as well."

"I signed up for that." Gray looked at Celia, a slow burn lighting up his eyes.

"Then we're all going." Rupert's features brightened with excitement.

As they'd been talking, the lounge filled up. It wasn't long before their cruise director stood at the front, introducing himself as Mario, his accent smooth and lyrical. "I want to welcome you all. I'd like to give you some brief instructions and let you know that tomorrow night we'll have our welcome reception here in the lounge, where you'll meet our captain and all our department heads. And every evening, also here in the lounge, I'll give a brief talk about the following day's excursions."

Cathe glanced at Celia, whose gaze was fixed on Gray. It certainly didn't look like she needed the captain, or even the cruise director. Though Mario was handsome, with silver hair and an inviting smile.

"But for now," Mario went on, "I will tell you about tomorrow's roster of events." He went through a slideshow of all the things they could do, including the thermal baths, which looked astounding. He detailed meal times and noted that all the tours allowed them to eat on the boat every day if they chose. "We will depart at nine o'clock tomorrow night, and you're free to go up on deck and watch the sailing. There will be plenty of photo ops for you." Then he added, "But tonight we will have our fire drill. Before dinner, please go to your rooms and collect your life preservers which are under the bed, then proceed to the main deck where we will make our head-count. You should know that the river is not terribly deep, especially since we have not had a lot of rain. Should the worst happen, you will all be fine." He looked at Rupert and his walker. "For any of you with disabilities, please ask for help." He clapped his hands. "And then you shall join us for dinner."

Turning in his seat, Rupert raised his hand. "So we won't have to get off the boat and be bussed anywhere because the rivers are too low?"

Mario smiled, his features broad and attractive. "Not on this trip. We have had a couple of very good rainstorms in the last week, so we will all be fine. Thank you for asking, sir."

He bowed, and everyone made their way to their cabins for the life preservers.

As they filed out, Rupert asked, "Would you ladies have dinner with us tonight?"

"We'd love to," Celia said, then looked at Gray. "I hope you'll join us."

He nodded. "It will be my pleasure."

As they separated for their cabins, Cathe noticed Rupert, Jack, and Gray heading to the hallway past the stairs, which meant they all had veranda staterooms. While she and Celia headed down the stairs to their aquarium room with only a window at the top.

"He's to die for," Celia whispered. "I put dibs on Gray."

Cathe smiled. "You can have dibs."

She didn't say she was very glad her dibs were already on Jack. Not that she intended doing anything outrageous, not even flirting. Nothing more than looking.

But he was hers.

THEY WERE TWO EXQUISITE WOMEN.

Gray didn't add those damning words, *for their age*. At sixty-five, he appreciated a mature woman from top to bottom.

He often thought that was his mistake, marrying a woman fifteen years younger than him. He'd waited a long time to meet Eva, had put her through law school. He wasn't even threatened when she began making more money than he did because he loved his job as counsel at a nonprofit organization.

But something happened when he hit sixty and she was only forty-five. It was as if she suddenly saw what her life could be like ten or fifteen years from now, when she was a vital woman. And he was an old man.

What she didn't get was that he was still vital even now.

Instead of telling him she had an issue, she began an affair, undoubtedly more than one over the next five years, until she found the perfect sucker. And *then* she wanted the divorce.

They didn't have kids, and they'd had only possessions to fight over in the divorce. But he damn well refused to give her the cruise tickets for the anniversary trip he'd planned.

Now he was a free agent, on a cruise all by himself, with the ability to flirt with whomever he wished. And a luxurious suite to which he could invite an attractive woman.

And screw Eva.

8

Rupert and Jack made their way to the main deck, their lifejackets securely fastened, to find the lounge filled with orange-clad travelers.

"Let's go out on the terrace." Rupert muscled his walker through the throng. "Hopefully, I'll have more room with this." He pointed disdainfully at the contraption. Dad didn't like the walker, but he'd had a couple of falls and agreed it made him safer. And he moved faster.

The terrace doors opened, letting in the sun and the river air. They could eat lunch out here, or sit on lounge chairs at the front to view the scenery. The ship sat just before the Elizabeth Bridge, with Buda Castle on the hill and the tower of Matthias Church beyond it. On the shore opposite their dock lay Gellért Hill and the Liberty Statue. Cathe had said they'd hiked to the top, and it was one heck of a climb. Dad would never have made it.

He looked for Cathe and Celia, but it was impossible to see them in the throng of orange-clad passengers.

An elderly woman's raspy voice rang out among the assembled passengers. "I don't see why I should have to put it on. We're not sinking, and it'll ruin my hair," she grumbled, patting her permed curls. She looked to be around Dad's age.

"Agnes, dear, you need to put on the life preserver because it's a drill." A pretty brunette with the patience of a saint smiled down at the woman. Maybe her daughter, her age was right, fifty or so if the few strands of gray indicated anything.

"For once, Agnes—" A sandy-haired man with gray at his temples attempted to force the life jacket over her head. "—just do as you're told." His voice was pleasant but his tone implacable. Maybe he was the son, and the woman was his wife.

"I'm old," Agnes groused. "And this thing will constrict my airways. I won't be able to breathe."

The younger woman smiled. And her husband, or whoever he was, laughed outright. "If you don't do it, I'll have Barbara stuff you into it."

Jack noticed her then, a nondescript woman in her forties standing in the background, her hair pulled back in a bun. In a soft voice accompanied by a gentle smile, she said, "Oh, Agnes, you do not want me doing it."

The old woman scowled, but a hint of terror glittered in her eyes.

Then Jack's dad stepped forward. "Dear lady, I've got mine on." He tapped the orange vest. "And as you can see, it's not constricting at all." He breathed in deeply, his chest puffed up. "And it'll only be for a little while."

The elderly lady looked at him. "But what if we sink? He said it's not deep, but I'm very short."

Dad said, his tone as serious as a philosophy professor, "I'm ninety-nine percent sure we won't sink."

The lady looked him up and down. She was a tiny thing, even shorter than Dad. "What about the other one percent?"

With a grave set to his mouth, Dad answered, "Then, dear lady, I'll be right beside you, holding onto you. But I doubt I can hold you up if you aren't wearing your life vest. In fact, you'd probably drag us both down, then we'll drown. And we don't want that."

The old lady harrumphed, but she let her younger male companion slip the life jacket over her head.

"Watch out for my hair," she squealed. Once the life vest was in place and tied, the little lady fluffed her hair. "There, it's perfect."

"It most certainly is." His dad smiled.

The man, looking at Dad, mouthed, "Thank you."

"My name is Rupert Kelly. And you're obviously Agnes. It's so good to meet you." He pointed behind. "My son, Jack."

She tittered like a bird. "It's so nice to meet you. Did you say your name was Egbert? And this one?" She pointed at Jack.

His dad said again, putting a hand to his chest, "I'm Rupert, and this is my son, Jack."

The lady beamed. "It's so nice to meet friendly faces." She turned then, pointed at the pretty woman, but she never got as far as saying her name.

"I'm Rose Delaney. And this is my husband, Declan." She smiled sweetly, as if the word delighted her.

Declan Delaney stuck out his hand. "Good to meet you. I'm Agnes's godson. And here we have Barbara, Agnes's friend."

There was something in the way he stressed the word *friend*, and Jack decided she was the old lady's caregiver, something no one wanted to say aloud. At least not in front of Agnes.

Agnes tittered again. "We're on their honeymoon trip."

Rose laughed. "We got married a month ago. And we couldn't leave Agnes behind. She's always wanted to do a cruise."

The old lady looked at her, eyes as wide as they could get. "Have I?" she asked as if it was news to her.

"Yes, dear, you have."

"Congratulations," Jack offered, and Dad echoed him.

Crewmembers made their way through the passengers, taking down room numbers and names, checking everyone off a list.

Jack asked the obvious question. "Where are you all from?"

"San Jose." Declan supplied. "It's south of San Francisco."

"Now, isn't that amazing?" Dad's white eyebrows shot to his hairline. "We're from Oakland. The Oakland Hills."

"Oh my goodness." Agnes clapped her hands. "What a coincidence." And then she looked at Declan, asking softly, "Where's Oakland?"

He smiled indulgently. "The East Bay."

"Oh yes, now I remember." Though she obviously didn't. Agnes was delightful. But Jack was thankful his father wasn't losing his memory.

Then, as if suddenly remembering the question from minutes ago, she said, "It wasn't a cruise I wanted to go on. It was to see the little town where they filmed *The Quiet Man*."

"Right. In Ireland. And we went there. Remember?" Rose asked.

Agnes sputtered a moment before saying, "Of course I remember. It was the trip of a lifetime."

A bell rang then, and Mario came on the PA. "Thank you all for participating in our drill. Everything went smoothly, and I am ninety-nine percent sure we will never have to use our life vests."

Agnes elbowed Declan. "You see, only ninety-nine percent. What about the other one percent?"

Rose merely smiled. "Rupert said he'd be there to hold you up. As long as you're wearing your life jacket."

"You may return to your staterooms," the cruise director continued, "and remove your life vests, and when you are done, the dining room will be open for your pleasure."

Dad jumped in then. "You must have dinner with us. Please. I won't take no for an answer."

Jack had to say, "Don't you remember we invited Cathe and Celia to sit with us?" He hadn't seen the sisters anywhere in the packed lounge.

His father waved him off. "I'm sure they have tables big enough for all of us."

Declan Delaney politely accepted. "We'd love to join you."

THEY'D ENDED UP WITH EIGHT AT THE DINNER TABLE. Celia had envisioned something more intimate, just the five of them, where she would let Cathe dominate Rupert and Jack while she worked her magic on Gray.

But it wasn't to be. Somehow, Rupert had found a family in the lounge while practicing the fire drill.

Still, Celia managed the only seating arrangement she cared about, making sure Gray sat next to her. It worked perfectly since one of the interlopers, Declan, took the head of the table.

She stifled the urge to laugh. Because, dear Lord, she sounded like a bridesmaid at a wedding who wanted to make sure she got the best man.

Jack, across the table, was conveniently seated with Cathe on his right. "Agnes?" he asked the elderly woman. "Your friend Barbara isn't joining us?"

Agnes, who was godmother or something to Declan, said cheerily, "Oh, she's having dinner in the room. She has to put up with me day in and day out." She put a hand to her chest and tittered. "I might look small, but I'm quite a handful. And she needed a break."

Seated next to the little lady, Rupert patted her hand. "I'm sure you're a pleasure to work for."

Rose, the newlywed who was on her honeymoon with an old lady in tow, smiled fondly. "I can assure you that Agnes is a delight to spend time with."

Declan folded her hand in his, looking at her all starry-eyed. "Rose was Agnes's caregiver. That's how we met."

Agnes clapped her hands with delight. "It's such a romantic tale. Like *Beauty and the Beast*."

With his movie-star features, Celia certainly wouldn't call Declan a beast in any way, shape, or form. His short blondish hair, with a smattering of distinguished gray at his temples, was the kind a woman would want to run her fingers through.

His bride Rose was a lovely woman who could pass for the beauty in *Beauty and the Beast*. Probably a bit younger than Cathe, she'd kept herself trim.

They'd done the obligatory introductions before their two waiters arrived. Jahz and Mihai would serve this section the entire cruise, and Agnes made them bend down to pinch their cheeks as if they were boys. They took it gracefully, even loving the attention, calling themselves brothers, though they looked nothing alike. Mihai was Slovakian, and Jahz was Filipino. Perhaps they were just brothers in spirit, especially with the long days they worked together, serving in the dining room for all three meals.

The boys, as Agnes called them, returned soon with their drinks, cocktails for the men, champagne for the ladies, Agnes included. "You don't mind if I get a little tipsy?" No one did.

Declan raised his glass as if he were the host of the evening. "It's a delight to meet all of you. And what a coincidence that we all live in the Bay Area. Here's to a fabulous cruise and making new friends."

They all raised their glasses, clinked with those nearest to them. Celia was happy to see that Jack's gaze lingered on Cathe.

"I'm the odd man out, being from Miami," Gray said when all the toasting was done. "But we've got great golfing."

Which probably meant he was retired. The bonus was that he lived on the other side of the country. Absolutely perfect for an onboard fling. She wouldn't have to worry about seeing him again. But they could have a lot of fun between now and the end of the cruise.

Cathe leaned around Jack to ask Rose, "So you only just got married a month ago? And this is your honeymoon trip?"

Agnes was a talker and didn't even let the couple answer. "I told them they couldn't bring an old lady on their honeymoon. It just isn't done. But they have their own suite. And I have a suite with... my friend?" She ended on a question as if she couldn't remember her caregiver's name.

Rose rescued her. "Barbara is a godsend. And despite all the things Agnes says, they adore each other. We simply couldn't leave Agnes behind. She loves to travel. Don't you, Agnes?" She looked at the tiny woman, who'd had Jahz bring a pillow for her to sit on.

Agnes piped up loudly. "I do, I do. And this boat is lovely. I hope the food is good."

Jahz and Mihai returned then with their salads and soups, remembering exactly who'd ordered what.

Mihai ground pepper on Celia's salad, then moved around the table. Cathe had the fisherman's soup called *Halászlé* off the regional menu, and Celia noticed Jack had ordered it as well. As they each took spoonfuls, they exchanged comments on the taste, creating their own world for a moment. Good. Very good. It wasn't flirting, but it was something.

Then Celia made her move, speaking in a softer voice just to Gray. "Tell me more about Miami. Is it terribly humid?"

"It's gorgeous in the winter, shirts and shorts all the time. But yeah, hot and humid in the summer. This was my first summer there. It took getting used to."

"Where did you move from?"

"Denver."

"Wow. That's a big change. From snow in the winter to sunshine all the time."

"I wanted a complete change from everything." He shrugged, looking down at his shrimp cocktail, as if he'd rather not remember all the things he'd left behind.

And Celia didn't need to know his baggage. She had enough of her own.

"So you wanted a change and retired to Miami."

"Not exactly retire." He shook his head. "I'm a lawyer. I do a lot of my work online or on the phone or on video chats. Though occasionally I fly out to visit clients. Especially in the beginning, when I need to learn their stories."

"Fascinating. You don't go to court all the time?" She had a knack for getting people to talk about themselves. And she wanted Gray to talk. His voice was like mellow whiskey drizzled on her tongue.

And she wanted more of it.

He speared a shrimp. "It's more about the research, talking with clients, going over documents. I let other people go into court." Then he turned the questions back on her. "And what you do with your time?"

She smiled, happy with how she spent her days. "I arrange charity fundraisers, mostly for a nonprofit organization benefiting homeless shelters for women, including unwed mothers and battered women. We help them get back on their feet and into the workforce, providing interview clothing and training on how to present themselves."

"That's very admirable."

Her smile felt as if it grew. "Not really. I love event planning. It's my favorite thing in the world. I get to help other women in bad situations while doing something I love."

"The best of both worlds." He gave her a look then. She wasn't sure what it meant. Until he said, "I'm sorry you came out of a bad situation."

He surprised her by picking up on that. Then she remembered her use of the word *other*, as if she had suffered the way those women had. Her ordeal was nothing in comparison.

"I'm divorced, but I didn't go through anything as bad as what many of these women have. It just... didn't work out." She wouldn't tell him her husband didn't find her desirable anymore. Or that he'd cheated.

He added, as if he needed her to know, "My marriage was the same. Good until it wasn't anymore."

She knew everything she needed to. He was divorced and unencumbered.

Exactly what she wanted.

9

"You've never seen *The Quiet Man*?" Agnes said with a round *O* of awe on her lips.

Cathe had liked her immediately. She might be a little dusty, as her mother would've said, but she had to be close to ninety. And she was delightful, always with a smile, always with a laugh.

Rupert, seated next to Agnes, said, "Of course I've seen *The Quiet Man*." He flourished a hand across the expanse of the table. "But I'm not sure about these youngsters."

Cathe had to jump in. "I've watched it. And loved it. John Wayne and Maureen O'Hara."

Agnes put her hands together and raised her head a notch, as if she were swooning. "It was the most romantic movie."

Keeping her voice extremely polite, Celia asked, "Didn't he drag her across a field by her hair?"

Agnes flicked her hand. "No woman deserves to be dragged by her hair. But he was proving a point, that her dowry didn't matter to him, only she did. It was the only way he could make her see the truth." Remarkably, the little lady remembered every detail of the movie.

Rose and Declan shared a look, then a smile, as if they'd already had this discussion with Agnes.

But Cathe had to agree that in today's cancel culture the movie would likely be banned. Yet she remembered the romanticism of John Wayne fighting for her. And Maureen needed that show of strength because until then she'd thought he was weak.

Agnes, however, didn't care about political correctness. "Right in the center of town, there was an amazing statue of him holding her in his arms. And we stayed in a real castle. They had a movie theater and played *The Quiet Man* for us. I saw it on the big screen again. They never show it on the big screen anymore." She rolled her eyes like a teenager, which she probably was when the movie came out.

Rose cupped Declan's hand in hers. "We stayed in Dublin, then toured the countryside. And there was a lovely dance at the castle on our last night."

Agnes snorted. "Then I almost ruined the entire trip."

Declan snorted, too, sounding almost like her. "You ruined nothing. As you can see, Rose and I found our happily ever after. Just like John Wayne and Maureen O'Hara."

"You know, they did several movies together. I wonder if they had an affair?" Agnes propped her elbow on the table, chin in hand. "Back then, we didn't talk about things like that. We only learned all the dirty details years and years later."

Beside Cathe, Jack chuckled, leaning close to murmur in her ear. "She's adorable. I'm in love."

Cathe laughed softly. "I'm in love with her too."

But what she liked best was Jack's smile, his warm breath against her hair, his eyes on her, his sexy male scent.

He jutted his chin at his father. "Dad's obviously smitten."

Cathe was happy, too, to see her sister engrossed in conversation with Gray, missing most of this little tête-à-tête with Jack. Good God, if she'd been paying attention, Celia might have given Cathe a thumbs-up or something equally embarrassing.

"Your father is such an open and gregarious guy. It must've been terribly hard on him to lose your mother."

Jack's smile faded for only a moment, then flared back. "They adored each other. It was hard watching her debilitation. But when someone's sick and in pain for so long, it's a relief when they finally let go and they're no longer in agony. After Mom died, I realized we'd both done all our grieving before we lost her. And afterward, we felt blessed that she was no longer suffering." He looked at her, his lapis blue eyes soft and understanding. "I don't know how your husband died. But I hope you found some sort of blessing in it."

She blinked, tears studding her eyelashes, then closed her eyes.

Jack covered her hand with his. "I'm sorry. That was callous of me."

She shook her head, eyes still closed. "It was very sudden. A heart attack two years ago. We had no idea anything was wrong. He was there and the next day he was gone. And it was so hard." She met his gentle gaze, his features soft with sympathy for her. "But for my parents, I felt like you did. Mom was so sick and Dad was so broken by it all. It was a relief for them both." She had to grit her teeth a moment, stopping the tears that threatened. "I tried to say the same thing about my husband. But we didn't even know he had a problem. I guess the blessing was that he enjoyed every moment of his life." The breath she took hurt her chest. "But it's still hard even though it was two years ago."

"I'm so sorry. I was insensitive."

She touched his arm. "It was very caring, in fact." She didn't tell him that Celia never let her fully grieve. She'd had to stifle it all. It was actually a relief to tell him how hard it had been. She glanced at Celia to make sure she wasn't listening, and thankfully, her sister was captivated by the handsome Gray.

"There were days when I couldn't get out of bed." Her voice came out low and soft, with a hint of the tears she felt. "I wandered around the house in my bathrobe. And there were all the estate issues to take care of. It's like you're grieving, but you've still got all that hanging over your head." She cut herself off, not wanting to go into a complete meltdown. "But my daughter was great. Sarah helped me with a lot of it. So did Celia."

He squeezed her hand. "I can never know how hard it was. I mean, you expect to lose your parents. But you don't expect to lose your husband so young."

She turned her hand over in his, gripping his fingers. "Every loss is terrible. It doesn't matter whether it's a parent or a spouse."

She didn't want to cry. Celia would see and have a fit. But she had to say, "And divorce is a big loss too. Sometimes it just wrecks you."

His answer was slow to come and soft when it did. "Yeah, it can. My wife and I didn't have a great marriage, obviously. Life was sort of hell for a long time. We stayed together for my girls." Just like Celia had stayed with Bart for the boys.

They might have let out all the secret feelings of grief and loss, but Jahz and Mihai sailed in with big smiles, whisking away their soup and salad plates and setting out the main course.

Jack looked at her salmon, juicy and pink. "I should have ordered that."

Laughing, because she had to or cry after that too emotional exchange, she held her hands over her plate. "Don't you dare try to steal it."

Jack ordered the chicken paprikash with the same noodles in sour cream she'd had last night, *spätzle*, she now knew.

His wink warmed her. "I'll give you by bite of my chicken paprikash if you give me a bite of your salmon."

Gosh, she liked this man. She felt comfortable with him. Which was probably why she'd spilled her guts over her fisherman's soup. "Deal." As everyone tucked into their meal, Cathe cut off a piece of salmon and slid it onto his plate. Jack dipped a forkful of chicken in the sauce and added it to her plate.

Only then did she feel Celia's gaze on her, a sassy thumbs-up glittering in her eyes.

Thank goodness she didn't follow it up with a gesture.

"WELL," CELIA SAID WITH A SUGGESTIVE TONE AND A wink. "You certainly had a good time with Jack tonight."

As hard as she tried, Cathe couldn't control the blush that rose to her cheeks. Turning away, she hid the color under the pretext of retrieving her pajamas.

Celia hip-bumped her, putting her off balance. And Cathe's voice didn't ring true. "It was nothing. I just happened to sit next to him at dinner."

"And sharing bites of food off each other's plates." Celia snorted a laugh.

Cathe tipped her head back and rolled her eyes. That was a huge mistake. Celia had eagle eyes.

Time to turn things around. "And I noticed you kicking up your heels with Gray on the dance floor." She shucked her blouse and bra, stepping into her pajama bottoms.

When she looked again, Celia was smiling. "The difference is I don't mind that you saw. And I hope it works on him. Because he's totally hot."

Cathe stifled a shiver. Sitting next to Jack in the lounge after dinner as they watched Celia and Gray dance to everything from Jim Croce's *Bad Bad Leroy Brown* to Elvis's *Hound Dog*, her skin had tingled with his closeness. Blondie, their pianist, a big Ukrainian with a shaved head, belted out song after song, the oldies they'd all loved when they were young.

Rose and Declan swayed in each other's arms the way a newly married couple should, though the music was too fast for slow dancing. Even Rupert and Agnes got out there, twirling their walkers around the floor. Drinking two champagne cocktails, Cathe had laughed with Jack. Though she wouldn't say she was drunk, she certainly wasn't feeling any pain. And she *was* feeling those tingles.

Even if she couldn't remember what she and Jack had laughed and talked about, she'd enjoyed every moment. It had been so long since she'd had the pleasure of a man's company.

Would Denny have wanted her to find another man?

Hands on Cathe's shoulders, Celia stopped her downward spiral. "I like seeing you smile. You don't have to sleep with him. Just have fun. Now I won't say anything else. I don't want you to feel self-conscious. Just know that I think it's great."

Cathe muttered a thank-you, but she knew Celia wouldn't stop. She might not say anything, but she'd flash those looks, winking, raising her eyebrows, a thumbs up.

She just had to get her sister off the topic. "Do you plan to sleep with Gray?"

Celia smiled, waggling those eyebrows she so loved to waggle, but at least it wasn't at Cathe's expense. "I don't know yet. We'll see how it goes. But he has a suite, and he's unattached." She clutched Cathe's arm, her eyes dancing. "Will you be mad if some night I don't come back to the room with you?"

"Of course not. I want you to enjoy yourself just as much

as you want me to have a good time. It's just that maybe our definition of good times is different. Can you just accept that?"

Celia looked at her for a long moment. "I can. As long as you promise to have fun."

"I'll try."

And her sister hugged her.

FIRST UP THE NEXT MORNING WAS A PANORAMIC TOUR OF Budapest.

It was no surprise to Celia that Jack and Rupert, as well as Rose, Declan, and Agnes were waiting for the bus. There was plenty of handicapped seating.

Gray stood beside her. "I'm not feeling like a bus ride today. I'd prefer to walk."

Suddenly torn, Celia sighed as he stepped back to let others get on. Cathe was taking the tour. Yet more than anything, Celia didn't want to. What came out of her mouth wasn't even a question. She didn't want him to say no. "I'll come with you."

Then she turned to Cathe. "Do you mind?" She should have asked Cathe first, but she didn't want Gray to get away. Besides, this would give Cathe time with Jack without her sister hanging over her and making faces.

She waited for Cathe's smile to falter, but her sister looked from her to Gray. And grinned. "I'll be fine. We made so many new friends at the dinner table last night, and I'll hang with them."

Celia could have squealed her delight like a teenager.

Stepping to Gray's side, she was giddy but still maintained control. "Where do you want to start?"

"Here on the Pest side. We've both walked Buda Hill." He

obviously knew she was the woman waving at him as he stood by the eagle near the castle. "And I'd like to check out the Parliament Building and St. Stephen's Cathedral."

He held up his guidebook, pointing to a few other places while she leaned close to look at the map, his aftershave tantalizing her. "You've certainly done your planning."

He smiled, his eyes deepening to dark chocolate. "Actually, I didn't sign up for any of the bus tours. I might not see as many things by walking, but I get to explore, which you can't do on the bus." He smiled, and it was so deliciously sexy that everything inside her seemed to melt. "And I'd been hoping you'd want to go with me."

Her heart pitter-pattered like that teenage girl she'd thought of. "Then I'm so glad I asked to come along."

He popped his sunglasses on the bridge of nose. "Let's head to the Church of the Blessed Virgin Mary."

"What a grand name."

Smiling, he took off toward the bridge. His stride didn't make her breathless. It was just his proximity.

"It was built in the Middle Ages."

As they arrived at the bottom of Elizabeth Bridge, the church's two towers rose above the trees surrounding the square. "Wow, it's in great shape."

"It's been restored a few times. It was even used as a mosque when the Ottomans invaded."

"Are you a history buff?"

He shrugged. "I just like to read about places I visit."

Inside, a chandelier hung over the central aisle tiled in marble, and a painting of the Virgin Mary with the disciples and Jesus covered the wall behind the altar. They took the elevator up the tower, and Celia snapped pictures of the river view and Buda Castle. Cathe would have glared if she didn't take at least a few photos.

Outside again, the sun was warm on her face. The

weather was perfect, not too hot. Sometimes, even in September, the Bay Area could see temperatures close to a hundred.

"Now where, oh leader?" She looked up at him, smiling, almost able to see his eyes behind his sunglasses.

"The promenade along the river, heading toward the Parliament Building. It's about a mile, maybe a little farther."

She pointed to her feet. "I've got my good walking shoes on."

The promenade ran along the river beside the tram tracks, with nearby restaurants and buildings of old architecture. Celia laughed when she realized the girl sitting on the edge of a large flower planter playing ball with her dog was actually a statue.

"I absolutely need a picture of that." She shooed Gray over to stand next to the bronze girl.

They found another bronze sculpture, a boy sitting on the tram railing, a long jester's cap on his head. From afar, she thought he was real. This time Gray took her picture with the statue. Monuments stood all around as they walked, the promenade peopled with other tourists snapping photos.

And all the while, they talked, about her event planning, about her boys, about his job, that he actually worked for a nonprofit helping people wrongfully imprisoned. "It can take years," he told her. "And, regretfully, we don't always win. But when we actually free someone, it's the best feeling in the world."

"My God, that's such a fabulous thing to do." It was heroic. She wanted to ask him if he ever got out to San Francisco to work on a case. But that would be too high school, almost like begging to see him again.

"No more admirable than the work you do."

"But I only do it part time, when there's an actual event. It's not a real job like yours."

"And you don't get paid for all your work?"

She shook her head. "Just expenses. I don't want to take money away from the good work this charity does. I believe in helping women in trouble."

"See. That's admirable." Then, before she got embarrassed, she asked, "So you're our goalkeeper now?"

He let out a laugh that delighted her. She wanted a man who wasn't afraid to laugh, to let himself go. She hoped it meant Gray could let himself go in other ways as well.

Scaffolding still covered the Chain Bridge and its famous lions, and the Four Seasons Hotel stood across the park. They were more than halfway to the Parliament Building when he asked, "So tell me about your divorce. Was it ugly?"

A chill shimmied down her spine. Because it *was* ugly. That had been her doing. She'd been so angry. But she didn't want to admit that to Gray, and she skirted the truth. "It wasn't the friendliest. But I had a fabulous divorce attorney. She believed in me, and she understood my feelings. Unfortunately, she died a little while ago. She was such a good person. So sad about that. I'm also sad she won't be able to help other people like me."

"Sounds like she was a friend."

"Carol was a friend to all her clients. But she didn't represent only women. She represented whoever she thought was the underdog, even downtrodden husbands with domineering wives."

Gray simply grunted, and for many long steps, he said nothing.

Finally, after she swore she'd said something terribly wrong, he spoke in a low voice she had to strain to hear over the happy tourists they passed. "I was the underdog."

Her step faltered. "No way."

He sighed. "Maybe I still am." He waved a hand as if the words were blasé, but the lines of his face tensed. "Nonprofit lawyers don't make a lot of money. And my wife was a lawyer for a large firm. She was the breadwinner."

She didn't say anything, letting him tell the story at his own pace.

"She was younger, and I worked at a prestigious firm to help her through university and law school. When she got out, she said she'd pay me back, because she knew I was tired of being a corporate lawyer. I looked for the job I wanted. And she got the job she wanted. It was great, but I thought we'd have kids. I should have realized that wasn't part of her partner track. But, well, life, it was okay."

He surprised her by stammering through his words at the end, something she wouldn't expect of him. But she realized his story had scarred him.

"I suspected she might be having affairs. Long-term ones. When she went away on business trips or overnight stays in the city while we lived in the suburbs, I should have seen she wasn't a suburban woman. I never caught her. I even told myself I was wrong." A long exhale sighed out of him. "But I sensed it."

She couldn't help herself. "I am so sorry. That must have been awful."

"Any more awful than your marriage?"

She gave him the truth. "I'm not sure. My husband had an affair at the end, and I think that was the only one. But he didn't touch me at all during the last five years of our marriage."

He stopped then, right in the middle of the pathway, with people skirting around them, and cupped her cheek. "He was an idiot."

His hand warm against her skin, she whispered, "And your wife was an imbecile."

10

Gray took her hand in his, and they walked again, the Parliament Building right ahead. Celia wanted to cry as she remembered the feel of his palm on her face and his words in her ear, in her mind.

Cathe had always said the same, but it was different coming from a man. Different coming from Gray.

But she couldn't let his understanding and empathy get to her, couldn't let her heart turn topsy-turvy. She wanted to sleep with this man. But that was all. She'd didn't want to feel anything for him other than friendship.

Swinging their arms, she said, "I feel like I'm only hearing part of the story. What happened? I mean, you're divorced."

He laughed, soft and sorrowful. "In the end, she divorced me. She was having an affair with a senior partner at her law firm. It had been going on for years, just as I suspected." He pressed her hand, almost like it was involuntary. Then he added, "I was a cuckold. The pathetic husband who let his wife do whatever she wanted, the laughingstock of her firm. They all must've known."

She laced her fingers between his. "I remember talking with friends, pretending my questions were hypothetical, that I'd heard it from a friend none of them knew." She shook her head and rolled her eyes at herself. "I said this woman's husband hadn't had sex with her for five years and asked what should she do about it." She wanted to squeeze her eyes tight shut even now at the painful memory. "One of them said my friend had to be lying. Because no woman on earth would live for five years with a man who refused to have sex with her. And another one said she needed psychiatric help if she continued to take abuse like that. They all unanimously agreed that my 'friend—'" She air-quoted. "—had to dump the guy immediately." She leaned forward to see his face. "You see, I was a laughingstock too." She smiled. At least she thought it was a smile. It felt like a smile. But it could have been a grimace.

"Is that when you divorced him?"

She wanted to groan, but held it in. "No. I didn't do that until I found out about the affair and I was so angry that I kept looking at the knives in the drawer and wondering if they were sharp enough."

He guffawed, real and heartfelt, as if he understood her emotions. "So you left before you killed him."

"Yes. I made the right choice. I wouldn't have looked good in *Orange is the New Black*."

He was still chuckling as he said, "Then you'll love the end of my story. With that team of high-powered lawyers at her firm, you'd think she'd be able to take me—" He stabbed a thumb at his chest. "—for everything I was worth, even if it wasn't much. But oddly enough, one of her colleagues called me and gave me the name of a very good divorce attorney. The colleague was a woman too. I guess she felt sorry for me while none of the men did."

"They were probably afraid of ending up just like you."

She was glad he smiled. "And did you take her for all she was worth since she made more money?"

His grin was as wide as his handsome face. "I shouldn't be gleeful. I probably shouldn't even admit that she has to pay me alimony, in addition to giving me half our investment portfolio." The broad smile remained on his face. "I also got the house, which I promptly sold, intending to move to Florida. And then there was this trip." He paused for effect. "She wanted the tickets for the cruise even though I'd paid for it as an anniversary gift, and of course, that meant she wanted to take her lover along. Her lawyer claimed I wouldn't need a suite, unless, of course, I wanted to admit I was having an affair and planned to take another woman in my wife's place." His laugh sounded hollow. "You should've seen her face when she suddenly thought I'd been playing around on her. Talk about someone's jaw dropping. My lawyer simply said that since I'd paid for the tickets, they were mine, and I could do whatever I wished with them." He looked at her. "There was a moment when I planned to cancel the trip, even though I'd have lost most of the money by then. But I realized the better way to pay her back was to go alone and enjoy the hell out of myself."

He pulled her close, hands entwined, bodies brushing. "And I have to say I'm having the time of my life."

Then, almost in the shadow of the Hungarian Parliament Building, he framed her face in his hands and kissed her.

It was a kiss to steal her breath, a kiss to make her knees weak, a kiss to liquefy her bones. A kiss to make her lean into him and grab his shirt in her fists to steady herself.

He finally let go, his hands sliding down her neck to her shoulders, holding her as he gazed into her eyes. "Thank you. That was the best kiss I've had in years."

He made her feel sexy and wanted, desired and adored. She wanted to beg him to kiss her again.

And he deserved the absolute truth. "That was the best kiss of my entire life."

They each laughed as if neither had meant it, yet both knowing they had, every word.

He held her close, his arm wrapped across her shoulders as they walked around the Parliament Building, with its red dome and arched columns and beautiful gardens.

But that kiss made her forget everything, Budapest, the amazing architecture, the Danube, the warm sun on her skin. There was just this man, that kiss, and his arm around her as they walked.

She should have taken pictures, but she didn't care if Cathe rolled her eyes when they got back. All she cared about was this moment. And Gray.

Once he'd gotten his fill of the monument, he tugged her toward the heart of the city. "Let's head over to Saint Stephen's Cathedral. It's supposed to be beautiful."

She'd follow him anywhere. "That would be lovely."

He opened a map app on his phone, and they zigzagged along cobblestone streets, many of them wide enough for only one car. Then the buildings opened up to a vista of the church, the grand entrance, the stained glass windows, the spires rising above the city. And to the crowds surrounding it. The plaza around the church was cordoned off and tours cancelled for the day, a special event planned. A podium and microphone sat before rows of chairs, the ones up front white, the ones farther back all in black.

"Maybe it's a special outdoor mass," she said.

"The front must be reserved for important dignitaries." Gray pointed at the white chairs. "While the rest belong to the unwashed masses."

She laughed. "I think we're the unwashed masses, since we don't even get a seat."

He wrapped his big hand around hers. "Since we can't get inside, how about a coffee and a croissant instead?"

She wrinkled her nose. "We can get a croissant at home anytime. We need Hungarian chimney cake." It was one of the treats her sister had mentioned.

"Coffee and chimney cake, it is."

He glanced at his phone map once more. "The Four Seasons should be that way."

The Four Seasons café was delightful, reminding her of a Parisian café, with small tables outside and counters full of delicious treats. The coffee was rich, with cream to sweeten it, and the chimney cake, shaped like a cone as the name suggested, had a crusty outside of caramelized sugar and cinnamon.

"Oh my God." She licked her lips. "That is so good."

He looked straight at her. "Oh yeah. Absolutely perfect."

And she knew he was talking about her.

She should have known from the moment she saw him at the Fisherman's Bastion that he was the one. He robbed her of speech when he offered to take their pictures, and her heart had raced when their gazes met from afar at the castle.

But she hadn't thought it would happen this fast. She hadn't truly believed she'd find the perfect man. She'd thought she'd have to settle for something far less.

But Gray had found her. And he was perfect.

CELIA WAS DELIGHTFUL. SHE RAVED ABOUT THE CHIMNEY cake, which Gray agreed was tasty. She gushed about the coffee as if she'd never had coffee before. The woman oozed enthusiasm about everything.

Gray couldn't pinpoint why, but she made him feel alive again. Probably because she made him realize, finally, that he'd been living half a life with Eva. The first years had been good, but it all went downhill when her high-powered law career outshone his, not because he cared but because she did.

She'd celebrated his victories, when an innocent man or woman was freed from prison. But he wasn't sure she'd believed in his calling. For Eva, everything was about money and more money, power and more power. Maybe she'd only kept him around for appearances, trotting him out at company functions, saying, "Oh my God, my husband is amazing. He defends the downtrodden and the innocent people who should be set free." It made her look good, as if she was the one doing the work.

Yet his work didn't have the prestige and power she craved. She'd climbed the firm's ladder as easily as she climbed the firm's partners, always reaching for the next rung, the next powerful partner. Until she'd made it to the top.

And then she didn't need Gray anymore.

Even as the story had escaped his mouth, revealing all the sordid details to Celia, he'd wondered at the wisdom of that. It turned him into the cuckolded husband who sat in the background and let his wife screw her way to the top so she could support him.

What did Celia think of him? A woman whose husband hadn't wanted to make love to her. Did she think he was weak?

The thought burned in his gut, forcing the words out almost unbidden. "I love my job. I love helping people who couldn't afford a decent lawyer and made a deal they shouldn't have or got railroaded by a DA looking to put wins on his resume."

She stared a long moment, and he had no clue what she was thinking. Which made him feel even lower. He wasn't an alpha male. He was the drab beta guy.

"I admire what you do." She propped her chin on her hand, gazed at him with a glint in her eye. "Tell me about the case that made you feel the best."

He closed his eyes. The wins all made him feel worthy. It was the people he couldn't save who crushed him. And there were far more of them.

"The one that gave me the most gratification was a case we finished last year."

Her expression was almost adoring, as if she were an acolyte who couldn't wait for her mentor's next words. And he was man enough to admit he liked it.

"Tell me everything." She gave him a rapt, blue-eyed stare.

"Our client had gone to prison for the murder of her three children by setting a fire in their apartment. They all died of smoke inhalation."

She put her hand to her mouth, gasped. "Oh my God."

She was a mother. It must have felt like the worst crime imaginable to her. "The kids were three, five, and seven. They all had different fathers. She'd worked as a prostitute. The DA thought it was a slam dunk from the beginning, and she had only a newbie public defender whose only goal was a plea bargain. The state's theory was that she had a boyfriend who didn't want the kids around so she got rid of them. An old lady died in the apartment as well."

"That's horrible." Her eyes blazed with intensity. "But why didn't you think she was guilty?"

"I always look into cases where the accused says they didn't do it."

"I thought all criminals said they didn't do it." She gave him a pretty half smile that almost made him forget his train of thought.

"You must watch too much crime TV," he said with a smile that couldn't be half as sexy as hers. "For some people, it's a badge of honor to admit the terrible crimes they've committed. But she wrote to us saying she hadn't killed her babies. And she couldn't live anymore letting people think she had."

"What made you believe her?"

"I watched the tape of her police interview. She could barely speak, and her eyes looked dead. She was poor, and she needed money. She'd even prostituted herself to get it. So maybe this boyfriend was the promised land. But I looked at that tape, and I saw a woman who'd lost all her desperation. Her desperation had been for her children. Now they were gone, she didn't care about anything." He said it as if each word was a separate sentence. "She knew it was ultimately her fault. And she pled guilty. Because it was three young children and an old lady, the judge slammed her. It was only later, when she saw the other women with their kids on visiting days, that she couldn't perpetuate the lie anymore. The one thing women in prison hate more than anything is a baby killer."

"Could she have been lying? So she wouldn't be attacked in prison?"

He loved her questions. He'd asked himself the same thing before he took on the case. But he remembered the woman's dead eyes that would never recover from the loss and couldn't go on letting everyone believe she'd killed her children.

"That was always a possibility," he agreed. "But no one had looked deeply into her case. The DA decided she was a terrible mother. Her public defender didn't care whether she was guilty or innocent, as long as he cleared the case off his desk." He sipped his coffee, still looking at her. "I took the case only after extensive investigation. I talked to the people who still lived in the apartment building and remembered her. They all said she was a good mother. The lady who died of smoke inhalation was babysitting the kids. Everyone agreed this woman never left her kids alone. Nothing I heard smacked of a mother who would kill her children and the old lady who babysat them."

He leaned forward, took her hand. "By the time I went to interview her, she'd been in prison for ten years. She was still grieving for her children and the old lady who died with them. I know there are people who can spin a tale so real you believe every word. I've seen it all. But I knew in my guts she hadn't set that fire."

"How did you save her?" she whispered, completely taken by the story.

He puffed out a sad, soft laugh. "Let me be clear, I never saved her. She'll live with the guilt of her children's deaths for the rest of her life. But I finally found witnesses willing to go on record that they'd seen three young men enter the building around the time the fire started. And they'd seen them running away even as smoke began pouring out the windows. One witness who was afraid to come forward originally finally identified one of the young men, and it turned out this guy knew my client's boyfriend. It took five years, but we finally proved that the boyfriend had paid those three hoods to torch the apartment. He'd planned to pimp her out once he got her completely enthralled. But that wouldn't work if she had children hanging around. He hadn't expected her to be accused, but he hadn't lifted a finger to help her either."

"What a tragic story. How's she doing now?"

"She has a job in a battered women's shelter where she's able to live as well. She's working on her GED, and her goal is to help other women like her. She volunteers at my nonprofit organization as well. She'll never forget her babies, and she still cries herself to sleep every night. But she's found a better path now."

Celia turned her hand over in his. "I don't understand why your wife wasn't enormously proud of you for that."

Eva hadn't wanted him to take the case, saying that it would be bad press to defend a baby killer. When they won, she'd simply said, "All's well that ends well."

It wasn't long after that she told him she wanted a divorce. She'd worn down the senior partner who'd given her both a partnership and an engagement ring.

He didn't try to explain the inexplicable, just shrugged his shoulders. "That's why I do what I do. Because people can go through bad things and come out reborn into better people on the other side."

"That's amazing." She sniffed, touched her eye, the glimmer of tears there. "I said your wife was an imbecile for leaving. But it's worse. She doesn't have a single worthwhile brain cell in her airhead."

His smile actually hurt his cheeks. "Is it pathetic to say that I appreciate that?"

She held his hand in both of hers. "It's not pathetic. I'm totally in awe of you."

As he was of her acceptance.

"ARE YOU EXPECTING ME TO PUT MY ALMOST NINETY-YEAR-old body in a swimsuit? Seriously?" Agnes could have been a valley girl. And she growled with an acerbic bite.

It was Cathe who pointed out, "I see lots of older women in the pool. They do water exercises and sit in the hot tub for their arthritis." She'd only been once or twice, but Agnes didn't need to know that.

Jack smiled. Beside Agnes, his father said, "I'm willing to get in the thermal baths if you are."

Jack had signed them up long ago, so Dad was going regardless.

They'd had a good morning on the bus, stopping at Hero's

Square, then a visit to an old church, and finally a walk through the Market Hall. Jack found it amazing, crammed full of goods and souvenirs.

Maybe it had been amazing because he was with Cathe.

They'd all had lunch on the boat, after which everyone at the table would head out to the thermal baths.

Jack had appreciated Cathe's help with his father. Dad didn't like to admit his decline, but Cathe had stepped up, helping Rupert on and off the bus, walking with him, talking to him. And Dad was a talker. Sometimes he even tired out Jack.

Thankfully, his father had become enthralled with Agnes, the two of them strolling side-by-side through the Market Hall, hanging onto their walkers, stopping occasionally to rest.

And Cathe's gentle voice had soothed Jack. "You remind me of my husband. He took such good care of his dad when he was ailing. And you're so good with your father."

He'd wanted to say he wasn't, but he took her praise. "He needs me." Dad didn't want a full-time caregiver, but he couldn't be left alone overnight. There would come a time when he couldn't be left alone at all.

And Jack clearly remembered Cathe's words as they'd watched Agnes and Dad. "I hope you're being good to yourself too." She'd held his arm, and the touch was electric. "Our parents can drain us even though they don't mean to."

"Is that how it was with your parents?" he'd asked.

She'd dipped her head as if she still felt the pain. "Yes. But at least I shared the burden with my sister." She'd squeezed his arm, and he'd wanted to tell her how damn good that felt.

If his wife Tina had been there for him like this, would they have stayed together?

Even now, at the lunch table, Cathe engaged his dad,

talking animatedly with both him and Agnes. Jack noticed the grateful gleam in Declan Delaney's eyes.

"How's your hamburger?" Cathe asked, as if she'd left him out of the conversation. But she made him part of it simply by sitting next to him. By breathing the same air he did. By entertaining his father.

For a moment, he ached to be alone with her.

It was impossible. He had Dad; she had her sister.

Although, Celia seemed to do very well entertaining Gray Ellison. They'd spent the morning wandering the city. And now she seemed to hang on his every word, surfacing only occasionally to add to the table's conversation.

Then lunch ended, and it was time to catch the bus to the thermal baths.

He felt a thrill imagining Cathe in the buff rather than a swimsuit.

How much longer before his thoughts turned entirely erotic?

The thermal baths were on the Buda side of the Danube, and they drove over the green Liberty Bridge to Gellért Square.

The morning bus tour with Jack had been wonderful. And with everyone else as well. She'd sat up front with Rupert and Jack, laughed and joked. Jack was a funny man, Rupert even funnier. In many ways, Rupert overshadowed Jack, but Jack allowed it, as if he understood that Rupert's only joy in life was being the center of attention.

The changing rooms were coed, but they all had separate cubicles and electronic bracelets to lock the doors.

In her bathing suit, self-consciousness threatened to overwhelm Cathe.

Celia sensed her trepidation. "That black suit is perfect for you. You look amazing."

A gold buckle glittered between her breasts and the material gathered down one side to give her a slimmer waistline. She'd tried on a million suits before the trip, and this was the only one that worked for her. She hadn't even balked at the exorbitant price tag.

"Thank you." She looked her sister over. "You always look fabulous."

Celia wore a flowered, teal one-piece that flattered her toned figure. She'd lost her baby weight right away and never gained it back, unlike Cathe, who'd struggled. Even twenty-seven years on, she still didn't like to look at herself in the mirror.

After showering, they headed out to the hottest pool, which was supposed to be around 103. Measured in Celsius, she had to convert.

The two pools—one slightly cooler than the other with a tiled walkway between—were in a cavernous room with mosaics on the walls and skylights in the high, curved ceiling. Fountains spouted water out of Cupid's mouth in one pool and a fish's mouth in the other. Young people flitted about the baths like butterflies, running, laughing, splashing each other. Couples sat in corners, briefly kissing, perhaps doing things under the water that no one could see.

"Oh my God," Celia exclaimed as she dipped down into the steaming water. "This is so good." Wading to the far side, she sat on a shelf below the waterline.

Cathe stepped down, the heat melting her bones and easing aches she didn't even know she had. The water only waist deep, she breast-stroked to Celia's side, hauling herself up on the shelf around the rim. "Where's Gray?"

"Still changing. And where is Jack?" As Celia waggled her eyebrows, Cathe was glad no one from their group was there to see.

She answered primly, lest a smile give anything away. Not that she'd done anything. "I'm sure he's helping Rupert into his swimsuit."

"He's a great guy." She patted Cathe's hand under the water. "Not many men would be so attentive to an elderly parent." Celia held her gaze. "He's one in a million."

Cathe knew it. "He's as good with his dad as Denny always was." Then she took the focus off herself. "Did you have a good time with Gray this morning?"

She'd never seen quite that smile on her sister's face, not even on her wedding day. Though it could have been her imagination. Or hindsight. But Celia said in a dreamy voice, "It was amazing." Then she laid her hand on Cathe's arm. "He's really quite a man. Caring and loyal. He's a nonprofit lawyer working to free innocent people from prison."

"Wow." That truly was amazing. "I thought he just played golf all day."

Celia laughed, a twinkle brightening her eyes. "He's in Florida, so of course he plays golf. But he does so much more." Leaning her head back against the tile wall, the smile still played on her lips. And Cathe sensed Celia knew so much more too.

Eyes closed, Celia seemed to relish the warmth. Or maybe it was the memories of her morning with Gray. "What about your bus tour with Rupert and his son?"

A brilliance unfurled in Cathe's chest. "There are probably similarities between him and Gray, kind and caring and loyal."

"Rupert?" Laughter laced Celia's voice.

Cathe slapped water at her. "You know I'm talking about Jack."

As if talking conjured them, Jack and Rupert entered the mosaicked cavern, and close behind were Declan, Rose, and Agnes, all of them wet from the showers. The two elderly folks wheeled their walkers as if they were chariots, both wearing water shoes to protect against slipping.

Declan's voice carried. "Take your walker right up to the edge, and I'll help you into the bath."

Agnes would have left her walker back in the dressing room, Cathe was sure, so no one could see her infirmities.

But Declan was having none of that. And Jack herded Rupert to the edge too.

Swimming toward them, Cathe flipped onto her back, looking at Celia. "This is probably too hot for Rupert and Agnes. You want to go in the cooler water?"

Celia just smiled. "I'll stay here. It's too good to move." Besides, Cathe knew, she was waiting for Gray.

Water sluicing off her, Cathe climbed out. "This one is really a hot tub." She pointed at the opposite pool. "That one's a few degrees cooler."

Declan smiled gratefully. "Good idea."

Rupert grumbled as Jack headed him to the cooler thermal bath. Looking over her shoulder, Cathe saw Celia slip down until the water covered her chin.

As Agnes stepped down into the warm water, she squealed and shrieked and laughed. "Oh my, this is hot!" She made a wonderful display in her lime green one-piece with a white ruffle and long sleeves.

Jack helped Rupert into the water—minus Agnes's shrieks and squeals—his swim trunks billowing as he dipped down.

Cathe called out, "I'll just move the walkers. There's a place by the showers."

Beside her, Rose wheeled Agnes's walker, both of them leaning over, a sign of how much the two elderly people had shrunk.

Finding a recess to store the two walkers, Rose said, "They must get a lot of people who need more assistance. I saw ramps and grab holds all the way along." Devices by each pool allowed physically challenged people to be lowered into the water.

"And these are mineral baths," Cathe added. "It'll be good for both Rupert and Agnes."

Rose smiled. She was pretty woman, a very happy woman,

who'd found her match in Declan. "It'll be good for all of us. Thanks for pointing out the cooler pool."

Returning to the pools, she found Gray had arrived, sitting next to Celia, their shoulders resting against each other. Cathe imagined their hands were linked beneath the water.

Cathe gave Celia the moment. There were so many tours they would take together; she didn't want to feel like a stone dragging her sister down.

Walking into the warm waters side by side with Rose, she dipped low and swam to their group gathered on the far side.

"Let's do a few water exercises." Rose squatted in the relatively shallow water, swishing her arms back and forth, hands cupped.

"Great idea." Cathe crouched, too, imitating Rose.

"Agnes and I often go to the local pool to do water exercises." Then Rose called out. "Come on Agnes. Let's show them what we do at home."

"It's too warm in here." Agnes harrumphed, almost an actual word.

Rose snorted. "No, it's not. Get out here." She waved her hand.

Rupert joined them first. "That sounds marvelous."

Agnes, not to be outdone by someone who might actually be younger than her, jogged through the water to Rose's side, Declan behind, just in case. Jack came last, a smile just for Cathe.

Short enough to do the exercises without squatting, Agnes mimicked Rose as she counted out the arm movements. Rose's gaze on Declan shone with love and adoration as he stayed close to the little lady if she should need him.

Beside Cathe, Jack murmured, "I should take my dad to the pool every day. He loves this."

Rupert frog-marched to Agnes, circling her, his steps steady as a rock with the water to buoy him.

Like a drill sergeant, Rose called out, "Now, arms down by your side, bring them up, palms cupped for resistance."

Everyone followed her edicts.

Jack, at his height, could barely get his shoulders under the water. He took Cathe's hand, saying to Rose, "It's too shallow for me. I'm moving over there where it's a little deeper."

He pulled Cathe, and lifting her feet, she floated along with him.

"Good idea," Declan said. But he didn't leave his spot by Rose and Agnes, his hand right there if Agnes had problems.

Cathe asked softly, "Rupert doesn't need you?"

"He's fine," Jack said. "If I stood by his side ready to grab him—" He shook his head, brow furrowed. "He'd have a fit. And he's having the time of his life. I had no idea we'd find someone close to his age. And with a walker. It's perfect."

"He seems a little smitten." Cathe smiled.

Jack returned her gaze solidly, without a glance at his father. "He's completely smitten."

A flush spread across her skin, and she was glad for the warm water, which had already turned her face hot. He wasn't talking about his dad and Agnes.

Somehow it made her feel terribly shy and insecure, and she stayed beneath the water, hiding her flaws. Because Jack was perfect, his stomach washboard flat, his muscles corded.

He was a man in his prime.

Whereas she'd had a child, and even the one-piece suit didn't cover her tummy bulge.

She repeated the mantra in her head. *I'm okay. I'm good.*

Then Rose called out again. "Now let's do some curls, bending at the elbows, palms up."

Cathe followed suit, her cupped palms slicing through the water.

"You're an expert," Jack said.

"I'm more of a hiker. But I might like to take a class at our local pool."

Rose changed it up once more. "Arms out to the side, let's go up and down, palms up, then down." Finally, she glanced at the clock. "We've been in this hot water for twenty minutes. It's time to dunk in the cold pool."

They groaned in unison, but followed Rose as she marched to the steps.

Cathe acted quickly. "I'll get Rupert's walker."

Jack's smile warmed her more than the hot water. "You're very sweet to him."

The cold pool, which was outside in the main hall, was refreshing, measuring somewhere in the seventies. Once again, there wasn't a deep end, and skylights filled the high, curved ceiling over second-floor balconies all around. Statues sat in alcoves, water cascading from urns held in their arms, giving the feel of a Roman bath. Rose set them to running laps around the pool, Rupert behind her, then Cathe and Agnes, Declan and Jack coming up the rear.

Until Rose called out, "Now we turn." Their jogging had created a wave in the water they had to push against.

After several rounds, Cathe pulled up. "I'd like to swim laps."

Once again, Jack joined her as she swam breaststroke one way, backstroke the other.

She turned to him as he kept pace. "We need thermal baths like this at home."

"I've never seen one where you go from pool to pool with the different temperatures. But we'll have to look it up online. It would be great for Dad."

She imagined meeting Jack every day at a thermal bath and enjoying a glorious workout.

Agnes and Rupert weren't the only smitten ones. Cathe was smitten with this beautiful man.

But was it because he reminded her of Denny?

THEY BECAME A CLIQUE. DECLAN, ROSE, AND AGNES, along with the two sisters, Jack and his father, and Gray. And sometimes Barbara, the caregiver, if Declan and Rose needed her.

They ate meals together, attended the welcome reception, laughed, talked, toured, danced.

Gray couldn't have imagined this was how the trip would turn out. He'd never dreamed of meeting a woman like Celia. A woman to whom he could bare his soul, a woman who didn't look down on him for his mistakes or the weakness he'd revealed. She empathized, sympathized, and looked at him as if he'd hung the moon and the stars.

Had Eva ever looked at him that way?

He'd been a means to an end, a husband who willingly put her through college and law school, a patsy to her desires. But he'd foiled her plans by wanting to become a nonprofit lawyer. Although perhaps she loved that, too, for a time, at any rate. She could wear the pants in the family and call the shots because, being the breadwinner, she was in control. That gave her, in her own mind, the right to do whatever she wanted.

As Jahz and Mihai spirited away their dessert plates, the captain announced they would sail in twenty minutes.

Gray took Celia's hand, and she smiled. He suddenly felt like the man he hadn't been in twenty years. Her accepting gaze rebuilt his esteem. It wasn't simply adoration. It was that he could expose his soul and still be regarded with that adoration.

Cathe stood up. "I want to find a place at the railing for some good photos. I'll stake out a spot for all of us."

Jack was already rising. "I'll come with you." Then he compared her diminutive size relative to his. "We'll need a big body to stake out that much space." He looked at his father. "You'll come up with Agnes?"

Rupert patted the old woman's hand. "Absolutely."

The old gal was a trooper. Though she'd groused about showing off her ancient body in a bathing suit, she'd done water exercises and even jogged around the cool pool. Then she'd plunged back into the hot pool with squeals and laughter to the delight of everyone.

If he had that much life in him in twenty years, even with a walker, Gray would be thrilled.

Agnes, and Rupert too, made him realize he needed to enjoy every moment he had left. Glancing at Celia, he knew he had to enjoy her too. After all, they only had a week.

She stood. "I'll come too," she said, looking down at him.

"Between the two of us—" He waved a hand between Jack and him. "—we'll make space at the railing for everyone."

Declan, Rose's hand in his, smiled. "We'll make sure Rupert gets up there. Thanks for saving a spot."

The sundeck was in darkness except for the fairy lights crisscrossing it, and already passengers were staking a claim to watch the sailing.

"Gosh," Cathe said. "We'll need both sides to get pictures of Buda Castle as well as the Parliament Building."

It was Gray's opportunity, and taking Celia's hand, he said, "We'll save a spot on the Buda side." He wouldn't be alone with Celia, but the more anonymous people around them, the more cocooned they would be in their own world.

Gray overheard Cathe's excited voice. "Let's find a spot up

front where we can get both angles. Oh look, the Liberty Statue is all the lit up. I wouldn't have thought it even had working lights after seeing the conditions up there."

She was already taking pictures, though they hadn't even left the dock.

The Elizabeth Bridge lay ahead, the Chain Bridge beyond that, then the Margaret Bridge lit up in the night, gleaming and white.

But the real beauty was Celia. He wondered what would have happened if he hadn't seen Celia and Cathe that first night on Fisherman's Bastion. If he hadn't stopped to take their picture. He'd found Celia charming, even alluring, as he'd watched them mugging for selfies before he'd offered to take the pictures himself.

Would Celia think he was a stalker for watching them? And he confessed. "The first night at Fisherman's Bastion, I saw you on the parapet and I took your picture before I approached you. You might think that's weird. I can delete them."

She looked at him. "More than one picture?"

A sheepish smile curved his mouth. "Yeah."

"Then I'll have to admit I looked for you in the hotel dining room while we had breakfast." She smiled and his heart beat faster. Harder. "Both mornings." She winked. "And we saw you at the castle too. But you already know that."

Raising her hand to his lips, he planted a kiss on her knuckles. "Then we're even. We both spied on each other."

This time her smile trickled all the way down to his belly and her husky voice turned him inside out. "I like it," she murmured.

And he loved it.

CATHE SMELLED SO SWEET AND FELT SO THIS PETITE beside him.

Jack could gaze at her all night, finding her brighter than any city lights laid out before them.

He loved her enthusiasm as she pointed out this monument and focused her camera phone on that church or castle or statue.

The rest of their group joined them at the front of the boat, people kindly making room for Agnes and Rupert at the railing. They squeezed together, Cathe's body pressed to his.

A cheer went up as the engines rumbled and the ship swayed, pulling out into the river. And they were off.

Buda Hill lit up the night sky, but he couldn't help thinking Cathe was the most beautiful sight right in front of him.

They passed the glory of Matthias Church, its tower bright above the Fisherman's Bastion. And finally, the Parliament Building loomed large beside them.

"This will be amazing." Cathe spoke almost to herself as she waited for the right moment, until the building's reflection was crystal clear in the water.

Then she concentrated on Margaret Bridge, bathed in light before they passed under it.

A cheer went up as they left Budapest behind and started their journey. Leaning close to him, her arm brushed against him, shooting an electric charge to every limb.

She opened her photo gallery, scrolling to the picture of the Parliament Building. "What do you think?" Her words came breathless in the night.

"Absolutely amazing." *She* was amazing. "You could sell that photo."

She tipped her head, her hair caressing his chin. "But there are tons out there just like it."

"But this one is perfect. Would you send it to me?"

She pulled away as he took out his phone, and he almost wished he hadn't asked the question. But she needed to know how good she was, so he reeled off his number as she typed into her phone, then dialed.

When his cell rang, he answered before quickly shutting it down. "There. You have my number."

He liked having her in his phone. And he loved that he was in hers. Moments later, a text pinged, and there was the picture. "Amazing."

He loved the way she blushed and smiled. As if she had no clue how incredible she was.

"You should think about selling to stock sites. You've got a good eye and the patience to wait for the right moment. You're very talented." Jack tried to impress that on her.

Cathe's skin flushed as if the praise embarrassed her, and she shrugged. "You've only seen one picture."

"Let's make a deal," he said. "You show me the ones you feel are good. And I'll tell you what I think." Not that he was an expert.

She cocked her head. "You'll be honest?"

He crossed his heart. "I'll always tell you the truth."

Pursing her lips, she finally smiled. "Deal. No one's ever said anything like that before. I just might try the stock photo sites. Thank you."

He didn't want her to feel gratitude.

He wanted other things. So many things. Things he hadn't wanted from any other woman in a long time. Just last night, he'd told his father he didn't want another relationship. Yet almost in the blink of her pretty eyes, Cathe had changed that for him.

12

Once the ship left the lights of Budapest behind, they'd all gone down to the lounge to celebrate.

Celia and Gray cut it up on the floor, dancing to their Ukrainian entertainer's renditions of Elvis's *Suspicious Minds* and *We Gotta Get Out of This Place* by The Animals. But Blondie singing Donna Summer's *Hot Stuff* had them laughing hysterically. Celia reveled in every moment.

When it was time to go, Gray kissed her cheek, looking at her as if he wanted to beg for more. Yet it was so good to wait, so sweet to lie in her twin bed and imagine his lips on hers.

She and Cathe lay facing each other, lights off, just the moonlight through the aquarium window.

"Did you have a good day?" Cathe asked.

Celia held the warm glow in her chest. "Amazing. We learned a lot about each other."

Thankfully, Cathe didn't ask for details because Gray's story wasn't Celia's to tell.

"I half expected you to go to his room, and I'd be sleeping alone tonight."

"I thought about it." Celia let out a sweet little sigh. She could have done it. She'd wanted to do it. Especially after bearing their souls and that kiss at the Parliament Building. "I'm biding my time. The moment needs to be just right."

"We'll have to make sure it is," Cathe said with a conspiratorial whisper.

"What about you? Good day?"

"Rupert and Agnes are a trip." Celia could hear Cathe's smile in the dark. "I see a romance blooming there."

They giggled together, then Celia asked, "What about Jack?"

"He's nice. And great with his dad."

Jack was also tall, his body toned, his dark hair turning silvery like Denny's. And he was so good with his dad, like Denny, who'd even helped relieve both Celia and Cathe when their mom was ill and their dad couldn't handle it.

But Denny was gone. Jack was here. She hoped Cathe could see that. For now, at least her sister was spending time with him. "You two seemed cozy up there on the top deck tonight."

Cathe laughed. "It's called the sundeck, even if there's no sun." Amusement laced her voice. But was there a hint of something else too? Then she added, "I showed him some of my photos. He thought they were good. He even suggested I put them on stock sites. What do you think?"

What a great guy to give Cathe that idea. "You should do it. Your photos are fabulous. Remember that one you took when we all went to Florida?" She didn't say it was before Denny died and Bart still seemed to want her.

"The one of the sandpipers on the sand at dawn?"

"That one. And the one with the pelicans flying across the water as the sun was rising. They were incredible."

Cathe seemed to be deep in thought. "Yeah," she said slowly, drawing the word out.

"And those desert sunsets over the golf course in Palm Springs."

She thought she saw a smile grow on Cathe's lips. "Yeah," this time more quickly, with more enthusiasm. "They were pretty good, weren't they."

"You should concentrate on taking incredible pictures while we're here. And maybe Jack can help us figure out how to put them on stock sites. Even those old photos too."

Cathe was still dubious. "I don't know."

"You said you don't know what to do with yourself. This could be a good thing. Like your volunteering. But that doesn't take up all your time." She shook her finger at her sister. "And I love the ones you took on the Sausalito side of the Golden Gate Bridge, with the spires and the fog over the city on the opposite shore."

She could almost hear Cathe roll her eyes. "Everyone takes those photos."

"But maybe someone will find yours. Promise me you'll do it."

"I promise I'll think about it."

"You said Jack thought you should do it."

There was just enough light to see Cathe's teeth as she smiled, and it was a strange smile, almost as if she were having secret thoughts about Jack. "I actually made a deal that I'd show him the best pictures and he'd let me know what he thought."

Celia wanted to punch the air. It was perfect. Between her and Jack, they'd help Cathe pry open her shell.

BY THE TIME THE SUN WAS UP, THEY'D DOCKED THE NEXT morning in Bratislava, the capital of Slovakia. Cathe slept through the night's sail without feeling more than the gentle rock of the boat lulling her to sleep.

Cathe and Celia had booked the free panoramic bus tour around the city and to the castle they could see from the ship. Their entire group was on the bus, except Gray, who'd headed out on his own. This time, Celia hadn't changed her plans to go with him, though Cathe sensed she'd wanted to.

Sitting up front near the handicapped seats Agnes and Rupert had taken, they drove the hills of Bratislava so quickly that Cathe didn't get even a single good picture of the castle. So much for showing Jack what fabulous pictures she could take.

But Bratislava Castle made up for it. They climbed the steep hill, Rupert and Agnes getting a ride in a golf cart. The castle, its white walls brilliant in the sunshine and its red-tiled roof visible for miles, perched on the hill overlooking the Danube. The gorgeous gardens stretched out before them, and a magnificent staircase led into the massive courtyard, the castle a big square surrounding it, with turrets on each corner.

Unfortunately, the bus tour didn't include the castle's interior. The most interesting part of the trip was Nela, their guide, who told them about her experiences when communism ended in the country.

A tall woman with a rough voice, she'd been a student, and her tale was riveting. "My parents were afraid for me," she said. "That I might cross the border into Austria and never be able to come back. They were reliving 1968 when our borders closed. But this was 1989 and we were students and we had to do it. My friends and I all marched to the border. And no one stopped us." She held up her hands as if she were still in wonder of it all. "An old man sat on a bench, and he told me he was waiting for his son, who'd crossed the border into Austria in 1968 before the Russians closed it, and he hadn't seen him since, not for twenty-one years. It was so incredible, so amazing, none of us could truly believe it. And we crossed back over the border to our homeland, back and forth, over and over. Just because we suddenly had the freedom to do it, and we couldn't believe it."

Standing next to Jack, Cathe murmured, "I remember when it all happened. It was unbelievable."

Jack nodded. "We were glued to the TV, watching it all unfold, history in the making."

And Cathe was grateful they'd chosen the bus tour.

After Nela's fascinating story, she kept thinking of the major events that shaped your life. Like the first day she'd seen Denny in her freshman year at university. In an accounting class, he sat up front while she took a seat in the back. He was so beautiful that she hadn't heard a word the teacher said.

Jack asked, "What are you thinking about? You have such a faraway look in your eyes."

Blushing, she told him the truth. "I was thinking about the first time I met my husband."

He nodded gravely. "A significant moment in your history."

That day had shaped her life.

Then Nela gave them fifteen minutes to wander the grounds before the bus returned them to the boat. With Jack by her side, she photographed the gardens and the castle and the battlements below.

But when Jack asked to see, she was suddenly self-conscious. "None of them are any good." They were just normal vacation shots she could show Sarah, nothing special.

"Maybe you're being hard on yourself," Jack offered.

She shrugged. "I'm being honest. But I promise, when I've got a photo I really like, I'll show you."

He smiled, almost as if he didn't believe her.

Then Agnes's hand shot up. "I need to use the restroom before we get back on the bus. Who's coming with me?"

Rupert raised his hand. "I'll accompany you."

The two oldsters climbed on an elongated golf cart bigger than the one that had brought them up the hill, and they were all shuttled over to the restrooms.

In the back seat, Celia leaned close to say, "I'm glad Agnes said it because I had to go too."

Giggling together, Cathe said boldly, "You didn't sneak off with Gray today."

Celia shuddered. "He did a bike ride, and I was terrified I'd look like an idiot if I fell off."

"God forbid you should look like an idiota." They laughed together at the memory of their airport driver.

They arrived back at the ship in time for a delicious lunch, and then they were the sailing again. The excitement for the afternoon was passing through the locks, and everyone went up to the sundeck to watch. The massive steel gates opened, and the ship sailed in, keeping so far to the left they were almost touching the high concrete wall as a second boat drew alongside them.

Standing up front, Agnes gasped. "I feel like I'm being swallowed down into the belly of the whale."

The ship's bumpers edged right up against the concrete wall rising high above them, and behind, the massive steel doors closed, shutting them in. Amid a subtle bubbling in the water ahead, the ship rose. Cathe couldn't actually see it or feel it, only detect its rising by the markings on the wall.

Agnes giggled. "It looks like the Loch Ness monster is down there trying to get up."

As it grew, the bubbling and roiling of the water filling the lock did look like a monster rising.

Cathe smiled and leaned close to Jack. "I think I'm as excited to watch this as Agnes is."

He nodded, smiled. "Me too."

The process took about fifteen minutes, and when they were near the top of the wall, the front gate lowered, its yellow caution stripes disappearing into the depths.

Agnes clapped, her eyes shining. "Wasn't that marvelous?" Rupert clapped with her. Then everyone at the front of the boat did as well.

In her excitement, Agnes kissed Rupert's cheek. And with the ship underway once more, she bounced on her toes. "Now we have to play Skip-Bo. It's my favorite card game. Let's go down to the lounge." She looked at Rose, a plea in her eyes. "You brought the cards, didn't you?"

Rose smiled indulgently. "I would never forget Skip-Bo."

Agnes beamed at the surrounding group. "All right, who wants to play?" She gave Rupert a twinkling smile. "I'm sure you do."

He smiled as indulgently as Rose had. "Of course."

Cathe looked at Jack. He looked at her. And they shared a secret smile. "I'll play," Cathe said.

Jack immediately followed. "I'll play too."

Agnes, clapping, said in a high, sweet voice, "Goody-goody. Let's grab a table."

She pushed her walker in the wrong direction until Declan put his hand on her shoulder and guided her to the elevator.

As Cathe turned to Celia by the opposite railing, Gray at her side, her sister waved her over. "Gray and I want to stay up here and watch the scenery go by."

Fluttering her fingers in acceptance, Cathe headed to the stairs, leaning close to Jack to say in a soft voice laced with a smile, "Right. Like they're really going to watch the scenery."

His answering grin said he knew what was going on too.

Rupert and Agnes, along with Rose and Declan, exited

the elevator just as Jack and Cathe stepped onto the landing, and they all headed to the lounge.

"Shall I get coffee for everyone?" Jack asked.

"A wonderful idea." Cathe jumped in first. "I'd like one of those lattes with extra sugar," adding, "I'll help carry," as everyone gave their orders, including tea with cream and sugar for Agnes.

By the time they'd made the coffee drinks, Rose had returned with the cards, and they sat at a round table in the center of the lounge. Barbara, the caregiver, took a seat by the window, opening her e-reader.

Shuffling, Rose explained the game. "You've got a pile of fifteen, and the object is to play that stack in order from ace to king onto the four piles in the center."

Agnes was giddy with excitement at the prospect of playing her favorite card game with all new people. "And when you get a Skip-Bo card, you can play it as any number." She patted Rupert's hand. "Don't you worry, I'll help you."

Rose dealt the cards only to Rupert, Agnes, Jack, and Celia. "If we try to play with the six of us, there's just not enough cards. That's why Barbara's not playing. Declan and I will show you how to play the game. Then let you guys continue."

An easy game to understand, there was still strategy to it. Agnes, while it was her favorite game, often missed playing the cards she should. Each time, either Declan or Rose made a sound like the buzzer in a game show, and Agnes looked up. "What, what did I miss?" Everyone waited patiently for her to figure it out. And when she did, she'd bounce in her chair. "Oh, oh, I know."

They let her play incorrect cards and take them back. They gave her hints. Rose and Declan were obviously used to helping Agnes play the game. And the little woman loved every moment.

"Oh my goodness," Rupert said, playing the last card in his stack. "I think I've won."

It was all good fun. Despite Agnes's lack of skill, she had a marvelous time, laughing and joking.

The game gave Cathe a chance to watch Jack in action with his father, with Agnes, with all of them. He was funny, trading wisecracks with Agnes, and eventually taking over the buzzer sound when someone made a bad move, usually Agnes.

"Now that Rupert has won the first game," Rose said, "you all get the gist of how to play."

Declan went on as if they'd rehearsed. "I'm tired after all the activity this morning and I'd like a nap, if none of you mind." He looked at Rose, a smile curving his lips. "Don't you need a nap too?"

With an adoring smile, Rose agreed. "A nap would be marvelous. The rest of you enjoy the game. We'll be back after a lovely nap. If you have questions, Barbara knows how to play."

Standing, Declan pulled Rose close, his arm around her shoulders, and kissed her temple. After stopping a moment to confer with Barbara, they strolled away.

The moment they were out of earshot, Agnes said in a loud sotto voce, "It's their honeymoon, and they seem to need a lot of naps."

With smiles all around, everyone understood the euphemism.

And they played on. When Agnes made a move she probably shouldn't, she'd say, "Oh, that's a rule we forgot to tell you about."

Rupert, laughing, would challenge her. "I really don't think that's something you're supposed to do."

And Agnes, grumbling, would put the card back.

It was a marvelous afternoon with the green grass and

vineyards and trees and hills sailing by outside the windows. Jack was so good with the two elderly people, patient, kind, fun-loving.

Then he said, "I'm ready for an alcoholic beverage. Can I get something for anyone else?"

Agnes clapped her hands, two of her cards falling to the floor, and Rupert was able to bend down from his chair to pick them up.

"I'd love a Grasshopper. I haven't had one for ages." Then she added in a loud whisper, "Rose and Declan only let me drink champagne. And not very much either."

Rupert smiled at his son. "Surprise me with a nice cocktail."

Finding that a fabulous idea, Cathe said, "Surprise me, please. Something delicious."

Jack winked. "I'll get something sweet and refreshing just for you."

He was back shortly, having given his order to the bartender, who would send the waiter over with the drinks. The cocktails arrived only a few minutes later, a Grasshopper for Agnes, something called a Toasted Almond for Rupert. And for himself and Cathe, Jack had ordered espresso martinis.

"What's a Toasted Almond?" Agnes sat forward eagerly to peer into Rupert's glass.

Jack explained. "It's a white Russian. Kahlúa, cream, and vodka, with amaretto added for the almond flavor."

"Yummy." Agnes fluttered her eyelashes. "I'll let you taste mine if I can taste yours."

Rupert pushed his glass over to her.

And Cathe tasted her espresso martini. "That is absolutely delicious." Then she laughed. "Will it make me completely wired?"

Jack chuckled, shaking his head. "I have no idea. But don't worry, I'll make sure you don't bounce off the walls."

Espresso beans floated on the top, and the coffee taste was strong, but the vodka made it sweet going down.

Agnes took charge. "We have to finish the game. I think I'm about to win."

The time passed quickly as Jack entertained the two octogenarians, charming Agnes and making Rupert burst into peals of laughter.

And melting Cathe's heart.

13

Many of the other passengers had gone to the lounge or their staterooms to sit on their private verandas and enjoy the sail, but Celia and Gray stayed on the sundeck, watching the scenery slip by. The ship rode higher against the riverbank after passing through the lock, and the waterway was bounded by levees and farms spreading out across the flat land.

Celia stretched luxuriously on the lounger, the breeze across the water keeping her cool. "It's gorgeous up here. I don't know why everyone's gone below."

Gray laughed. "Afternoon cocktails."

She smiled, closing her eyes. "But we can order afternoon cocktails up here and still have the view."

Their chairs nestled close together, he took her hand, his touch warm, comforting, inviting. "I'll call over the waiter. What would you like?"

It was on the tip of her tongue to say the only thing she wanted was him. But it seemed too soon for that. She didn't want to feel that Gray was one of her quickies. She said instead, "A champagne cocktail."

He raised his hand, signaling the waiter. "Two champagne cocktails, please."

She stretched again, the feeling sensual as well as relaxing. "I have to tell you how jealous I am that you have a suite with two rooms and two verandas."

Gray chuckled. "There's only one veranda. The bedroom has a French balcony with a sliding glass door, but there's no actual balcony you can step onto, just a railing so you don't fall in the water."

She huffed a breath and gave him a look. "Well, Cathe and I are in an aquarium room with only a long window high up at water level."

"At least you have light."

She sighed, "There is that." When their champagne cocktails arrived, she toasted to having two large windows and a balcony.

He smiled with what could only be a wicked glint. "Why don't I show you what the room is like?"

She thought he'd never ask and returned the smile, hopefully with a glint as wicked as his.

Naturally, his stateroom was far more spacious than the aquarium room she shared with Cathe, where they had to suck in their stomachs when they passed each other at the foot of the beds. Outfitted with a sofa, two armchairs, a coffee table, and a minibar, the sitting room of Gray's suite was awash in light. The two floor-to-ceiling sliding glass doors opened onto a wraparound balcony with a spectacular view of the river and shoreline.

"Wow. You made it sound like you had one tiny veranda."

Leaning against the wall by the doors, he shrugged, but his smile was as wide as the amazing veranda. He'd totally splurged on his anniversary trip, booking the biggest suite on the boat. No wonder he didn't hand over the tickets so his cheating ex-wife could take her lover.

She put her hands together in a plea. "Show me the rest."

The bedroom was lit up through the French balcony window, and the bed seemed huge, or maybe it looked bigger because there was room to walk around it. But it was the bathroom that made her gasp. "You can actually fit two people in here."

He laughed. And she really did love his laugh. "I most certainly can."

"Our cabin is tiny in comparison, with not much room to move around." She lifted her shoulders, tipped her head, and smiled. "But that forces us to get out to meet new people."

He raised his champagne flute. "Here's to amazing new meetings."

She liked it, the perfect toast, and she tapped her glass to his.

Then he flourished a hand. "Let's sit on the veranda and watch the river go by."

The day was gorgeous, not too hot, the breeze perfect, and just as they had on the sundeck, they watched the river flow past verdant vineyards and lush farmland. Villages popped up along the shore, with boat docks proclaiming the name and two churches per town. They chatted about tidbits from their lives; she gushed about the last gala she'd planned, and he told her about the time his buddy drove their golf cart into a sand trap, rolling them over, luckily without injury.

When they'd finished their champagne, Gray rose. "Time to order another glass?" he asked, looking down at her.

She nodded. "Please. Can I use your restroom?"

He waved his hand. "You know where it is."

Gray was just closing the door after the arrival of their champagne when she entered the sitting room again. "Wow, that was fast."

He'd ordered a bottle of the best, and it came chilled in an ice bucket. He tore off the foil and the wire cage.

"Allow me." She held out her hand. "I'm an expert at popping the cork without spilling a drop."

Smiling, he handed her the bottle. "Then I need to learn from an expert. I have to admit I drink beer more than champagne."

He certainly didn't look like a man who sat in front of the TV all weekend watching sports and drinking beer, not with that physique.

"We can all learn new tricks." She sounded almost coquettish.

Twisting the cork, she held it tightly in her hand until it came out with a pop and the barest whoosh of bubbles. "Like I said, not a drop wasted."

He grinned. "That was pretty amazing. Though I missed the cork flying across the room and out the veranda window."

"It would have gone through the window." And laughing, she began pouring. "There's a technique to this so you don't overflow. Tip the glass to the side, and pour slowly so there's fewer bubbles."

She handed him the first glass, poured her own, and snugged the champagne bottle into the ice. They saluted, sipped.

Then Gray slipped his fingers beneath the hair at her nape. And kissed her. Long and sweet, laced with the heady champagne taste of him, the kiss sizzled through her blood and started a fire low in her belly.

When their lips parted, she whispered, "Is this what you invited me here for?"

His rogue's smile was infectious. "Hell yes. Because yesterday's kiss was just an appetizer. Do you want more?"

She loved the sexy smile on his lips, and she answered by setting her glass down, taking his also and putting it on the sideboard. Then she rose on her toes to wrap her arms around his neck. She kissed him for long, lingering minutes, his body hot and hard against her. Delicious, glorious, momentous.

Not one kiss since her divorce had felt like this, tasted like this, joining her with him until she didn't know where she ended and he began. Had there been anyone like him? No, not in a long, long time. She thought the boat rocked beneath her feet, but she knew it was him, rocking her world.

He slid his hands beneath her tank top, his fingers warm on her skin, his palms sliding around her sides, his thumbs caressing her through the lacy bra. Then he whispered, "I'd love to make love to you."

She murmured against his lips, "I'd really enjoy that."

Never taking his hands off her, he walked her backward into the bedroom with the slow, luscious glide of his hands on her, his lips on her. Until the backs of her knees hit the bed. Standing slightly back, fully concentrating on her, he slowly tugged the tank top up, up, up, and off her shoulders.

A sounded vibrated deep in his throat as trailed his fingers over her skin, murmuring, "Pretty. So pretty."

The words fed her soul. The roughness of his voice bathed her in what she'd needed since Bart stopped making love to her. The heat in his eyes gave her what she'd been searching for with those other men she'd taken to her bed, a feeling she'd never quite found, not until this moment with Gray. That she was beautiful, that she was truly wanted, genuinely desired, exquisitely craved.

He traced the line of her bra across the upper swell of her breasts. Then he leaned close, planting a trail of kisses from her shoulder to her neck. "You smell so good."

She loved that he understood she needed the words.

"Your skin is so smooth." He licked her. "And you taste as sweet as champagne."

She lapped up his praise, her nipples pebbling, her body

turning liquid. Unsnapping the clasp of her bra, he pushed the cups aside. Every move was slow, as if he had to savor her.

Then he held her breasts in his hands. "God, yes, you are so perfect."

He slid his thumbs over her nipples, and finally he bent his head, taking one pearl in his mouth, sucking luxuriously. Her knees went weak with pleasure, and she moaned, her hand on the back of his head, holding him to her.

He rose again, cupped her face, kissed her, their tongues melding, going deep. Arching into him, she let the bra straps fall down her arms and whispered, "Your shirt. I need it off."

Reaching behind, he pulled at the neck, the polo ruffling his hair as he tugged it over his head and threw it aside. She wrapped her arms around his neck, held him close, kissed him with the thrill of his warm skin against hers. A hand between them, he popped the snap of her crop pants, and his fingers delved into the waistband, pushing them down, over her hips.

For one instant, a flicker of fear chilled her. He would see her whole body, the stretch marks, the skin that wasn't as taut as it used to be.

Her heart thundered, and she suddenly remembered all the logistics. "I can't get pregnant. But I didn't bring a condom."

Why hadn't she? This was what she'd wanted, but she'd followed him to his room without it. And she said weakly, "I have one, but it's in my purse back in the cabin." For the first time since she'd been with a man after the divorce, she was embarrassed, and a little ashamed that she hadn't waited for a man like him.

But Gray laughed softly. "We think alike. I bought some this morning." He rubbed his lips against hers. "I was very hopeful."

Then her crops dropped to her ankles, and he helped her

step out of them. "I want to touch you, taste you, kiss you, fill you up."

She didn't have another moment to think about her flaws or the necessities or embarrassment. There was just this, his desire for her, her need for him. Tugging on his cargo shorts, she pushed them down. Until he was outlined against his boxer briefs.

He slipped his hands inside her panties, slid them off, and finally pushed her gently onto the bed. Standing over her, he shoved his briefs over his hips.

And she lost her breath. God, she wanted him. She wanted to feel him inside her. He was big and bold and beautiful. How could his wife ever have preferred someone else? This man was everything any woman could want.

She leaned back on her elbows, her legs dangling off the bed, and she looked at him, finally raising her eyes to his. "You're beautiful," she said without embellishment.

"I dreamed about this," he whispered. "The night I took your picture at the Fisherman's Bastion. I've dreamed about it every night since."

How did he know just the right thing to say?

He went down on his knees at the edge of the bed, shoved his hands under her bottom, and spread her legs around him as he pulled her in. Then he put his mouth on her. And God oh God, his tongue on her was so damn good. Even better when he slipped his fingers inside her. His touch pushed her to the peak so fast, she gasped, then she moaned, and finally, she tangled her fingers in his hair, hearing her chant as if it came from outside of her. "So good, so good."

Sensation flooded her body. She writhed and rocked and cried out when her climax blasted through her. Rolling up slightly, she panted, her eyes squeezed shut as wave after glorious wave of perfect pleasure shuddered through her.

She didn't feel as if she was quite back in her body when

he helped her farther up the bed, lifted her head to put a pillow under her. She felt him lean over the bedside table, heard the rustle as he grabbed a condom.

She laughed as if it were a release. "Oh my gosh, you really are prepared."

He smiled down at her, the tiny crinkles at his eyes endearing. "Like I said, I was hopeful you wanted the same thing I did. I wanted to think you were dreaming of me as much as I dreamed of you."

Propping herself on her elbow, she looked at him, the laughter gone, just the need remaining. "You can't possibly know how long I've dreamed of this."

And he whispered, "It can't be as long as I've waited for you."

She let the sweetness of his words caress her as he climbed between her legs. On his haunches, he rolled on the condom, but instead of coming down on top of her, he pulled her thighs over his.

"You'll like it this way," he said, reaching for a pillow to push beneath her hips. "It'll hit you in the perfect spot, I promise."

Then he slipped inside her, easily, smoothly, because she was so wet, wetter than she'd been in years. Instead of going deep, he rocked slowly, barely inside, but hitting just the right spot.

It was crazy how good it was. "Oh my God," she whispered.

"Touch yourself," he murmured. "It'll be even better."

Living with a man who didn't want her, she'd given herself her own orgasms. But she'd never done it in front of a man. Yet she wanted to for Gray.

Hand between her legs, she circled, her fingers brushing him as he moved. And yes, God, it was good, so good, and he was so right. She was already climbing to another peak with her touch and the slow, relentless stroke of him inside her, caressing her G-spot.

In what seemed like only moments, she climaxed, the pleasure drowning her. As if he could feel every pulse of her body, her tight grip around him, or maybe it was just her wild cries, he abandoned the slow rhythm, thrusting deep and hard inside her, the way she needed, the way she craved. One orgasm rolled into another, on and on, almost without end.

His breath puffed harder, faster, and he came down on her, arms around her. He growled and gasped, his body hard, and she felt him pulse and throb as he filled her up.

Her only wish was that they hadn't used a condom. She wished it was just skin on skin, everything in him filling everything in her.

He shuddered once more, his breath sliding out, and she opened her eyes to see him looking at her. "Jesus, that was good." Braced on his elbows, he held her head in his hands and kissed her. Her taste lingered on his lips. "That was so damn good."

She held him in, her legs wrapped around him, not wanting him to pull out.

Stroking her chin, he murmured against her ear, "Nothing has felt like that in a long, long time."

She smiled up at him, her heart feeling tremulous and needy. "Is that like saying I'm the best you've had in the last few months?" Yes, she was fishing for compliments.

"I haven't been with anyone since my divorce." He framed her face in his hands. "And you are the best ever."

He hadn't been with another woman since his wife left him? It was too hard to believe. "No one else since your wife?"

He shook his head. And smiled. "I was waiting for you."

She slapped his arm playfully. "You didn't know you'd meet me."

"I was hoping for the perfect woman, not necessarily on this trip, but sometime. And there you were."

His words touched her deep inside, but she was too afraid to take them to heart, even as badly as she wanted to. "The truth is," she said with a pause, "you were busy moving to Florida, setting up your career there, finding the right golf club, making friends. And you couldn't have been divorced all that long."

He laughed. "That's true."

"But I'm honored you chose me as the first woman you wanted to make love to." She didn't mind using the words. She'd had only sex with other men since her divorce. This was the first time she'd made love. What they'd done was special. It wasn't love, but it was special. She couldn't put it in the same class as those other men.

She wanted to hold this time with Gray close, savor it, keep the memory alive.

Still holding him inside her, she fell asleep in his arms.

WITH CELIA ASLEEP IN HIS ARMS, HE FELT... SUBLIME.

He'd probably rushed her into making love, but they only had a few days, and he didn't want to waste a single one of them. Though he should have pulled out and gotten rid of the condom, he relished the feel of her body around him, enjoyed her warmth, her sweet scent, her lingering taste on his lips. He was glad he hadn't had time for another woman or a relationship since the divorce. Maybe he truly had been waiting for her. He'd uttered no lies when he said he'd been dreaming of this since the moment he'd seen her. She was special. Like him, she was damaged by her partner in life. He wanted to show her how beautiful she was, how desirable, how flawless.

He wanted to show her how perfect he could be for her.

14

Celia woke just before the cocktail hour to the sound of Gray in the bathroom. She climbed out of bed, looking for her clothing, stepping into her panties, fastening her bra. Instead of making her feel bereft or ashamed or even let down, as it sometimes had in the past, getting dressed filled her with bliss. What they'd done had been so good. She was still walking on clouds.

Fully clothed, her hair smoothed, she peaked into the bathroom. Craig stood before the mirror over the sink wearing only his boxer briefs and brushing his teeth.

"I'll just pop down to my room and freshen my makeup," she told him.

He gave her a toothpaste-covered smile. "Meet you in the lounge?"

She would meet him anywhere. Smiling, she nodded, but before she could leave, he stepped close to plant a kiss on her.

Laughing, she wiped off the residual toothpaste. "You're bad."

"I didn't want you to forget me while you're gone."

She couldn't forget him. Maybe never.

Cathe wasn't in their cabin, and Celia quickly fixed her makeup. Thinking about changing, she discarded the idea. It would be obvious to everyone what she and Gray had been doing. Besides, she'd packed nothing dressy for dinner. All she did was make sure her clothes were free of wrinkles, then headed up to the lounge.

Gray had found the others in the lounge and saved her a seat next to him.

Before her sister could say anything, Celia asked, "So what have you been up to all afternoon?"

"We played Skip-Bo with Rupert and Agnes." Her sister's smile lit up her face.

Cathe was happy. It had to be Jack. Or maybe it was just being away from home without all the reminders of Denny.

"And I won," Agnes said, her eyes bright.

Rupert added with a cheeky grin, "And she cheated."

Agnes gave him an indignant glare. "I never cheat. I simply pretend I've forgotten how to play and you all let me get away with it."

Everyone laughed, and Rose said, "She's very sneaky. But I'm glad you all had a good card game."

Agnes gave her a knowing wink. "I hope you and Declan had a lovely nap."

Rose blushed, but Declan, holding her hand, saved her. "We're not over our jet lag yet."

It was their honeymoon, after all, and jet lag would probably last the rest of the cruise.

Mario, the program director, went through his spiel on the upcoming events for the next day. They would arrive early in Vienna, and she and Cathe had signed up for the morning's walking tour. Celia, however, hadn't been interested in the afternoon visit to Schönbrunn Palace, the summer home of the Habsburg queens and kings, so Cathe would take that one on her own. Celia didn't have plans except to wander around Vienna.

She leaned close to nudge Gray. "What's on tap for you tomorrow?"

He looked at her, smiled. "I actually signed up for the walking tour. And the e-bike ride in the afternoon. What about you?"

She glanced at Cathe, who was laughing with Jack. That's exactly what Celia wanted, for her sister to find someone to hang out with, a man who would make her feel like a woman again. She'd never forget Denny. He was her first and only love. But there were other men out there, men who would find her attractive. Men like Jack. The more time Cathe spent with Jack, the more her sister would realize that.

Of course, it was also a good excuse for spending time with Gray. And Mario had said there was still space on the bike excursion. "What a coincidence. I'm on both the walking tour and the e-bike ride as well."

He squeezed her hand. "Wonderful."

As everyone went into dinner, she excused herself to use the restroom and headed to the front desk instead, booking a place on the bike ride.

Their group sat at the same table again, Agnes and Rupert keeping them all in stitches, Rupert obviously taking a shine to the elderly woman.

Cathe ordered everything off the regional menu for Slovakia, a sour cabbage soup called *kapustnica* to start.

"I don't like the sound of *sour*. Isn't that sauerkraut?" Celia made a face at Cathe and ordered a salad instead.

"You can have a taste of mine," Cathe said good-naturedly, knowing Celia wouldn't take it. "And I'm having the *bryndzové halušky* for my main course." She laughed, obviously botching the pronunciation.

"I'll have the same," Jack agreed.

But dumplings and sheep cheese, the description for *bryn-dzové halušky*, didn't appeal to Celia. "I'll have the lamb stew." Maybe she just wasn't adventurous. At least not in her food.

Beside her, Gray gave the menu one last glance. "More power to the two of you for ordering Slovakian favorites." He smiled at Jack and Cathe. "But I'll take the salmon, please."

And though the two enthused over both the sauerkraut soup and the dumplings, Celia shook her finger at Cathe. "I know you're salivating over my lamb stew."

Cathe, smiling, shook her head.

They lingered over dessert and coffee, all of them choosing the *marillenknödel*, a sweet Austrian apricot dumpling. And *these* dumplings were delicious. A meal on board took at least an hour and a half, and afterward, they all met in the lounge for cocktails and more of Blondie's oldies.

Agnes pointed at Rupert. "I want one of those drinks you had this afternoon."

"A Toasted Almond?"

She nodded her head so hard her curls bounced. "Yes. I want to try that."

Rose gave her a wide-eyed look. "Don't you want to champagne or a Grasshopper?"

Lips in a prim line, she tipped her nose in the air. "I want something different."

"I'll order the Grasshopper," Rupert offered. "And if you don't like the Toasted Almond, we can switch."

Cathe ordered an espresso martini.

Celia looked at her askance. "Won't that keep you up?"

"I had one this afternoon." She raised her eyebrows, her smile wide. She really was smiling a lot. "And it didn't seem to do anything."

"I'll have one of those too," Celia told the waiter. Why not?

Gray's turn came around. "I'd like a dirty martini, but make it really, really dirty."

The server smiled, an older man, his silver hair slicked back. "You mean you want a filthy martini."

Which had them all laughing uproariously.

When the waiter left, Agnes asked, "What's in a dirty martini? I might want one of those." She wrinkled her nose. "Maybe I'd even like a filthy martini."

When the second round of laughter died down—really, what else could you do with a wonderful woman like Agnes?—Gray explained, "It's a martini with extra olive juice. So a filthy martini would be a lot of olive juice."

Agnes screwed up her face. "I'll just go for dirty and not filthy." The lady was quite the character.

The floor in front of the bar wasn't huge, but that didn't stop everyone from dancing as they had the two previous nights. Blondie, who was bald rather than blond, belted out *Dancing Queen* by ABBA. And Agnes was definitely the dancing queen as she and Rupert twirled their walkers around the floor. Celia was actually worried for Agnes until she saw the smile on Rose's lips. And Declan's. They were obviously conscious of the elderly woman's abilities.

For Elvis Presley's *Can't Help Falling in Love*, Agnes sat on her walker, and Rupert turned her around the floor. It was lovely to watch.

Gray pulled Celia to the dance floor, and there was nothing better than his arms around her.

Except his afternoon kisses in that big bed.

THE FEEL OF CELIA AGAINST HIM WAS LIKE THAT FIRST blush of romance, when you couldn't take your eyes off a woman and her fragrance stayed in your head long after she was gone. When you anticipated the next time you'd see her, the next time you'd touch her, the next time you'd taste her.

Holding her close to the rhythm of Elvis's song, it almost felt as if the words could be true. He could fall for her. He *was* falling for her. He couldn't get enough of her.

With Celia in his arms, Gray imagined long, luxurious nights, her skin against his, their bodies sated after hours of incredible lovemaking. He wondered how often he could fly out to California to see her and how often she could fly out to Florida?

And he whispered in her ear, "Will you spend the night with me?"

Though her body was still pliant and warm against his, he felt the slightest withdrawal. "Not tonight," she said, dashing all his hopes. "I need Cathe to get used to the idea." She gazed up at him with brilliant blue eyes. "Rain check? Tomorrow night?"

He didn't go down the rabbit hole, just held her tight. "Rain check. But you should know I'm ready already."

She laughed, a sweet tinkling sound that splashed over his nerve endings.

"I can tell you're ready." She swished her hips against him as they swayed to the music of their bodies. "I'll take care of you tomorrow."

He shivered with the promise in those words.

Maybe they should skip the bike ride and spend the day in bed.

He could only hope.

Cathe removed her makeup in front of the cabin's long mirror while Celia washed her face in the bathroom.

When the water shut off, Cathe called out, "Looks like you and Gray are getting on like a house on fire."

Her sister laughed. "Or something like that."

After throwing her makeup remover in the trashcan, Cathe smoothed on her night cream. "Where did you both disappear to this afternoon?"

Celia leaned out of the bathroom, her tone saucy. "Where do you think?"

Hand on her hip, Cathe looked at her sister's reflection in the mirror. "Don't tell me you slept with him?"

Celia melted with a faraway smile. Or maybe that was just the distance in the mirror. "I wanted to see his suite. And let me tell you—" She hung out the door again and looked at Cathe before going back to the mirror. "It was amazing. We really should've gotten a suite."

"But I'm too cheap," Cathe said for her. They would always be different in how they spent their money. But even Celia hadn't wanted to pay double the price for the upgrade. "And?" Because *just* seeing his suite didn't take the entire afternoon.

"Let's just say that one thing led to another."

"And you slept with him?"

"We fell asleep." A sexy smile curved Celia's lips. "Eventually."

Putting her moisturizers away, Cathe left the bag on the counter and strutted to the bathroom door. "How was it?"

The look in Celia's eyes could only be called dreamy. "Let's just say I wouldn't kick him out of bed for eating crackers." They laughed at the old saying they'd used many times.

Then Celia turned, suddenly, stepping out of the bathroom to put her hands on Cathe's shoulders, her eyes bright, her smile gentle. "It was so good, Cath. He made everything about me and my pleasure."

"Oh my God." Cathe gasped. "Don't tell me you're falling in love?" But would it be so bad if she was?

Celia clucked her tongue. "Of course I'm not falling in love."

"I mean, he lives on the other side of the country. You'd have to move."

For a moment, she worried about Celia moving away. Even though Cathe had her daughter close by, they had their own lives. She couldn't bear for Celia to be that far away.

"Don't be silly," her sister said, breathing in, then letting it out on a long sigh. "I want a fling. But this is the absolute best fling I could ever imagine. He's just so attentive. He says the sweetest things. He calls me beautiful and gorgeous."

"And you are." Her sister was a beautiful woman, but Bart had messed with her psyche, sucking away all her self-confidence. And Cathe was glad Gray was giving some of it back.

"I know," Celia agreed, even though Cathe didn't believe her. "He's just..." She shook her head, shrugged her shoulders. "I don't know how to explain it."

"He's adoring," Cathe said for her. "And he makes you feel like he can't get enough of you."

Celia looked at her a long moment. "That's it exactly." She paused a beat before asking, "Is that how you felt with Denny?"

Feeling the ache in her chest, Cathe managed to say, "Yes. And I miss it."

Celia hugged her close. She didn't say that Cathe would find someone else to make her feel like that, whispering instead, "Bart never made me feel that way. Not even before those last five years."

Cathe held her in a tight embrace. "I'm so sorry."

Swiping at her eye as if she might have a bit of dust in it, Celia smiled. "It's going to be better."

Cathe, thinking of Denny, of the past and the future, of Jack, said, "I hope it will be."

She just wasn't sure how much she really believed that. This was just a holiday, a vacation from her real life. And then she'd have to go back.

THEIR ENTIRE GROUP HAD SIGNED UP FOR THE WALKING tour of Vienna, but they broke into two sets, those who wanted a faster pace, and those who needed a little extra time. Rupert and Agnes chose the second group, along with Rose and Declan.

Jack planned to stay with his dad, but Declan said, "We'll take care of Rupert. You should walk with the others." He looked pointedly at Cathe.

Glad for the offer, Jack had actually thought of asking Cathe to join him with his father. But it was a whole different dynamic when he was with Dad. Jack loved him, wanted to take care of him, but he relished the moments with Cathe where he could focus on her.

"What do you think, Dad?"

"You go on." His dad patted Agnes's hand. "Agnes will take care of me."

You go, Dad. Maybe they both deserved a little romance on this trip.

"We'll take the Metro into the city," their guide said, a pretty blonde woman in her fifties. Inga's speech was tinged with only a slight Viennese accent. "I'll show you. It's very easy. If any of you would like to stay longer, you can come back on the subway."

As Inga marched them along the riverfront, Jack noticed Gray take Celia's hand. Something had happened between them yesterday afternoon if that glow they'd both worn at dinner meant anything.

A twinge of envy circled his gut. He wished he could be that easy with Cathe, not in a sexual way, but comfortable enough to take her hand because he wanted to feel her touch. And why the hell not? Walking beside Cathe, he curled his fingers around hers. Looking up at him, she smiled. And didn't pull away.

He enjoyed the warmth of her hand in his, her touch making him feel giddy, like a guy who'd finally asked out the girl of his dreams. And she'd said yes.

Bustling people filled the sidewalks, a mixture of languages floating on the air. Their group of fifteen followed Inga into the Metro, swiping their tickets and finding seats close together on the train. It was much like BART back home.

"If you return on your own, remember it's the Red Line," Inga instructed.

The streets were clean, the beautifully ornate buildings antiquated but well-kept, giving Vienna the old world feel it was famous for, even with the modern streetcars. Inga pointed out Café Sacher with its long line of tourists outside waiting for the Viennese treat *Sachertorte*.

They followed narrow streets, past a shop touting Wiener souvenirs on its awning. Cathe stifled a laugh. "I know Wiener means Austrian, but I can't help thinking they're selling hot dog souvenirs."

Pulling her close, he laughed with her. "Don't let Inga hear you say that."

Inga took them through a covered alley fronting the Lipizzaner horse stables. "This isn't where they perform," she told them. "But you can see the beautiful horses inside."

There were several tour groups in the small alley, all of them plastered against the Plexiglas to get pictures.

Jack muscled his way to the gate. "You can see them feeding on hay back there." He protected Cathe with his body as she took her time to get just the right shot.

He closed his eyes to breathe in her fresh scent and savor the heat of her body until they moved back to give others a chance.

"Here," she said, holding out her phone. "I think I got it."

She'd zoomed in on the brilliantly white horse just as it turned its head for her.

"Fantastic." And he meant it.

She gave him a high wattage beam at his praise. "Have you ever seen the Lipizzaner stallions perform?"

When Jack shook his head, she said, "I saw them in San Jose. They're beautiful and amazing."

"I'll have to put the show on my list." He could have added that he'd love to see them with her.

There were a lot of things he'd love to do with her.

They moved on down wide esplanades and past beautifully ornate buildings that could have been palaces. Until Inga brought them to another café.

"I showed you the most famous place where you can get the *Sachertorte*," she said with a big smile. "But I much prefer this place to the other café. This one serves very moist *Sachertorte*, which is a dense chocolate cake with apricot jam between the layers and dark chocolate icing." She closed her eyes and shuddered as if she were enjoying a piece right now. "You might think about that if you wish to stay a little longer."

The esplanade opened onto St. Stephen's Cathedral, its interior glittering in gold and stained glass. But the surrounding crowds were too immense, almost claustrophobic, and they moved on quickly to the concert hall where Mozart played his first concert as a child. It was a beautiful city, many of its buildings having survived World War II.

As they came full circle, Inga stopped again. "You now have half an hour of free time, and we'll meet here to return on the Metro." She pointed to the station where they'd arrived. "But you can stay in town for the rest of the day, if you'd like, and take the Metro back on your own." She repeated the line to take and the station to get off.

Cathe said to Celia and Gray, Jack included, "Do you want to get a coffee and a *Sachertorte?*"

With a smile, Celia declined. "I'd like to get back to the boat so I have time to change for the bike tour this afternoon."

"Me too," Gray agreed. "I've got the same tour."

Jack had the feeling that's not all they'd do back on the boat. And he felt that same stab of envy. But now he'd have Cathe to himself. He wanted time to talk with her, time to share coffee and a *Sachertorte*.

Time alone with her.

"Instead of just a coffee and treat—" Cathe took his hand as Celia and Gray headed off. "Let's have lunch and head back to the boat on our own. We'll still have time to make the Schönbrunn tour."

"My thoughts exactly." Just the two of them.

They found a restaurant around the corner with outdoor seating in the beautiful sunshine.

"This looks so good." She turned the tabletop sign for him. "It's like an English tea," she said, excitement brightening her features.

The picture was of a two-tiered cake plate filled with tea sandwiches, dill-sprigged salmon on toast, brie with a dollop of jam, cucumber and cream cheese, ham and cheese.

"We could share if you'd like," she said hopefully.

Jack laughed. "The sandwiches are barely more than a mouthful."

She wasn't daunted. "Then we can each order one. Unless you'd like something else."

Her. That's what he'd like. But he said, "Then we'll share dessert too?" he asked.

"Deal. What dessert do you want?"

He pointed at the table next to him, a woman seated alone reading her newspaper, a heart-shaped raspberry tart on her plate.

"Don't you want the *Sachertorte*?"

"How about this?" he teased. "We'll get one of each and share. Then decide which is better."

In the end, they decided on one savory plate and two desserts, plus a café au lait each.

After ordering, she beamed at him. His heart turned over. God, she was so beautiful. She was everything he wanted. Even if he barely knew her.

Even if he'd thought only a short time ago that he'd never want a woman in his life again.

Meeting Cathe changed everything.

15

J ack was right. The sandwiches were barely more than a mouthful. But they were delicious, and she savored each one. Jack demolished his in no time.

Her tone rueful, Cathe said, "I guess we should have gotten one each, like you said."

But Jack just laughed. She liked that about him, his ability to laugh over anything.

"I could definitely have eaten both tiers myself," he agreed.

Their café au laits arrived with the two dessert plates. Cathe leaned close to sniff as if the scent would tell her which was best. "We should each take a bite of the tart. Then a sip of water to cleanse our pallets. Then a bite of the *Sachertorte*. And we'll compare."

"Deal."

Jack was so easy. She suggested something, he said yes. If it didn't turn out exactly the way she'd planned, like the savory plate, he laughed it off.

Denny had been easy like that too. Not that they didn't fight, but it was always the big things, like money and kids.

Denny said she was too soft with Sarah. And she said he gave in too much on whatever Sarah wanted.

Jack was already drinking his water before she'd finished her forkful of tart, and she hurried to catch up. Then they dug into the *Sachertorte*.

"Definitely the raspberry tart," Jack determined.

"Yeah. The cake is a tad dry."

"Guess we should have gone to Inga's favorite café for our *Sachertorte*."

She shrugged. "But then we wouldn't have had the raspberry tart, and this is so good." Eyes closed, she savored the buttery pastry and the sweet raspberry. "Yum." Then she looked at him again. "But we can't waste it." She stuck her fork into the cake.

They demolished both desserts, then sat back to enjoy their coffee.

Jack insisted on paying the bill, and she argued. "But I suggested lunch. It should be on me."

He held up a hand. "Absolutely not. I got you to stay behind and miss lunch on the boat."

She didn't remember it that way, but she gave in. "Thank you very much." Clasping her hands together, she set her elbows on the table. "I wish we had another day in Vienna. There's so much to see."

He breathed in deeply, held it a moment. "If you like, we can skip the palace and wander around the city for the rest of the afternoon."

The idea was so appealing. Just Jack and her, strolling hand in hand the way they had during the tour, wandering the streets, maybe getting lost but enjoying it all anyway. It was a crazy idea. And she wanted it.

"We could watch a video of the palace," she suggested, her pulse racing. "I'm sure there must be one out there."

He didn't hesitate to pull out his phone, as if he wanted

more time to tour Vienna as badly as she did. "Let me call Dad and make sure that Rose and Declan are okay with taking him."

He was so caring. She'd seen that every day of the trip. If Rose and Declan hadn't been so willing, he would have taken the slower walk with Rupert.

She winked. "I'm sure your dad will love more Agnes time without you hanging over him."

Jack let out a belly laugh. "You're so right. I feel romance in the air."

She felt slightly giddy with it too.

Of course, Rose and Declan were fine with the change of plans. So was Rupert. And it was a glorious day. The sun shone brightly without being uncomfortable, not even with Jack holding her hand. They parted only when a crowd surrounded them, or kids rode between them on electric scooters.

They didn't enter any of the sites, not even the Albertina Museum, stopping only for photos of stately architecture and beautiful gardens. There were just so many places to see. The Hofburg Palace, the winter residence of the Habsburgs—imagine having a winter and a summer palace in the same city—St. Peter's Church, the Vienna Opera House, and all the way out to Belvedere Palace. She took pictures of everything, many times putting Jack in the frame for perspective.

"I was afraid I'd regret missing Schönbrunn Palace. But here, we've got so much." Even as they walked their feet off.

He bumped her shoulder. "I agree. Besides, we'll see everyone's pictures tonight."

She tipped her face up to laugh. "Of course, they'll try to make us jealous that we didn't go."

"They can't possibly make me jealous." He raised her hand to his lips, kissing her knuckles. Her heart doing a backflip, she wondered if she was enjoying the day far too much.

It was late afternoon when Jack pointed across the street. "Isn't that the café Inga said had the best *Sachertorte?*"

Cathe clapped a hand over her mouth. "We've been going in circles."

Jack gave another of his big laughs. "Not entirely. But that is the café." He twisted his wrist to look at his watch. "And it's teatime. Shall we share a *Sachertorte?*"

"Absolutely." After being seated, they ordered coffees and cake.

Cathe chewed thoughtfully, wanting to taste and compare. "This is way better than the one we had for lunch." Then she winked. "But that raspberry tartlet wins the prize."

Jack pulled the Vienna map from his pocket and figured out exactly where they were. "We can spend at least another hour here and still make it back for dinner at seven."

"I have to be back before dinner. I've left Celia alone all day."

Jack gazed at her a long moment, and she saw the wheels of his mind working, wondering if he should speak. Then he did. "I don't think she's feeling the pinch of not having you around. She and Gray are getting on like a house on fire."

She rolled her eyes at him. "That's such a cliché." Especially since she'd already used it. "Think of something better."

"They're getting on like..." He drew out the word, thinking. Then his eyes turned flame blue. "They get on like oil and balsamic on sourdough. Just soaking each other up." He closed his hand into a fist like he'd won the contest. "They're just lapping each other up."

She smiled, let it grow until it was a full-fledged grin stretching across her face. "Now that's a pretty good one." She pointed her finger at him. "Because I love balsamic vinegar and oil with all those herbs drizzled on French bread."

He groaned. "You're making me hungry. Maybe we need an Italian restaurant."

Secluded in their corner, they smiled together as if they were sharing a secret.

Jack once again insisted on paying the bill. "On the way back to the Metro, we could stop at the café where we had lunch and get the raspberry tart." Outside the café, he took her hand again, looking down at their fingers. "But I'd rather hold your hand than carry a raspberry tart back to the ship."

He made her laugh so hard. But mostly, she liked the feel of his hand around hers.

Even though it was September and most schools were back in session, Vienna was obviously a destination. Sightseers crowded the streets, especially with the lovely day, and they dropped hands several times as other tourists broke them apart.

"Let's take a shortcut where there's not so many people." He led them into a narrow street.

He was right. It was much quieter. "I like this better," Cathe said in relief. "You want to see all these fabulous places, but the problem is everyone else wants to see them too."

"We just have to find places that are just as beautiful but off the beaten track, so no one knows about them."

"Do places like that even exist?"

"Sure. Instead of Rome, you could go to a little town in Spain called Mérida which has an amphitheater, aqueducts, Roman bridges, a theater, a temple. And there's a town in Croatia that has one of the most well-preserved amphitheaters.

"Have you ever been?" she asked.

Jack shrugged. "I just read about it in one of those blogs that says instead of visiting this crowded tourist spot, visit here and see all the good stuff without all the crowds."

"Someday you and Rupert will have to do it." She'd gone to Rome with Denny, but the town in Spain sounded lovely.

He grew quiet as they walked, and she thought perhaps it was something he'd planned to do with his wife.

They made a left, and Jack consulted his map. "We should find the main road back to the Metro just down here."

But after another turn, the area became more residential, with few shops and no tourist attractions. Finally, they found themselves in a narrow alley, and Cathe said, "We must have made a wrong turn when we went off the beaten track."

Jack looked at his map, frowning, then eyed the street placard on the wall of the corner house. "I'll find that street name on the map. That'll straighten us out."

She shifted a little, studying the map along with him, but she couldn't see the street either. "Maybe we're lost."

Without looking at her, he said, "I promise we're not lost."

He sounded so like Denny whenever they were lost. Waiting a couple of beats, she suggested, "We could find a busier street and asked directions."

He turned the map as if that would help. "No worries. I'll figure it out."

Hearing Denny's words in Jack's voice, she couldn't help smiling. "I can speed walk down to the intersection and see if there's anyone who can direct us."

He looked at her. "No, no. I don't want to lose you in the crowds down there."

Laughter laced her voice as she asked, "Why don't men ever want to ask for directions?"

He looked at her deadpan for a second. "Because it's written in our DNA not to ask for directions."

She waited, the smile on her lips.

And he added, "Way back in prehistoric times, men were the hunters. They couldn't ask other hunters, 'Hey, do you know where the next woolly mammoth is that I can kill to feed my family?' They would've lost face. They might even have been tossed out of the clan and have to go it alone. But women, they were gatherers. It was fine for them to go up to another woman and say, 'Where's the closest gooseberry bush so I can feed my family?' And that's why men are genetically predisposed not to ask for directions and women are." He shrugged like she should know this. "It's in the DNA."

He was so utterly serious that she couldn't help her burst of laughter.

She laughed so hard she had to hold her sides as she leaned against the wall. Finally, she managed to say, "You're joking, right?"

She saw he was laughing with her. "It sounded pretty good, right?"

"But you were so serious, like you actually believed it."

"It's gotta be true, don't you think?"

Through her laughter, she said, "Well, you certainly made it sound good."

He leaned in to wipe a tear from the corner of her eye. "I've never made a woman laugh so hard she cried."

Smiling, she tapped his chest. "There's a first time for everything."

He was so close she could see the flecks of gray in his blue eyes, so close she smelled the spicy-sweet scent of his after-shave. So close she felt everything inside her shift.

It was as if their bodies were magnets, drawing them to each other. She wanted the taste of him on her lips.

Then his kiss filled her up. His lips were gentle, providing her with a warmth she hadn't known in two years. He went deeper, taking her with him without meaning to, without thought. On her toes, she wrapped her arms around his neck, and he pressed her against the wall, his hand hot and sensual on her waist, his body touching hers everywhere. She felt what she did to him, his hardness, his need, and the same need rose inside her. Moaning softly, she held him tight, his chest a caress against her breasts. Her nipples tightened, wanting his touch.

She pulled back, needing to breathe, needing to tell him exactly what she wanted. "Oh my God, Denny, please."

Instead of giving her what she needed, he stiffened. Her skin was cool where his warm hands had been, his lips inches away, and she was leaning against the wall, her arms falling from his shoulders as he looked down at her.

And the echo of her words filled her head even as Jack said, "I'm sorry. I shouldn't have done that. I got carried away."

She wanted to tell him she'd liked it. That she'd wanted it.

And yet, standing there, hearing herself say Denny's name, grief assaulted her. The pain, the loss. All the lonely days and nights.

And now this, using Jack to fill the gaping hole inside her.

The terrible wave of guilt pressed her flat to the wall. Not for betraying Denny. He'd been gone for two years, and he would never begrudge her finding another man.

No, it was for what she was doing to Jack. Her heart wasn't free to give. It would always belong to Denny. And right now, she was just assuaging a physical need. The need to be touched and held and kissed and loved. The need for physical and emotional connection with another human being. Yet it was so wrong for Jack. She sensed he was a man who would need more. And all she had to give was this holiday.

Because she would always belong to Denny.

JACK WATCHED THE TURMOIL ROLL ACROSS HER FACE, THE emotions pooling in her eyes. Guilt gnawed at his insides. He shouldn't have pushed. He'd wanted more, but now obviously hadn't been the time.

The sound of her husband's name on her lips had killed him.

Yet he tried to soothe her. "I am so sorry." Cupping her cheek, he leaned in to whisper words of apology in her ear. First, he couldn't touch her. Now, he'd touched too much. "That was all my fault." He stopped short of saying she wasn't ready. He added only the last part. "I couldn't help myself." She needed to know how desirable she was. "But I'm so sorry for putting you in that position."

She blinked, and a single teardrop ran down her cheek. She opened her mouth with something she needed to say, but closed up again, as if the words couldn't come.

"I am so, so sorry," he murmured, as if she were a child he needed to comfort.

He wanted to wipe her tears away, but she did that herself, and finally said, "Please don't apologize. It was a mutual kiss. And I enjoyed it." She breathed heavily. "I just don't want you to get the wrong idea."

That she'd wanted his kiss should have made him feel better, but his heart begged him to ask what the right idea was. One night or a few days on the boat? Or even a few weeks? He'd take whatever he could get. Even as he had the thought, he saw how pathetic it was. Is that what he'd done with his wife? Taken the scraps she offered until he had no more scraps to give?

He took her hand in his. "Come on. I'll walk you back to the Metro." He wanted to say they could do whatever she wanted. But he wouldn't humiliate himself that way again.

With her hand in his, he led them out of the maze he'd created, the map suddenly becoming a living thing in his head, showing him the way.

Then they were on a main street he recognized. "We turn here."

She drew a deep breath. "It wasn't fair to you. It's just that I can't let go. You deserve someone better."

He knew what she meant. She could never let go of her husband. But he held her hand tight in his, not about to let go, not here where he could lose her. "I don't expect anything from you." He was about to say it was just a kiss. But it was so much more than *just* a kiss. "I understand how hard it is for you, how much you loved your husband."

She dipped her head, watching her feet as they walked.

He admitted to his bruises, if only to himself.

"I know you don't have expectations, Jack, and this is just a river cruise. But I also don't want to hurt you. I like you."

His battered heart started to hope again. "I like you too. And we're okay. We're still friends. But I enjoyed that kiss, even if you're not ready for anything else."

She stopped in the middle of the sidewalk, forcing him to turn back to her even as people flowed around them. "What if I'm never ready for anything else except a fling?" She hesitated after the word, as if using it was a terrible crime.

He smiled, wanting to ease her tension. "I'm totally up for a fling." Something changed in her gaze, though he couldn't say what, and he added, "I'm also perfectly content to be friends."

"I just don't want to hurt you."

"And I don't want to hurt you. But I'm an adult, and you don't need to worry about me." He palmed her cheek, her warmth seeping into the cold places inside him. "I know what I want. Even if it's just a night, or a few days. But I won't take anything you don't want to give."

He turned, started walking again, her hand in his binding them. "Neither of us has anything else to castigate ourselves for. We enjoyed that kiss." He knew it, felt it; she'd enjoyed that kiss as much as he had. "There's nothing to feel guilty about. And I'll always count you as a friend."

Yet a fist closed around his heart and almost stopped its beating.

What if she never wanted anything more than friendship?

16

"**O**h my God, it was so funny."

Celia sat next to Gray at the dinner table. "You should have seen Celia's face."

"My jaw was hanging open," she admitted to the group.

"I almost fell off the bike trying to reach over and close her mouth."

Everyone laughed with her. She didn't feel self-conscious at all. "I mean, the guide didn't even warn us we'd be biking through an island nudist camp."

"To be fair, she told us the name of the park. She assumed we all knew what it was."

Celia widened her eyes with the same astonishment she'd felt on the bike ride. And embarrassment. "A man just walked across the path with everything hanging out. And a woman sunbathed on the grass with her legs spread right in our direction." She practically gasped the words.

"There were more men than women," Gray said dryly. "Celia got far more jollies than I did."

Agnes clapped her hands. "Maybe we can go there after dinner? I've never seen a naked man."

Declan said, even more dryly than Gray. "You were married, Agnes."

"I meant naked men out in the wild." Then she clasped her hands as if she were praying. "Besides, in my day, everything was done under the covers." Her dry tone matched Declan's.

Rose tried to end the argument. "I'm not sure I could actually take the sight of naked men with everything hanging out."

Undeterred, Agnes looked at Barbara, her caregiver, seated on Rupert's other side. "But you'd like to go, wouldn't you, dear?"

Barbara stifled a smile. "The shock might stop my heart."

Agnes waved a hand. "You silly girl. It's just a man."

Rupert patted her hand then. "I would take you, my dear, but I have the feeling we wouldn't get anyone here to drive us."

Agnes's eyes brightened. "Would you actually go, Rupert?"

It amazed Celia that Agnes didn't remember anyone's name except Rupert's. Maybe she remembered exactly what she wanted to.

What Celia didn't admit was that they'd left the group to bike back on their own, with their guide's agreement. After their cohorts were far in the distance, never to return, she and Gray had removed their clothes and lain on the grass. It had been glorious, the sun on her bare skin, her hand in Gray's warm grip. And she whispered to Gray exactly what she'd do to him if they'd been alone out there.

Gray had rolled over, murmuring, "If you don't want everyone staring in my direction, you better stop that right now."

She'd wanted to touch him, only the thought of the police calling the cruise captain to say they'd been arrested for indecent conduct stopped her. Gray had stayed on his stomach, hiding his disreputable state even as she continued to bathe him with dirty talk. The day had been amazing fun. And tonight, she'd do every single thing she'd talked about.

Of course, she'd have to tell Cathe she'd spend the night in Gray's stateroom.

She hoped her sister wouldn't mind. Maybe she'd enjoy the alone time. She could wash her hair, read a book, write notes in her journal without worrying about when she needed to turn out the light.

After tonight's dancing and a couple of champagne cocktails, along with brief kisses no one would notice, she'd work Gray up until he dragged her to his stateroom and begged her to stay.

She couldn't wait to repeat all the magical things he'd done to her yesterday. She couldn't wait to do all the things she'd made up as they lay naked in the sunshine on a nudist island.

GRAY KNEW HE WAS DONE FOR. HE'D KNOWN IT THE moment she sat next to him in the lounge tonight, her scent curling around his head like champagne bubbles. He'd known it as she whispered her naughty thoughts while they danced to the slow numbers. He'd known it as he held her close, letting her feel what she did to him.

He loved how turned on Celia became. He loved the way she toyed with him. And when they got to his suite, it would be his turn. He'd make her scream, without caring one damn bit who could hear.

He felt young, almost whole again. He was glad he hadn't let Eva take this trip as part of the settlement. And he was so damn glad for the big bed and the expansive shower large enough for two.

Celia was perfect for him. He wanted her, but he'd go even further to say he needed her. He wasn't about to let her go when the trip ended.

He just had to figure out a way to get her to see that too.

❀

CELIA HAD WHISPERED IN CATHE'S EAR, "DO YOU MIND IF I spend the night in Gray's cabin?"

They'd already talked about it, and Cathe wouldn't tell her sister no. Celia had said long before this trip began that she intended to find a man. And Cathe liked the way Gray looked at Celia, as if she were the most desirable woman on the planet. Even if it was just for a week on a cruise, she was happy for Celia. After everything Bart had put her through, she deserved a man like Gray who made her feel special.

"I don't mind at all," she whispered back before Gray had whisked Celia away for another slow dance.

But now, alone in their room, Cathe looked out their aquarium window at the lights bobbing on the opposite shore. The tall buildings lit up the newer part of Vienna.

And God, it was so terribly lonely. She hadn't expected to feel that. She'd thought she'd write in her journal and tumble into bed. But once all that was done—without a single mention of Jack—she couldn't sleep. Thoughts of Celia and Gray and everything they were doing up in his stateroom consumed her.

Because she knew what she was missing.

Jack. His hand on her waist. His kiss. His arms around her as they danced. The fact that she hadn't felt a man's touch in two years.

Until today.

She wanted Jack so badly it hurt.

In the early days, she'd wanted Denny just like this, with

an ache in her belly. And after Sarah went to college, those good times had come again for a while. But then the frantic, heart-pounding, breath-stealing need had waned.

Until Jack kissed her with such overpowering passion. And all those needs for everything she'd been missing flooded back.

Maybe she should take a page out of Celia's book, just do it, take the edge off this need roiling inside her, quench the fire Jack had ignited.

But it would wrong. She wasn't even sure she could climax with Jack. And this afternoon, in the middle of that passionate kiss, Denny's name slipped past her lips.

Denny would understand she had needs.

But she wasn't sure Jack would understand that she only wanted it once. Or twice. Or maybe through the end of this trip.

But then it had to be over. She could never love anyone the way she loved Denny. And Jack, with his looks so like her dead husband's, with his gentle manner and his gentle voice and his gentle touch, needed more than half a love. She didn't have it to give. He would always be a substitute for Denny. And she couldn't do that to him. He was too good. It wasn't fair.

He'd said he had no expectations, but dancing with him tonight, slowly, in each other's arms, she'd felt his expectations overwhelming her.

She'd wanted him so badly, wanted his arms around her, his lips on her, his fingers inside her, his *everything* inside her.

And now her nerves jangled with need and her breath came fast, her fingers clutching the edge of the bed as her body reacted. She was hot and wet in a way she hadn't been for a long time.

She looked at her phone on the bedside table. Celia was

gone for the night. Jack had given her his phone number. She could call.

But he couldn't leave Rupert alone.

She jumped up to pace the room, running her hands through her hair. It was dry now, but she could smell the body wash on her skin, feel her hands on her body as if they were Jack's, taste his kiss on that narrow Vienna street. He'd tasted so good, his body pressed hard against hers.

It was as if her feet and hands decided before her mind could, her legs carrying her to the bedside table, her fingers fumbling with the phone, finding his number.

Calling him.

JACK SAT ON THE VERANDA, UNABLE TO SLEEP EVEN AS THE boat rocked him gently.

His father had fallen asleep over an hour ago, his snores echoing in the cabin. But the sound hadn't kept Jack awake.

Cathe kept him awake.

He hadn't thought it would happen for him again, not after the marriage he'd had. He certainly hadn't thought this need for a woman would come over him so quickly, after only a few days. But Cathe's kindness, her caring, and her laughter had burrowed under his skin. And now he wanted her so much his gut ached with it.

Still, he had to respect her wishes, had to accept her belief that she'd never be over her husband. Even if holding her in his arms as they danced tonight put the lie to her certainty.

He'd told her he had no expectations. But he'd lied. If he made love to her once, he'd beg for twice. And twice would turn into four times. If he had her for a week, he'd want her for a month. And a month would make him need a year. It would go on and on.

There was heartache in his future. But did he want to miss being with her for the sake of missing the heartache? He knew heartache intimately, and he could live with it.

He wanted her any way he could have her, even if it was only one night. At least then he would have a memory to carry with him. If she let him, he would make it the best memory of her life. And of his.

His phone rang on the small table beside him. Without even looking, he knew it was her. And his heart leaped, not caring one damn bit about heartache.

When he answered, she didn't say hello, just, "You said you didn't have any expectations."

"I don't. Except to make you feel good." He had so many expectations he couldn't even count them. But he hoped only for this one night.

"I don't want to hurt you." She repeated her mantra of the afternoon.

"I won't be hurt. Because this will be so good. For both of us." Before she could put up another roadblock neither of them truly wanted, he said, "Just tell me you want me. And I'll be there."

The silence killed him. Until she whispered, "Can you leave Rupert?"

"He's sound asleep, and he'll be good for three hours. He's like clockwork, so I'll have to come back to help him then."

"Do you want to come to my cabin?" she asked.

He wanted to shout out his joy. But he held it in, answering softly, "I would love to come to your cabin."

This time, she didn't hesitate. "Then come now."

He would make her come so many times she'd never be able to forget him.

And she'd need him again.

❀

THOUGH SHE'D BEEN EXPECTING THE SOFT KNOCK ON THE door, Cathe still jumped. Her nerves assaulted her the moment she'd set down the phone. The cabin was too small, there were only twin beds, she didn't have a sexy nightgown.

In the end, she'd dressed again, not wanting to be in her pajamas when he arrived. Her palms were sweating as she opened the door.

Then her breath whooshed out of her lungs. He was so beautiful. Even if she felt bad that she might hurt him, her whole body melted at the sight of him.

And there was no going back.

"Will Rupert be okay?" She stepped back to let him in.

"You can set an alarm by Dad." He looked at his watch. "I need to be back by two, which is when he gets up. He says I make him feel like an invalid, that he can't do anything on his own. But he's unsteady without his walker. I left it sitting by his bed, just in case."

She wondered if he was overexplaining, maybe feeling guilty. Or nervous like she was.

But she had her own guilt. "I just don't want you to get hurt."

He didn't touch her, at least not with his hands, but his gaze traveled the contours of her face. "I'm fine. As long as this is what you want. I don't want to pressure you into anything."

She put her hand over her mouth to stifle the ridiculous laugh. "You aren't pressuring me." She swallowed hard, then her thoughts burst out. "I'm just so lonely," she said on a near sob.

It didn't take a moment for Jack to gather her into his arms. "You don't have to be lonely. At least not for tonight."

He held her tight the way she needed him to. His arms around her were so strong, so soothing, so safe. She melted into him, and they held each other until all her butterflies flew away.

She leaned back to look up at him. "As long as I'm not the one pressuring you." Jack was the kind of man who couldn't resist helping a needy woman.

He smiled, stroked a finger down her cheek. "You don't know how long I've dreamed of holding you in my arms. It seems like forever. I saw you over breakfast that first day in the hotel dining room. Then later at the café."

She suddenly knew how her sister had felt for those five years when her husband refused to make love to her as if she'd were invisible, nonexistent. Cathe had been invisible for two years without even knowing it. With just a few words and a passionate kiss, this man turned her into a woman again, feeding her everything she needed.

All her questioning rushed out of her head, and she reached up, her hand on the nape of his neck, pulling him down.

Jack kissed her, a sensation like no other, as if she were drowning and he was breathing life into her. He made her feel beautiful and wanted. Desired.

Greedy for a man's touch, she wanted only this man's touch. It couldn't be the same with anyone else.

She went up on her toes just as she had that afternoon against the wall and wrapped her arms around his neck. He hauled her up against him, holding her tight. He kissed her with all the beauty she knew lived in his soul. Parting her lips, she took his tongue into her mouth, savored his taste, sweet and minty. She relished his spicy scent enveloping her.

Settling down on her feet, coming back to the real world, she looked up at him.

And he said everything she needed to hear. "I want to touch every inch of you. I want to run my hands over your skin, feel your heat. I want to taste you." His voice dipped down to a harsh whisper. Then he licked his lips. "I don't have a condom, but there's so many other things we can do. Is that okay?"

"I'm too old to get pregnant. And I haven't been with anyone since my husband. You don't have to worry."

He shifted slightly, his eyes roaming her face. "I want to protect you. And I haven't been with anyone else for a long time. Even before my divorce. She wasn't interested in me."

How similar his situation had been to Celia's. She cupped his face. "I'm so sorry."

He shook his head. "I'm not. I feel like I've been saving myself for you." Smiling, he leaned down to kiss her swiftly.

Her heart soared. "I want you. All of you."

Suddenly, his hands were on her bottom, hauling her up until she wrapped her legs around his hips, locking her ankles behind him. She kissed him from above, deliciously slow and sweet and deep, filling her up.

When they took a breath, he asked, "Which is your bed?"

"By the window." She pointed over her shoulder.

He carried her there, and she slid leisurely down his body, feeling how hard he was.

Kissing her as his hands snaked beneath her top, he pushed it up over her breasts until she raised her arms. He left her lips long enough to pull it over her head.

She didn't even feel self-conscious, not with him so close and the heat of his body reaching deep inside her. Her hands under his shirt, she tugged it up, and he pulled it over his head.

With his beautiful chest tempting her, she leaned in to kiss his nipple. He sighed as she traced her tongue over his skin, then sucked him gently. This time, he groaned. His chest lightly covered in soft hair, she caressed him, twirling the soft strands until she followed the line down his abdomen. Her fingers tucked into his shorts, she waited, looking up at him. "May I?"

She wanted to be bold and say she needed him naked, but she wasn't sure of herself yet, wasn't sure of him. But even now, even before she felt him inside her, she knew once would never be enough.

"Please," he murmured, a crack in his voice. Laying his hands over hers, he helped her unbuckle the belt, tug open the snap, and pull down the zipper, letting the shorts fall.

Stepping back, he toed off his shoes. And she took in the full glory of his body, toned as if he worked out every day and sexy in the tight briefs outlining everything. He was big, thick, and her mouth actually watered.

She hadn't tasted a man in so long.

Could she confess this to him, tell him how much she loved the feel and taste of a man in her mouth? What would he think of her?

She looked up, his eyes like fire, and knew she didn't have to say anything at all. Easing her fingers inside the briefs, she slid them down, going to her knees as she helped him step out of them.

There he was, bold and beautiful. She wrapped her hand around him, looked up.

And whispered, "I want this."

He groaned as she wrapped her lips around him, tasting the salty-sweet pearl on the tip. He was ambrosia. His taste made her feel like a woman again, brought her to life as if she'd been sleeping for a hundred years.

"Jesus," slipped out on his breath as she slid down on him. "Christ. Cathe." Two separate words, not a sentence.

Cathe pulled all the way up, down again, until Jack tangled his fingers in her hair and guided her to the rhythm he needed.

The erotic sensation of him in her mouth and his soft

grunts and growls strummed her nerve endings. She hadn't felt this alive since those frantic days as newly minted empty-nesters. She'd forgotten how good it was. And God, she needed it now.

She let herself go, planted both hands on his flanks, taking him all the way, deep in her throat, back up, matching the rhythm he wanted. She wasn't sure how she could live without this again. He'd reminded her how good a man tasted, how sensual his hard flesh felt in her mouth, how delicious the tiny drops on her tongue.

Until finally he pulled back, his eyes hot on her. "I can't take anymore or I'll lose it. When I come, I want to be deep inside you."

hen I come, I want to be deep inside you.

Never had there been more erotic words. They set all her cells buzzing, needing, wanting.

Jack hauled her to her feet, and his hands under her armpits, he turned, lifted her, laid her on the bed. "But first I need to taste you."

She'd never put on shoes. All she wore was a skirt and her bra and panties.

After peeling off the skirt and throwing it aside, he snapped the clasp of her bra, and pushed aside the cups until he could devour her breasts. Sucking, licking, pinching her nipples, he turned her into a quivering, crazy hot mess.

Without sliding the bra off her shoulders, he crawled down her body, trailing warm kisses in his wake. His fingers inside her panties, he pulled them over her hips. She rose to help him, the silk skimming her legs. She'd never been more glad of her taste for silky lingerie.

What if she'd been wearing cotton granny panties?

She laughed. He looked up at her as he kissed his way to her mound. "Does it tickle?"

"No. It's tantalizing. So good." Then she smiled. "I was just glad I chose nice underwear."

He laughed deep in his chest, the vibration rumbling against her thighs where he lay. "I don't care what you wear. I want you any way, anyhow, anywhere."

She trembled with the depth of his words, and a fresh wave of heat flushed her body.

"I want the taste of you on my tongue. I want to feel your climax as you tighten your legs around me when you come."

His words took her to a new level, and she thought she'd come with his very first taste.

But no, not yet. She wanted to feel so much more. "Touch me," she whispered.

Shifting lower, he spread her legs, kissed her all over, blowing warm air on her until finally he parted her. The first touch of his tongue made her shudder, almost shatter.

She fisted her hands in the duvet. "So good, so good. Please. More." Not even realizing she spoke until he looked at her, raising only his eyes, his mouth still buried against her.

She'd never seen a more beautiful sight, never felt a more sensual touch, his tongue on her, swirling, licking, his mouth sucking her.

Then he slowly eased two fingers inside her.

"Jesus, you're wet," he whispered in wonder and need.

She was wetter than she'd ever been, needier, wanting so much more.

Maybe it was the length of time since... *No, don't go there, not now.*

He stroked her slowly, his tongue rolling over her, slow, then faster, faster. A quiver started in her legs, rose up her torso. She only remained on the bed by holding the coverlet tight in her fists. Her hips rose to his rhythm, her legs quaking to his touch. Breath puffed from her lips, fast, jerky.

And finally, she cried out his name. "Jack, Jack, Jack." The tidal wave hit her, rolling her under until there was nothing but sensation, nothing but the fire in her blood, nothing but his mouth on her and his fingers inside her.

Climbing her body, he fit himself between her legs. Then he was in her, slamming hard, pounding, thrusting, like a bighorn sheep rattling his horns and fighting for her, claiming her.

And somehow her climax went on and on with each deep thrust of his body.

He growled, he groaned. Then he kissed her.

Their tongues melded, their breaths mingled, his taste sweet and salty with her. And it started all over again, the quaking of her limbs, the flash of heat through her body. He throbbed deep inside her, intensifying every sensation. Until finally she felt his heat everywhere, deep within, over her skin, straight up to her heart.

She clasped him tight, her ankles locked behind him, and she came endlessly, messily, beautifully.

When his body shook, she opened her eyes to his throat stretched above her, his teeth gritted, everything in him filling everything in her.

She would need this over and over. She would need *him*.

And for this short time, she wouldn't think about Denny and everything she'd lost.

HE FELT AS IF HE'D ENTERED ANOTHER REALM, MAYBE another world. Rolling to his side, Jack brought her with him, staying deep inside her. He wanted to feel every quake, quiver, and throb of her body, just as she would feel his. When she climaxed, her body had clamped so hard, so deliciously around him. Even as he wanted to make her come endlessly, her body had worked him until he couldn't hold out. He'd flooded her, just as she flooded his senses, his consciousness.

He couldn't let her go yet.

"That was exquisite. I wish I was a writer and I could find all the right words."

She clasped her arms tightly around him, and he never wanted to leave her embrace, didn't even want to look at the clock on the bedside table or twist his wrist to see his watch. He never wanted to go anywhere without her, not ever again.

Tipping her chin, he kissed her, enthralled by her taste, a little bit him, a little bit her, a whole lot sexy.

"I want to stay the night." He punctuated that with a kiss. "To wake up with you in my arms and make love to you again in the early morning."

"I know." She didn't tell him he couldn't, didn't remind him about Rupert, didn't tell him when her sister would return. She simply clung to him.

Maybe it was all he needed, words to tell him she wanted exactly the same thing. Even if life intruded, she wanted him.

He fell asleep still inside her, and it was glorious.

His internal clock woke him at one thirty. He could stay a little longer.

Then a brilliant idea bombarded his senses. "Come with me. I'll help Dad, get him back to sleep, then we'll share a glass of champagne and talk. And I can kiss you again."

He was afraid she'd say no, afraid he'd have to leave her.

But she pulled him down for another kiss, and when their lips parted, she whispered, "I'd love that."

He could have wept with the warmth that swept his heart and soul.

AFTER JACK TOOK CARE OF HIS DAD, THEY SAT ON THE veranda, watching lights twinkle on the opposite shore. Though her body was sweetly sated, she thought she'd need him again tonight.

His minibar was stocked with liquor. They'd found two champagne splits and sipped in comfortable silence, the harmony after making love.

She wouldn't call it anything else. She didn't think Denny would mind. If she'd gone first, she would have wanted him to find happiness again. And yet she would never stop loving him. Even as good as it had been with Jack, Denny would always be first.

So how could she do this to Jack, who was so caring, so loyal, so beautiful?

It was a useless question, and she'd have to live with it. Because there would be more nights like this, every night until the trip was over. She would give in to the guilt when she was home. For now, she wished they were like Gray and Celia, spending the entire night together.

But this would have to be enough.

"Are you going to the Abbey tomorrow?" he asked.

"Yes."

"We're going too." And tomorrow afternoon, they would sail again.

She smiled to herself. "I wonder who we can get to play Skip-Bo with Agnes and Rupert."

Jack knew what she was thinking. "We'll find someone. There's Barbara, her caregiver."

"And Declan and Rose."

He laughed softly. "They'll be thinking along the same lines as us." Oh yes, he knew exactly what she was thinking. "Have no fear, we'll find someone." His eyes twinkled as brightly as the lights across the river. "Then we can slip away."

"I'll have to make sure Gray and Celia are on the sundeck."

Winking, he added, "Or in his suite."

The ideas were so tempting, her body melted. She wanted him again. "Maybe we should sit inside and close the bedroom door." Reaching over, she cupped him. "I want you in my mouth again."

"And I want my mouth on you."

They ventured back inside, leaving the veranda door open for the warm breeze off the river. And closed Rupert's door to cover the sounds of pleasure they were about to make.

CELIA WOKE TO THE FEEL OF A MAN'S ARMS AROUND HER, a sensation she hadn't been able to relish in far more than the five years Bart hadn't touched her.

For a long time, he claimed that sleeping in each other's arms overheated him. But lying in Gray's arms, she no longer cared if that had been an excuse not to touch her. Now she had *this*, and it was made all the more glorious because it had been so long.

As he moved, she realized he was awake and turned to face him. "That was amazing."

He'd made love to her twice. When was the last time she'd made love with a man twice in one night? She couldn't remember and didn't want to destroy the moment by thinking too hard.

He pulled her in, tugged her leg over his hip, his hardness against her core, making her want him again. She slipped a hand down between them, wrapped her fingers around him. "Don't tell me ready *again*?"

He grinned. "Where you're concerned, I'm always ready." Then he turned sober, his eyes dark chocolate as they roamed her face. "I can't get enough of you. If I could, I'd keep you imprisoned here day and night."

Her heart thrilled at his words. Of the lovers she'd had since leaving her husband, none had asked for her number, not that she'd have given it to them. But with Gray, it was all different. She wanted more and more. "Maybe I'll trap you here for the entire voyage." Squeezing him, he grew rigid in her grip.

"We should start right now." Then he rolled her beneath him, spreading her legs, tasting her, and driving her wild.

THEY SHOWERED BEFORE BREAKFAST, GRAY ENTRANCED with her body. Under the tingling spray, he searched all her erotic nooks and crannies, made her come again. This would have to hold him most of the day. No matter what she said about keeping him prisoner, she couldn't completely desert her sister.

She was so different from Eva, empathetic, sensitive to others feelings, fun-loving, and yet even with the damage she suffered, she wasn't bitter.

So he would steep his senses in this moment and dream about the night to come, all the nights to come.

And he'd plan ways to make it last far longer than this cruise.

CATHE MANAGED SURREPTITIOUS TOUCHES DURING breakfast, her thigh pressed to Jack's, his hand on her knee, her foot running up his leg and making him twitch.

She'd returned to the room long before Celia came in to change, and not a single sign of what she'd done in the night remained. Except her smile. Maybe she should have shared with her sister, but for now, she wanted to keep her feelings close. Besides, Celia had her head in the clouds after her night of lovemaking, and Cathe didn't want to bring her down. She wanted her sister to glory in the night she'd had while Cathe gloried silently in hers. There would be time enough to share later.

On the tour bus, Celia sat with her, as if they'd decided not to spend every waking moment with their lovers. It was a sweet gesture on Celia's part, when Cathe knew she'd rather be holding hands with Gray while he whispered sweet nothings in her ear.

But then, Celia didn't know what Cathe would rather be doing.

Today's tour, included with the cruise, was a visit to Göttweig Abbey, a monastery sustained by monks in Lower Austria's Wachau Valley. Cathe was happy for a window seat, which enabled her to take an amazing photo of the fog-enshrouded abbey, its church steeple rising above the misty layer. Her first thought was to show the picture to Jack.

Once they arrived, an introductory film talked about the abbey's history, how it had burned down and was rebuilt, but they'd run out of money and windows had been painted on one of the facades to make it look complete.

Obviously produced for the cruise line, the film mentioned them exclusively, and when the show ended, their guide expressed her thanks. "We are self-sustained, selling our wine and nectar, but we were having a tough go of it. I'm not sure how long we could have stayed open without the help of your cruise line by bringing you all here. And I assure you will not be disappointed." The woman was a civilian docent, and there were no nuns at the gothic abbey, only monks.

"From our tasting room," she went on, "we have samples

of our apricot nectar and our champagne. Please, indulge yourselves."

Celia groaned, tasting the sweet champagne. "Oh my God, this is good." And she asked their guide, who was also serving, "Is the champagne for sale?"

Older, her gray hair permed, her smile slightly coffee stained, she said, "Of course. We have champagne, wine, and brandy. And the apricot nectar." She held up a tasting glass. "You may even buy a sixpack of our glasses."

They both smiled and tasted the apricot nectar. Cathe echoed Celia's groan. "Oh my goodness, so good. It would be even better in the champagne."

The woman sent them away with apricot nectar drizzled into the champagne tasting glass, and Cathe was dying to have Jack taste it. As she approached, his eyes danced with hints of what they'd done last night.

She wished they could have stayed together. But after he'd treated her body to another luscious exploration and wondrous orgasm, she'd returned to her cabin. Snuggled deep in the bed, she relived every moment with him until she fell asleep.

Jack's eyes widened with appreciation at the taste while she was much more vocal. "This is delicious. We have to buy some."

Celia gaped at her since Cathe was the tightwad.

"Yes," she repeated. "We need this."

Rupert poured his nectar into the half-empty champagne and agreed on the first sip. "Now *that* is good."

Of course, Agnes had to follow suit, squealing and squeezing her eyes shut, uttering, "Yummy."

"They sell it in the gift shop at the end," Cathe told them all, Rose and Declan already nodding.

Then she showed Jack her photo of the fog over the

abbey. His appreciation warmed her, and her heart felt like a melted puddle in her chest.

She turned to Celia but her sister had already moved to Gray's side, letting him taste the juiced champagne. There was something significant in the way they looked at each other. Celia had lovers since her divorce, but none had been special. Other than telling Cathe the bare-bones, Celia usually said little more about them, and she was pretty sure her sister never saw any of them again. But there was something special about Gray, something glowing around them. Cathe didn't think it was just good sex, but she didn't want to ruin it for her sister by trying defining it. Instead, she'd enjoy watching it grow over the next few days.

She and Jack were different. The thought of anything growing between them scared her because she knew it had to end.

So why had she rushed to show him the abbey photo and have him taste the champagne?

JACK FELT AS IF HE WERE A PUPPY FOLLOWING HER AROUND, but he couldn't get enough of Cathe, didn't want to even let her out of sight. Especially when everyone was around and he couldn't touch her.

They separated only when he took Rupert and Agnes in the elevator to the abbey's second floor. There, the group viewed the magnificent ceiling frescoes.

Many of the rooms felt more like they belonged in a palace rather than an abbey. Monarchs had stayed here, treated to the luxuries they expected. The docent—he hadn't heard her name—showed them the intricacies of old-fashioned life without electricity or forced-air heating. Massive porcelain stoves stood floor-to-ceiling in each of the rooms, the fires fed by servants through trapdoors in the hallways.

"When these fires were blazing day and night in the winter," she informed them, "the porcelain of the stoves was so hot, it could burn."

They toured rooms filled with magnificent tapestries, elaborate paintings, and exquisite chinoiserie, a collection of artwork with Asian motifs. Everything from vases to paintings to furniture, the pieces came from a time when Europe had become fascinated with Asian art.

The king's chamber was kept sacrosanct, for the monarch alone.

Cathe leaned close to whisper, "They all must have been short because that bed is small."

He closed his eyes, drinking in her scent. "You'd be surprised what can be done in a bed that size." He remembered every single detail of their lovemaking in her cabin's twin bed.

She gave him a smile, stopping short of swatting him, just in case someone saw. But that smile warmed him.

She snapped pictures, and Jack looked forward to reviewing them with her, helping her see how good her photography was. The photo she'd taken of the abbey from the bus window had been amazing.

After more wine tasting at the end of the tour, Jack resolved to buy the champagne and nectar. He wanted to toast Cathe in her cabin while Rupert slept. The sales lady talked him into buying the tasting glasses too.

Out on the terrace with beautiful views of Austria and the Wachau Valley, Jack stood close to her, taking her hand for just a moment, squeezing with a furtive touch.

It remained unsaid between them that they'd keep their relationship a secret for now. He didn't want anyone telling them they should or shouldn't. He didn't want intrusion.

All he wanted was to enjoy these amazing days with her. And the erotic nights.

And he didn't want to think about what came after when the trip ended.

But as he had the thought, he knew exactly what he wanted. Even after the harrowing days of his marriage, after the months of divorce, after believing he'd never want to love again, he knew he never wanted to let Cathe go.

The afternoon's entertainment comprised watching the castles, vineyards, and churches in the small towns of the Wachau Valley flow by as the ship chugged along the river.

Stretched out on a sundeck lounge chair next to Gray, Celia closed her eyes to soak in the serenity. "It's beautiful out here." She'd expected the sun to beat down, but after the morning fog wore off, it was a perfect temperature.

Gray tucked her hand in his, tacit agreement to the serenity. Neither of them mentioned the storm ahead, far in the distance, dark clouds roiling in the sky.

Beneath the canopy, Cathe and Jack played cards with Rupert and Agnes. The old lady's voice rang out across the sundeck. "Why should we watch the scenery? We've got a cutthroat game of Skip-Bo going. And I plan to win."

The murmur of laughter and agreement followed her statement. It was sweet the way Cathe and Jack took care of the old lady. Barbara, her caregiver, stood at the railing, fascinated by the verdant hills and row after row of grapes, and Celia wondered if this was her first trip abroad.

The entertainment Rupert and Skip-Bo provided for Agnes obviously allowed Rose and Declan to enjoy their honeymoon.

Celia lowered her voice. "I know this is a slow-paced cruise for old people, but I've never felt so relaxed. Onboard, it's okay to lie on a lounge chair and do nothing. I love it."

Gray raised her hand to kiss her fingers. "And I'm not working on a case or playing golf. It's perfect to lie here with nothing to do but watch the beautiful scenery."

"You don't have a case going right now?"

He laughed softly, without humor. "There's always a case. But sometimes we have a lull. And I have good people working with me. It's not all on my shoulders. They can always contact me if they have a question. But that's how I get away for golfing. If I didn't have such confidence in my colleagues, I'd be at my desk round the clock."

"That's why I chose a September trip. We've finished the summer events, and I haven't started arranging the holiday gala. Plus, like you, I have good people I work with. And it helps a lot that I'm a volunteer. I can take the time I need to get away and recharge."

"Do you travel a lot?"

"Oh my God, no." She snorted out a laugh. "My husband had IBS, and he didn't want to go anywhere." She clapped her hand over her mouth, looked at Gray. "Oops," she said between her fingers. "I shouldn't tell you that." She squashed the laugh and added, "I'd have liked to travel with Cathe, but she always had Denny. And I didn't want to be the third wheel. But this trip—" She nodded to herself. "I thought she should get away." Over the past two years ago, Cathe had simply closed up. "I'm not sure how I got her to agree."

She looked at her sister now, laughing, smiling, leaning close to whisper in Jack's ear. They were probably colluding on how to make sure Agnes won. Celia leaned into Gray. "It's doing her a world of good. Look at her smile. She and Jack have really hit it off. He lives in the Bay Area too." She stroked her thumb over the back of Gray's hand. "This could be a love affair that lasts."

Gray watched her with an indefinable look on his face. Was it sadness? Or just thoughtful? "You've never been to Barcelona or Seville? Or Rome or London or Paris?"

She followed his train of thought. "Or Venice or Rio or the Bahamas. I haven't been to Hawaii since I graduated from college."

"You'd love Barcelona. All the Gaudi architecture."

"I've seen pictures of his whimsical Park Güell. And I'd love to see his cathedral, La Sagrada Familia, once they've finished it."

His lady-killer smile weakened her knees. "We should plan a trip to see it as soon as it's done. And visit Seville and the great Alcazar."

She laughed at his dreams. "The Alcazar. They filmed parts of *Kingdom of Heaven* and *Game of Thrones* there."

His eyes turned that deep chocolaty brown she adored. "You definitely have to see where they filmed parts of *Game of Thrones*. It's a date then, 2026, or whenever they finish Gaudi's cathedral."

Her breath quickened as she imagined it. What would it be like to meet him once or twice a year for a fabulous trip? Maybe a cruise to the Bahamas. What glorious sex they would have. She wouldn't need other men, only him. It would the most amazing time of her life. "I'd love that."

Agnes squealed with delight when she won the game, and Celia felt like it was an exclamation point for the plan.

Gray stroked a finger down her cheek. "Spain in 2026." As if he'd read her mind, he added, "There's no reason we can't make a few trips between now and then. Maybe a Caribbean cruise."

"A two-week cruise would be fabulous."

Two full weeks. She imagined the excursions they'd skip to stay in the cabin making love. Was it possible? Could they really do it? Or was it just a daydream?

Yet the thought filled all the aching, lonely crannies of the last five years of her marriage.

CATHE NOTICED GRAY AND CELIA RISE FROM THE LOUNGE chairs long before the cocktail hour. She knew where they were going, and her heart turned over with delight. Celia might claim this affair was just for the trip, but Cathe had never seen her sister so happy. She didn't begrudge her a moment of this time.

Agnes had just won another game, after Cathe and Jack schemed to make sure she did, when the first raindrops hit the canopy. Cathe had seen the storm brewing ahead.

Barbara left the railing. "We should get inside, Agnes. You can continue the game in the lounge."

Agnes groaned. "But if I move now, I'll break my winning streak."

Rupert calmed her down. "Your winning streak might get even better, sweetheart, especially if you have one of your special Grasshoppers."

Agnes beamed and finally agreed.

You couldn't hustle elderly people. While Jack and Barbara gathered the walkers and helped Rupert and Agnes out of their chairs, Cathe pulled the cards together. Two deckhands rushed to their sides with huge red umbrellas as the raindrops fell harder. The elevator could hold only the two elders and Barbara, so Cathe and Jack headed down the stairs.

Waiting outside the slow elevator, he leaned close,

planting a kiss on her lips. "You smell so good. You were driving me crazy up there."

The all-over flush wasn't a hot flash, not even embarrassment. It was all Jack.

Once they had Agnes and Rupert settled, they ordered Grasshoppers for the two and champagne for themselves. The game began over a beautiful view through the lounge windows of the dark sky behind the green hills.

Amid laughter and Agnes's wonderful snark, a woman in her early sixties passed by the table and gasped. "Oh my God, you're playing Skip-Bo. I love that game. We played it all the time as kids. Back then, we called it Spite and Malice and played with decks of cards."

Agnes echoed the woman's gasp precisely. "My dear, that's exactly how we used to play." Then she grinned. "But this is much better because it has so many more wild cards."

The woman crowed. "You're a lady after my own heart. I'm Gloria, and it's a delight to meet you."

Waving her in, Agnes said, "You must join us, dear." She looked at Jack. "Can we deal in this lovely lady?"

Cathe wondered how they'd manage it. With five players, there weren't really enough cards.

Jack came to the rescue with a brilliant plan. "Why don't we let Gloria take our place?"

Gloria smiled in gratitude while Agnes grimaced. "But then we'll have only three."

Rupert piped up to save the day. "Barbara can join us."

Barbara jumped up as if she'd been listening to the entire conversation. Maybe she always had one ear trained on Agnes. "I've been dying to get in the game." She'd probably been happy to sit by the window and cull the photos on her phone, but it was sweet of her. "And I can do all the shuffling." She held up her hands, showing them arthritis free. "I haven't gotten to play a single game on this boat," she said indignantly, laughter in her voice as she pointed at Jack and Cathe. "These two have been monopolizing the entire Skip-Bo playtime."

Then she winked.

She couldn't possibly know why Cathe and Jack wanted her to step in. Could she? Cathe decided not to think about it.

"We're so sorry to have monopolized Skip-Bo." Jack's grin spread across his face as he drawled, "We need some down-time to relax in the library anyway."

Barbara gave him a look. And Cathe waved. "Have fun."

Once they were out of sight, Jack took her hand and led her to his stateroom.

Rupert would be engaged for quite some time.

And Jack put the Do Not Disturb sign on the door.

THE CLOUDS OUTSIDE DARKENED THE STATEROOM, AND THE rain on the river sounded like a waterfall as Cathe slid open the veranda doors. With a sultry feel to the air, the rain wasn't cold.

When she turned again, Jack had pulled a bottle out of the small refrigerator and held it up. "Apricot nectar for our champagne." He pointed to the two tasting glasses from Göttweig Abbey.

She gave him a smile as sultry as the rainy atmosphere. "You have the best ideas."

He'd bought it to please her, she knew. And please her, he did. In so many ways.

Slowly pouring the champagne, he made sure the juice didn't overflow the glasses.

"I have just the thing to go with it." Cathe reached into her small clutch. She'd been waiting for this surprise, and the moment was perfect as she held up a marzipan fox covered in chocolate. "I told you I'd let you have one piece. And marzipan is perfect with champagne."

"Thank you." Smiling, Jack took the offering, unwrapping it. "I hate to bite off its head."

She leaned in and bit it off for him. "There, the rest is yours."

It was gone in two bites. "Delicious." Then he handed her a glass, and they clinked, the chime ringing through the room.

As she sipped, a moan rose up her throat. "This is so good."

And he was so good. Without thinking, without analyzing, without guilt or fear that she might be using him, she went up on her toes and wrapped her arms around his neck. "There's only one thing that would be more delicious than champagne and marzipan."

She kissed him.

She was afraid she might think of Denny, even after last night, but as he parted his lips, as their tongues met and their breaths melded, there was only Jack. There were only his lips on hers, only his kiss shooting thrills through her body, only the taste of champagne and almonds and chocolate and Jack. When she set down her glass and reached for the hem of her top to pull it over her head, she wasn't thinking of Denny at all.

"Make love to me," she whispered.

All she wanted in this moment was Jack, his hands on her, his lips and tongue all over her, his body thrusting deep inside her.

And for the moment, she didn't even remember the meaning of the word *guilt*.

CELIA SHOVED HIM INTO THE BEDROOM AND DOWN ON THE bed. She loved taking charge.

Gray leaned on his hands. "Are you planning to have your wicked way with me?" A slight breathlessness trimmed his sexy drawl.

As he sat on the bed watching her, she whisked the tank top over her head. "Like what you see?"

"You damn well know I love what I see." His voice was guttural.

She unsnapped her bra, tossed it aside, and cupped her breasts for him.

"Pinch your nipples. Make them hard and rosy."

When she did, a shaft of sheer pleasure shot down to her center. She was wet. She was ready.

Then she kicked off her sandals and shimmied out of the capris.

His eyes widened. "You're perfect," he said in a reverent whisper.

Under his gaze, she felt beautiful. She didn't feel almost sixty years old. She felt young and alive, beautiful and perfect.

Then she stepped close to him, took his hand and laid his fingers on the elastic of her panties. "Take them off," she demanded.

He pulled them down, his face breathlessly close to her, and he blew warm air, sending shivers through her entire body. She kicked the panties away, and in the drawer, she found the condoms, removed a packet.

Stepping back, she tossed it on the bed beside him, then went to her knees, hands on his belt buckle. And she looked up at him. "I sure as heck intend to have my wicked way with you." She dropped her voice to a sexy growl. "And you'll love it."

He laughed, if a little shakily. "I sure as hell will."

She unbuckled, unsnapped, unzipped, then shoved her

fingers in the waistband of his cargo shorts. He raised his hips to help her pull them off, and she threw them aside before she tugged off his deck shoes.

He was already hard, bulging his boxer briefs. And she whispered, "You make my mouth water."

The anticipation was like nothing she'd ever known. Tearing his underwear down, she heard a few stitches rip. She didn't care, and when she looked at him, neither did he.

Then he was tall and proud before her.

She wrapped her fist around him. "I love doing this to you. I want you to talk to me while I'm doing it. I want your voice. I want to know if you like it, if you want me to change something."

His voice came out in a raw, strangled gasp. "You're doing everything right."

She stroked him for long, delirious moments, then took him in her mouth, closed her lips around him, sliding down as far as she could.

And he groaned. "Christ. So damn good."

She sucked hard on the way up, ending with her lips around the tip, swirling her tongue over his crown. And he whispered how beautiful she looked with him in her mouth, how sexy, how perfect. Then finally she took him with short rapid strokes, her hand moving on his shaft in the same rhythm.

An animal sound welled up from deep within him. "Jesus. You're so damn good at this."

Her heart thrilled. She made him crazy, and she loved it, needed it. She'd needed those words, this feeling, this power. For so many years, she'd been denied it. But Gray gave her everything as he tangled his fingers in her hair and whispered, "Take more," then gently pushed her down.

She took him so deep he tickled the back of her throat

and she had to come back up. "Squeeze me here." He wrapped her fingers around his sack.

His groan was manly and guttural, filled with desire and need. For her. And he swore. Over and over. Letting her know only she could do this for him. He was in the palm of her hand, literally and figuratively.

"Christ, you're so good. Holy hell, you're the best there ever was. The best there ever will be." He chanted words, filled her up with them.

She took him faster, harder, matching the rhythm he set with his hands in her hair. Then he trembled and throbbed, his body bucking.

Grabbing her under the armpits, he pulled her off. "Not yet. I need to be inside you."

Clutching the condom she'd tossed on the bed, she tore it open, rolled it on him. And as he sat on the bed, she climbed on top, sliding down, down, down. Until he filled her up all the way. Without moving, she tightened her muscles around him.

Until he groaned, "Christ, do it now."

He groaned as she began to move, up and down, holding him just at the crest of her sex, using him to ride her G spot.

"God. So good." Her words were a mere whisper.

She rode him that way until her thighs quivered, and her orgasm built, intensified. "Just like this, until I come. Touch me."

He found the hard nub of her sex, using her moisture to swirl around it. She'd never been so wet, never been so hot, never been so needy.

It came as a cataclysmic wave, starting at the top of her head, then barreling down, through her arms, her fingers, her torso, and slamming into her sex. Sensation burst out in a wave of agonizing pleasure.

As if Gray knew—of course, he knew, with her body

clamping down on him—he grabbed her hips, rolled her over and pounded into her. It could have been rough, but instead it was perfection, his body grinding against her, into her, the climax going on and on. She crested another wave as he trembled and throbbed deep inside her. His cry was harsh, and the cords of his neck stretched taut as he filled her.

And nothing had ever filled her heart like the sight of his pleasure in her.

❧ 19 ❧

Gray listened to the patter of raindrops on the veranda, Celia in his arms.

Satiated and relaxed, he floated in a blissful neverland where she was a permanent fixture in his arms.

She was so giving. And not just through her organizational skills in running fundraisers.

Eva had been a selfish lover. If he gave her all the orgasms she demanded, she'd tell him to finish himself off. She'd claim he'd tired her out, but she liked three or four orgasms, and when she was done, she was done with him. He learned to give her only two, providing her third and fourth while he was buried deep inside her.

From that minor aspect of her, he should have guessed where it was all going.

He was a dupe. A cuckold. An idiot. But maybe he'd liked their way of life, where he could do the work he loved while she brought in the money and kept them in a style to which she was accustomed.

Her parting shot had been that she'd worked her fingers to the bone so he could do the job he wanted. When granted alimony, he'd also received vindication. He knew damn well she thrived on being the shark she was. If she'd worked her fingers to the bone, it had been because she loved sticking it to the other side. It had nothing to do with him. When he became inconvenient, she'd squashed him like a queen bee kills her drone. She might have done it sooner, but he was absolutely sure she'd wanted her hooks in the other guy first.

He sounded bitter. Yet all his bitterness had drained away in these last few days with Celia. It wasn't just the sex. It was the way they sat hand in hand on the sundeck watching the scenery. It was the way she looked at him, as if she thought he might actually hang the sun, the moon, and the stars. It was her smile, her laugh, her sadness and sorrow, even her anger over her husband's treachery.

Celia made him feel worthy again. She made him feel as if his love was healing her.

It was love. He knew what love was, having loved Eva. And he didn't care how fast this thing had grown between them, inside him. Celia was his lightning bolt.

He just wasn't sure if she was there yet. In fact, it was safe to say she wasn't there at all. But that didn't mean he couldn't guide her to see things his way. He wanted to be a part of her life. He wanted to be the only one in her bed.

He wanted so damn much.

He trailed his fingers up and down her arm. "I've been thinking about the trip we imagined. We need to do it. Just you and I."

When she opened her mouth, sucking in a breath, he knew the words wouldn't be the ones he wanted to hear. He put the stall on them. "I know we were just daydreaming. And I know you can't go for Christmas, not with your gala coming up."

She tipped her head back to look at him, and he hoped that gleam in her eye was a good thing.

And he went on. "This trip has been so damn good. I want to do it all over again. With you. A cruise. Or a flight somewhere to a city you've always wanted to see. I don't care where. Paris. Rome. London. There are so many choices."

"Barcelona," she said.

He laughed, yet that city was a sharp kick to his heart. "I can't wait until 2026. And it might take even longer to finish Gaudi's cathedral."

She smiled up at him, and he decided that was a good twinkle in her eye. "We could go in the spring, see the church the way it is." She leaned up to kiss his cheek. "Then we can go again when it's all done and do our own comparison."

"I like the way you think." The kick she'd given his heart subsided, and like chains falling away, he felt it soar. "The spring. I can get away."

"What if you have a big case?"

"I don't do the courtroom gig. I'm more of an advisor. It's all good work, and it gives me gratification when we get someone freed from jail. But there's nothing I have to be in the country for as long as I can do video calls."

She licked her lips, and he wondered if she could still taste him on her tongue. The thought made him hard again. "Do you have any spring galas?"

She snorted a soft laugh. "There's always a gala. But like you, I have good people working for me. I can do a lot of the arranging over the phone and online. I just need to be there the last week before an event. And I'm sure—" She grinned, wicked and seductive. "—I can get away for a fabulous trip." She leaned up again, kissing him, her tongue darting between his lips. "I can certainly get away for more of this." She put her hand on him, squeezed.

He was hard, ready, and he rolled her beneath him, falling into the lee of her legs. "Then I think we should practice a little more right now."

She wrapped her arms around him and pulled him close. "I'm so glad you're up for that."

Then he took her to heaven all over again.

THERE WAS SOMETHING IN HER SISTER'S GAZE, CELIA WAS sure, and when Rupert said to Jack and Cathe, "I hope you enjoyed your time in the library." His eyes twinkled.

The library? Boy, did that sound like a euphemism.

"We had such a marvelous game of Skip-Bo." Agnes paused, then added, "With that lovely woman. She used to play Skip-Bo when she was a child."

"That's wonderful." Rose smiled at the elderly woman. "I'm so sorry we missed it." She shook her head, a twinkle in her eye. "That jet lag again." Declan kissed Rose's knuckles, giving her a look meant only for her.

Celia smiled to herself. They'd all been getting their groove on. Fabulous.

Rupert and Agnes had played cards in the lounge while Declan and Rose took care of their jet lag and Jack and Cathe supposedly went to the library. Yeah, right. She'd have a talk with her sister. Celia wanted every scintillating detail.

She and Gray had been late for dinner, but only by ten minutes after she'd dropped by her cabin to freshen her lipstick, makeup, and hair. There was nothing like just-had-sex hair. She'd almost wanted to leave it as is.

She could safely say she'd never felt better in her life. And she lifted her glass. "Here's to lazy shipboard afternoons watching the scenery float by and playing oodles of Skip-Bo."

Gray chuckled softly. "I second that toast."

Declan, that handsome devil, raised his glass. "And here's to Barbara." He saluted Agnes's caregiver. "Who is always right where we need her."

Rose clinked her glass to his, and they smiled that not-so-secret smile together. It was obvious to everyone at the table exactly what they'd been doing. Yet neither of them cared.

What else were you supposed to do on your honeymoon?

Barbara smiled her appreciation. "I'm always here to serve. And Agnes and Rupert—" She tapped Rupert's arm gently. "—are an absolute delight to spend time with." Then she held her glass high. "Here's to wonderful friends."

Agnes, who may or may not be tipsy, it was hard to tell with her, raised her Grasshopper. "To all my friends." She laid her head on Rupert's shoulder. "And to very special new friends."

Everyone joined in the toast with a chorus of, "To good and special friends."

Good Lord, was the old gentleman getting it on with the even older Agnes? She whispered in Gray's ear, "I think Agnes might be a cougar."

He was still laughing as their dinners arrived. She had grilled char fish, whatever that was, with warm potato salad and red cabbage.

Gray, having ordered the same, looked up the fish on his phone. "It's similar to trout."

"Well, it's scrumptious."

Though nothing could be as scrumptious as Gray.

She thought about the conversation in bed, and even the earlier one up on the sundeck. He wanted to travel with her. And he was already thinking about arrangements. A long-distance lover would be fabulous. A more perfect scenario couldn't possibly exist. She'd have freedom to work long hours on this fundraiser or that gala, no one to report to, no cold shoulder in bed at night. And every two or three months, she'd indulge in a lovely trip with an amazing lover. Thank goodness her lawyer, Carol, had gotten that incredible divorce settlement for her. She and Gray would never have a

chance to tire of each other. There wouldn't be all the arguments you have living with somebody day in and day out.

She had so many plans, every one of them as delicious as
the next.

There was the rest of this trip too. And she had some very
hot and wicked plans for Gray.

THE BUS FLEW DOWN THE ROAD THE NEXT MORNING TO
Český Krumlov, a medieval town just across the Austrian
border into the Czech Republic. And Cathe experienced the
oddest feeling, almost as if a limb had been cut off her body.
It was ridiculous. She wasn't losing Jack. This was nothing
like Denny leaving her.

Yet Cathe couldn't stop the irrational feeling of being
abandoned.

Celia was talking, having no clue to all Cathe's turbulent
thoughts. "It only makes sense. I read there are some terrific
hills to climb in this village. Rupert and Agnes could never
have made it."

Okay, so she was talking about why they were alone on
this trek. Jack and Rupert, along with Rose, Declan, and
Agnes, had chosen the panoramic bus tour of Linz, the Upper
Austria state capital, where they'd docked early in the
morning.

She and Celia had booked this tour long before the cruise
even began. A medieval town had sounded fun.

And really, she didn't like this needy feeling and pushed it
away, asking, "What's Gray doing today?"

Celia smiled, a sexy, satisfied smile. Her night had obviously been good. "He booked the walking tour of Linz.
Supposedly, the group will walk fairly fast."

"Why didn't you go with him?"

Celia looked at her, head down, nostrils flared slightly. "We aren't tied at the hip. Besides—" She draped an arm around Cathe's shoulders. "I've been neglecting you. We need some sister time."

Their guide started her monologue then, detailing what they'd see in Český Krumlov and the history of the town. She talked about the kings and queens who'd ruled it, then Czechoslovakia as a communist state, the country's liberation, and finally the split into the Czech Republic and Slovakia. Just as she had in Bratislava, Cathe soaked up all the historical details, especially the woman's tale of her own experience.

Once the bus had dropped them off in a lower parking lot, they climbed the long, steep road up to the castle and medieval village.

Lacking any golf carts or motorized vehicles that could shuttle tourists, Agnes and Rupert would never have made it up the hill.

The climb was well worth it, with spectacular views of the town laid out below, church spires rising above the houses, and a river meandering through. Walking the cobblestone streets, they passed through the castle gates into a courtyard surrounded by medieval homes. The castle had been occupied for centuries, with a covered passage over the road linking the different parts. Many of the exterior walls were painted to look like brick, a technique used during the Renaissance. Now most of the buildings contained museums.

Cathe took some amazing shots, immediately deciding which ones she'd show Jack and deleting the less-than-stellar images.

Passing through yet another gate, their guide pointed out the large moat beneath the bridge. "This is the bear moat. In ancient times, it was filled with bears, most of them starving, so that if any hapless invaders fell into the pit, they were immediately devoured."

Resembling a rock quarry, trees and shrubs sprouted around the edges. As everyone else moved on, Cathe stayed behind for pictures.

Beside her, Celia leaned on the parapet. "They don't actually keep bears in there anymore, do they?"

Cathe pointed to the heaps of raw vegetables scattered on the rocks below. "If they don't, who's going to eat all that?" She suspected the bears had already been munching.

They wandered down the steep hill to a souvenir street bursting with small, quaint shops selling jewelry and candy, clothing and leather goods. Cathe stopped by a window with an array of pretty ruby necklaces. Reading the small sign in English, she found the jewelry was made of garnets and moldavite, a black stone mined in the area, which turned to a lovely shade of green once it was polished.

"Why don't you buy it?" Celia urged her.

Cathe checked the price, doing a quick calculation in her head. "It's too much money."

"How much?"

"Two hundred dollars."

Celia snorted. "Buy it."

But Cathe had never been an impulse buyer. "I'll think about it."

Celia snorted again, louder. "And that means you'll never get it. You really should enjoy life and get yourself some pretty things."

Cathe stared at the array of beautiful necklaces in the window. Maybe Celia was right. Maybe she deserved something pretty. Then, without letting her usual hesitancy stop her, Cathe opened the shop door. "You're right. I want it."

Celia almost tripped following her. Probably because she couldn't believe Cathe would actually do it.

But she did, choosing a heart-shaped pendant of garnets with the pretty green moldavite in the center.

Cathe wondered if Jack would think the necklace looked pretty on her.

THE TOUR GROUP HAD LUNCH AT A LOVELY RESTAURANT AT the bottom of the castle hill, taking a long table on the terrace overlooking the river. Eating family-style off platters heaped with Czech delights, they dug into chicken drumsticks and skewers, potato pancakes and dumplings, with salads passed all around. Then, after flan with blueberry sauce for dessert, their guide granted them an hour of free time.

They split off to stroll the streets, wandering in and out of the small shops. Celia bought macarons from a cute store where she picked her own flavors, pistachio, lemon, even lavender.

A lady Celia had seen in the ship's dining room stopped them halfway up the cobblestone street, her eyes glittering with excitement. Older than Celia and Cathe by at least a few years, the woman was still in good shape, her calves muscled from what could only be daily walks. "We went back through the castle, and there were bears in the moat."

Cathe nudged Celia. "We really need to see the bears." Then she added to the lady, "Thanks so much for the heads up."

Celia wasn't terribly interested in the bears. But she'd go for Cathe. And they trudged up the hill to the bear moat. Sure enough, two bears slept on rocks in the sun, probably having eaten their fill of the raw vegetables.

"I guess these guys are vegan." Celia pointed to the big bear lying on the ledge. He rose just then, stretched, and trundled down off his perch, turning his backside to them to take a big pee.

Celia, laughing, shot a video of it.

"I cannot believe you're taking a picture of that bear in such a personal moment." Cathe's voice would be perfect on the video.

"How often do we see a bear peeing? This is a classic."

Then the big guy lumbered back up to his perch and stretched out again.

"At least he didn't pee where he's sleeping," Cathe noted, taking a few more pictures of the two bears.

"Let's go find a coffee shop and eat some of these macarons." Celia looked at her watch. "We've got another forty minutes."

They headed back down the hill to a cute café above a candy shop and ordered lattes. Celia decided it was the best time and place for the conversation she'd been wanting to have for a couple of days.

Cathe chose the lavender macaron, and while she chewed, Celia hit her with it. "So, tell me what's going on with you and Jack."

Her sister tried to play it cool, but Celia picked up on the little start she gave, dropping macaron crumbs to the table. Then, of course, she had to chew and swallow, taking a couple more seconds to think of an answer. "What makes you think something's going on?"

Celia gave her a withering look, seeing right through her. "I see the way he looks at you. He adores you. And don't think I've missed the handholding."

Cathe pressed her lips primly. "I don't know what you're talking about." Picking up her latte, she studied it before she sipped.

"Don't give me that crap," Celia pressed. "I think it's

great. I told you to have fun on this trip. That's what it's all about."

Flexing her fingers, Cathe set her cup down again. "You're the one who wanted that kind of fun."

"I was hoping we'd both find someone to have fun with."

Cathe grimaced, and she gritted her teeth as if she were trying to stop tears.

Celia touched her hand gently. "It's okay. I'm sorry. I didn't mean to upset you."

"I'm not upset. It's just..." Cathe pursed her lips, silent a moment as she pondered the right words. "I... We..." She dropped her voice to a whisper. "We slept together."

Celia's heart raced like she'd sprinted up to the bear moat, and joy wanted to burst out of her. If the roles were reversed, she would have asked if he was good, but that wasn't important to Cathe. Her sister needed reassurance. And Celia kept her voice soft. "That's really wonderful. You deserve a little happiness."

Clamping her teeth again to hold in her emotions, Cathe finally said, "It doesn't feel right. It feels like I'm using him as a substitute for Denny."

Her fingers wrapped around her sister's hand, Celia gently squeezed. "That's not such a terrible thing. I'm sure he enjoys being with you too."

"But I don't want to hurt him." Tears wobbled in Cathe's voice, even if they didn't fall. "I don't want to give him any expectations."

Celia sure as hell hoped Jack had expectations. Maybe once they returned home, he'd pursue Cathe. Little did her sister realize how much she needed it.

Denny had been a great guy, no doubt about that. He was irreplaceable. But that didn't mean Cathe couldn't find happiness again. That was the difference between them. Cathe knew how good marriage could be, and it was those people who found happiness and wedded bliss again.

But not Celia. She knew the worst of marriage. Well, not the worst. Bart had never hit her, nor abused her mentally or physically. He'd simply ignored her. She often wondered if that was just another form of abuse, reducing a person to begging for attention, to doing anything to get him to look at her, debasing herself, wearing sexy clothing, only to have him turn his back on her.

She'd even purchased an expensive corset from an exclusive shop in the city, handmade and fitted exactly to her shape, waiting six weeks for it to arrive. Only to have Bart say, "I hope you didn't spend a lot on that." He'd crushed her with the comment, but she'd made it even worse by asking, "Do you like it?" And his answer was like a thousand pounds of stone laid on her chest. "It makes you look overweight."

She'd wanted to scream and stomp her feet and throw things.

But she was over that now. Gray was helping her learn that it wasn't just her. She was an attractive woman. Still, she'd learned her lesson about inviting another man completely into her life and giving over all her feelings and her battered psyche. No, she'd never do that again. But she would enjoy each moment with Gray. Until it didn't work anymore.

Cathe was an altogether different matter. "Jack's a big boy," Celia said. "He can look after his own feelings." She inhaled deeply, let it out through her parted lips before adding, "Would it be such a bad thing if he wanted to see you again once we're home?"

Shaking her head vehemently, Cathe's hair flew across her face. "I can't see him. My heart is taken. If he wants to see me after we get back, it will only be because he's grown attached. And I can't afford to hurt him. It just wouldn't be right."

"Maybe, if you give things a chance, you'll develop feelings for him too."

Cathe studied her latte as if it had all the answers written in the foam. Celia guessed she already had feelings, but felt too guilty to acknowledge them.

"Just promise me this," Celia pleaded. "If he asks for your phone number, give it to him. And don't erase it."

Still engrossed in the cup's contents, Cathe sighed. "He already has my number. I texted him a few photos I'd taken."

Celia wanted to punch the air. There was hope. "Then wait and see. Don't put the kibosh on everything right now. Just enjoy these few days together."

Finally, Cathe looked up. "There's only two nights and one full day left."

Celia recognized the misery in her sister's gaze. "Then enjoy yourself." Only two nights left. She hadn't been counting. But Cathe had. Was that good or bad? But she needed to warn her sister. "I'm spending these last two nights with Gray." It might be news to Gray, but she didn't think he'd mind. She laid her hand over Cathe's. "As long as you don't mind."

Cathe shook her head, her eyes still misty. "I'm happy for you. And I want to be the one to say that if he calls you after this trip, don't cut him off."

Smiling, Celia thought about her sweet little secret. And now she needed to tell her sister. "He's asked me to see him again. In fact, we're planning a trip in the new year, maybe spring."

Cathe smiled like a beam of sunshine. "Oh, thank God. He's good for you. I'm so glad you're seeing him again."

Making a face, Celia held up a hand. "Don't get your hopes up. This is like—" She raised her eyes to the ceiling, then back to Cathe. "—a booty trip. We don't have any obligations to each other. But maybe it's something we'll do a couple of times a year. I enjoy his company." Then she leaned close. "And he's fantastic in bed."

She knew better than to ask Cathe about Jack.

The smile on her sister's face didn't lose its hopefulness. "I'm happy for you. And if you enjoy those trips, you might want him around more often. Maybe even start a relationship."

Celia snorted, shaking her head. "I know what I want, and it's not a relationship. And especially not another marriage. But Gray is good fun." She tapped Cathe's finger on the handle of her mug. "That's what I want for you. To have fun."

"Please don't put that on me. I just can't think about the future."

"But you will enjoy these last two days together? Especially the nights? Right?"

The tabletop stole all Cathe's focus. But she finally admitted, "The time left is so short, and I want to enjoy every moment before it's over." Then she met Celia's gaze a long moment. "And I'll invite him into our room." She shrugged, as if it meant nothing, when actually it meant everything. "He can't spend the night because he has to take care of Rupert. But I'll enjoy what we have."

Celia hoped for so much for her sister. And it wasn't over yet. Jack had thirty-six hours to convince her. Even if he couldn't accomplish that during the rest of their holiday, Celia would harp on Cathe once they were home.

And maybe, when the trip was over and Jack was gone, her sister would realize how much she needed him.

20

Celia had missed Gray during the trip to Český Krumlov, and now, in the warm darkness of his stateroom, she loved his weight on top of her and the exquisite pleasure of his skin against hers.

He was so right. They couldn't let this go. She needed to see him again, touch him again, taste him again. Their arrangement for holidays together every few months would be the most perfect in the world.

After long, luxurious lovemaking, he rolled to his back, pulling her with him. She rested in his arms, the thump-thump of his heart against her ear as she twirled light circles in his chest hair.

Had she ever felt like this with her ex? If she had, the years had wiped away the memory. Now there was nothing to compare with the way Gray made her feel.

Somehow, even in her bliss, maybe because of her bliss, she thought of Cathe and Jack, of how badly she wanted Cathe to have this same thing. "I need to figure out how to get Jack and Cathe together."

Gray's deep voice vibrated through her. "You don't need to do anything. They're already together. Can't you tell?"

She nodded, his chest hair soft beneath her cheek. "I meant after the trip is over. She needs love in her life." The ease she felt with Gray amazed her. She could say anything to him, as if they'd been together for years. And she wasn't telling her sister's secret since he'd already guessed. She didn't want to keep secrets from him. The delicious nature of their relationship was that they had nothing at stake but good, hot sex.

"I still need to give them that extra push. Cathe was so happy with Denny. It's people like her, who had a good marriage. They're the ones who can find love. She just doesn't think she can. But I know better."

Gray chuckled. "We always think we know better. Maybe you should let them find their own way."

She shook her head. "You don't know my sister. She gets something stuck in her head and won't let go."

"You mean stuck in her heart," he said for her.

See, they were so good together they could finish each other's sentences. She didn't mind that he contradicted her. Even if she knew better. "She's stuck thinking there can only ever be one love of her life. It was terrible when Denny died, and you don't recover with just a snap of your fingers. But two years is a long time. And she and Jack are so good for each other. I know in my heart that she can find happiness again if she'll just accept it."

Gray seemed to hold his breath before saying, "Is that what you truly believe? That there's a second chance for love?"

She snorted softly. "Cathe can absolutely find love again if she lets herself."

After another quiet moment, he asked, "But what about people in general? Is there a second chance?"

She laughed, tipping her head back to look at him. "Of course there is. Look at us. We have this really hot thing going." She nuzzled his chest, licked his nipple, and felt a tremor shimmy through his body. "Good, hot sex," she whispered. "We'll meet for fabulous trips and indulge our senses." Then she grinned. "Kill ourselves with pleasure." Wrapping her fingers around him, she found him already hard again. "You're absolutely amazing."

Then she climbed on top to show him just how good they were together. And how good this arrangement would be. She could definitely do this at least four times a year.

The taste of him burst on her tongue.

And she decided once a month would be even better.

CELIA DRAINED EVERY DROP OF PLEASURE OUT OF HIM, AND now he held her in his arms as her breath evened out and she slipped down into a gentle sleep.

She hadn't understood. He wasn't talking about a second chance at good, hot sex. It wasn't enough. He wanted what Cathe had found with her husband. And he believed in it.

The problem was that Celia no longer did. Her ex's ignorance had damaged her. While she could see clearly what was right for Cathe, she couldn't admit the same was true for herself.

He'd have to show her. Even if it took months. Or years.

But in the end, he would prove that she deserved a second chance at love as much as her sister did.

JACK LAY AWAKE IN THE CABIN, THE EVEN RHYTHM OF Cathe's sleep the only sound. He traced a finger around the pretty heart-shaped necklace at her throat without waking her. She deserved pretty things. She deserved so much.

Her body was warm and soft in his arms. He'd never felt this kind of bliss after making love. Only with Cathe. He saw now that his marriage had been a dried-out husk, revealing all the things he'd lacked.

Now he'd found them with Cathe.

She was sweet and tender and thoughtful. She was a balm to his soul. He hated having to leave her in the middle of the night, craving the feel of her in his arms in the morning light. The gentle rock of the boat in the water and the warmth of her breath across his chest lulled him. But he knew soon he'd have to go to his father. He'd have to leave her.

It had been less than a week, just a matter of days, and yet she'd crawled inside his soul and wrapped herself around his heart.

But he knew that for her, there was only one man.

And that man was dead.

How did you fight a memory? How did you battle a ghost?

How did he make her believe that there was room enough in her heart for him?

He had only twenty-four hours left to show her how perfect they were together.

CATHE HAD WOKEN WHEN JACK LEFT HER BED LAST NIGHT. She'd known he had to go. Even as she wanted to beg him to come back to her, she kept her lips sealed. For his sake. She would only end up hurting him in the end.

The ship had sailed into Germany overnight. The quaint town of Passau rose up the hills on both sides of the Danube, as if the river had cut a path through the two halves of the city. A castle dominated the skyline on one side, and on the opposite shore, a monastery sat atop the hill overlooking the town square. The morning hike started at the monastery and ended on the top of the hill at the castle, and the afternoon bike ride toured the surrounding countryside. Cathe and Celia had signed up for both.

Breakfast was bacon, eggs, potatoes, even fried tomatoes, fried mushrooms, and fried bread, a full British breakfast.

And the entire gang had turned out.

Celia came back to the room this morning only to change clothes. She'd seemed almost manic with happiness. And when Gray showed up in the dining room, her sister glowed. Now, sitting across the table, Cathe saw how they fit together like puzzle pieces.

Beside her, Jack's body heat filled her up.

"Gray and I are doing the bike ride through the Passau countryside," Celia said. No one looked askance at their linked hands on the table as she turned to Cathe. "I can't handle both the hike in the morning and the bike ride in the afternoon, in addition to packing. I'll skip the hike and pack this morning. If you're good with that?"

The reminder hit Cathe in her belly. This was their last day. Tomorrow, they'd board a shuttle bus at seven thirty in the morning to catch an eleven o'clock flight. Their bags needed to be outside the cabin by six. The dining room would open early so they could eat breakfast before they left.

Then the trip was over.

Whatever she'd been doing with Jack, that would be over too.

Her heart hurt. But she had her life to go back to. She had the house where she'd lived with Denny. She had Sarah. She had her volunteering.

Life would return to normal, and she'd forget about Jack. They'd had only a few days anyway. The week would feel like a dream, like vacations always did when you returned home.

And maybe, over the years, the ache she felt for Denny would lose its hard edges, and she'd learn to live without him.

Yet for a moment, a very traitorous moment, she was afraid she'd never forget Jack's touch, his kiss, his taste. She was afraid the feel of his arms around her would grow in her mind, take on a mythical quality. Then she'd ache to kiss him again.

Wanting to cast off the thoughts, she spoke a little too loudly. "That sounds great. I'll still do the hike this morning and skip the bike ride. And that way we won't trip over each other trying to pack at the same time."

Under the table, Jack folded her hand in his. She wondered if he heard the hysterical edge in her voice. "I'd like to do the hike too. Dad, what do you think? Can you handle the bus ride with Agnes and Rose and Declan?"

Before his father could answer, Agnes jumped in. "We'll be fine. We don't need any old fuddy-duddy chaperones."

There were several chuckles around the table, and Cathe looked at Barbara, who was the main chaperone, fuddy-duddy or not. She smiled along with the rest.

And Cathe's heart beat faster. The warmth of Jack's fingers slipped inside her as she thought about the hike with him through the hills. Just her, Jack, their guide, maybe a few others from the boat. But they really hadn't talked with the other passengers. Being with strangers they didn't have to talk to made it feel like she would have Jack to herself, his aftershave tantalizing her senses, his body heat arcing between them, his hand around hers as they walked.

"I'd like to do the hike too," Rose said. "Is that okay with you, Agnes?"

The old lady snorted like a grumpy mare. "I said we don't need any old fuddy-duddy chaperones." She patted Rupert's hand where it rested on the table. "Right, Rupster?"

Rupster? Jack looked at Cathe. She looked at him. They smiled. Agnes was definitely a hoot.

"Good," Declan said. "We'll hike this morning, and we'll do your packing this afternoon."

Agnes looked at him, blinked her lashes, then turned to Jack, smiling coquettishly. "And if you'd pack up the Rupster's stuff, that would be marvelous. Because I really want him to sit up on the sundeck with me this afternoon so we can take in the rays."

Jack smiled, obviously stifling a laugh. "It would be my pleasure."

Yet Cathe's stomach sank, mourning the loss of those few brief moments when she thought she'd have Jack to herself. Not that she didn't enjoy Declan and Rose.

It was just the last day.

Maybe wanting him to herself was asking too much. She'd have to make the most of what she got.

THE HIKE WAS AMAZING. THEIR GUIDE WAS A COLLEGE history professor who provided interesting tidbits about the area's past. Because the town was of little strategic value during the Second World War, it had suffered only minor damage and most of the old buildings were intact. But the most interesting facts were about Napoleon. While history considered him a monster and the scourge of Europe during the early 1800s, he had, in fact, done some good. Inside the city walls of Passau, sanitation had been terrible, many people dying from diseases caused by the filth. What medical attention they received had come from the church and was inadequate even for the times. Napoleon had torn down the walls, introduced the concept of good sanitation, and instituted healthcare for the poorer citizens.

Leaning close to Jack, she murmured, "There are always two sides to every story."

Holding her hand, he agreed, "You're absolutely right."

There were only five on the tour, the two of them, Rose and Declan, and another woman, Maria, younger than Jack and Cathe by at least ten years. Beneath the canopy of trees as they approached the monastery, it was quite cool, the air fragrant with the last of the season's flowers. Their guide stopped on the trail at a statue of Jesus seated rather than hanging on a cross, in a pose that reminded Cathe of Rodin's Thinker.

"He seems like a very sad Jesus," Rose said.

Cathe took a picture, showing it to Jack. He gave her a thumbs up for the way she'd captured the statue's melancholy.

The monastery, when they reached it, had a small chapel, nothing like the magnificent churches of Budapest and Vienna. And yet it was charming, with gold leaf in the adornments and a painting of the Madonna over the altar. Beside the chapel, the professor pointed out descending concrete stairs, covered like a long walkway. Holy paintings, mosaics, crucifixes, and rosary beads hung on its walls. The wide steps weren't deep, each of them perhaps three inches in height, with landings every ten or so steps.

"These are the pilgrim stairs," he told them. "There are three hundred twenty-one steps, and the pilgrims climb up from below on their knees."

Maria gasped, wrapping her arms around her waist almost like protection. "You're kidding. On their knees?"

The professor nodded.

"They could have at least laid down carpet for them," Declan said dryly.

Jack coughed. "But it's supposed to be a hardship."

Cathe would have liked to walk down the stairs, but certainly not climbing back up on her knees.

"What do pilgrims do if they use a walker?" Rose mused, obviously thinking of Agnes and the Rupster. It seemed to be the one answer the professor didn't have.

But thinking of Agnes's moniker for Rupert once again made Cathe laugh.

Back on the trail heading down, Cathe let distance grow between her and the rest of the group, giving her time with Jack. "Do you and the Rupster go to church?" she asked.

He laughed. "The Rupster. Where does Agnes come up with this stuff?"

"She's too funny."

He nodded in perfect agreement. "We don't go to church. And I don't see myself climbing over three hundred steps on my knees."

"They all must have terrible knees by the time they reach old age."

His chuckle sent tendrils of warmth through her. "What about you... and Denny?"

She noticed a hesitation when he added Denny's name. "My mother took us to church when we were kids. I was confirmed. We were Episcopalian, which is only one step away from being Catholic. We had communion too."

"You only went when you were a kid?"

She shrugged. "Mom stopped forcing us when we were teenagers. Although I went with her on Christmas because I liked the Christmas hymns. But Denny wasn't religious at all. We didn't raise our daughter that way either."

"And you were a stay-at-home mom?"

She nodded. Below them, the professor led Maria, Declan, and Rose onto a road. But Cathe didn't hurry to catch up.

"Tell me what you wanted to be when you were a kid. Always a mom?"

Cathe laughed at that. "I wasn't the baby doll type. I wanted to be a dancer."

"Wow. And why didn't you become a dancer?"

"I wasn't good enough." Then she tipped her head, shrugged. "That's not quite true. I might've been good, who knows? But I didn't practice enough. You've got to be driven, and I never was." It didn't bother her to admit that about herself. Sometimes it was just better to know yourself. "What you what about you? What did you want to be?"

"I wanted to be an archaeologist. I saw myself as Louis Leakey and finding the missing link. Or Howard Carter, unearthing the next King Tut's tomb."

"So why haven't I heard about you on the news finding the next big missing link?"

He laughed at that. "Because I realized that the few minutes of glory didn't outweigh the long days or weeks or months of tedium, and I'd probably end up being a professor. That wasn't how I saw myself."

"I guess we both had broken dreams," she said.

He grinned, shaking his head. "I don't look at it that way. We were realistic and knew the parts of the profession that we didn't want."

"I like the way you think."

They joined the waiting group just beneath a bridge over the road, as the professor was saying, "And this is a portion of the pilgrim stairs." He pointed up to what Cathe realized wasn't a bridge but part of the covered walkway, windows all along it.

"That sure is a long way for somebody to crawl on their knees," Maria mused.

Making their way down into the town, the professor showed them the innocuous doorway at the bottom of the pilgrim stairs. Cathe would never have noticed it, but looking up, she had a view of the long, covered stairway climbing up the hillside.

Strolling along streets with buildings from long-ago eras, everything was clean, the sidewalks narrow with flower boxes in bloom.

Once again, the professor stopped, this time beside markings on the corner wall of a building. "This shows you where the floods of 2013 and 2014 rose over the banks of the Danube."

"Good Lord," Rose said.

It reminded Cathe of Sarah's height measurements they'd marked on the kitchen wall as she grew. But this, while measured in meters, had to be at least thirteen feet high.

"As you can imagine," the professor said, "there was extensive damage. But we have repaired it all."

Cathe, wanting to document the ravages of mother nature, waved her hand at Jack. "Stand right there so we get a perspective." The markings appeared more than twice his height. And they weren't even down at the Danube's level yet.

They walked on, through the gates of the old city which still stood, two ancient guard houses nearby. Around the next corner, they crossed a bridge where the professor showed them the meeting of the three rivers, Danube, Inn, and Ilz, the colors of the water diverse coming from each of the three inlets.

Cathe took Jack's hand in hers. They had so little time left, and she wanted to act like a couple, even if Rose and Declan were with them.

Along the riverfront, stairs led down to the water every hundred yards or so, where small boats could moor or kayaks could slide into the river. Several kayakers paddled along the river's edge, out of the way of passing ships. Just ahead, a great flock of birds swirled close to the pavement, and as she drew closer, Cathe made out a woman tossing seed for the birds.

The professor, in a low voice, said, "She really shouldn't be feeding those birds."

But Cathe loved it. The pigeons' feathers shone iridescent in the sunshine as they circled, dive-bombing to the ground to grab what the woman had thrown, while ducks and even two swans pecked around her feet. Cathe took a short video and a couple of photographs as the woman smiled at her.

They passed breaks in the wall with stairs leading up to narrow roads lined with houses. Cathe snapped photos of the picturesque homes and some of a group of children on swings and a seesaw in a playground.

Heading into the town square surrounded by coffee shops and patisseries, Maria asked, "Can we stop for a coffee?"

Their guide gave her a stern professorial look. "We really don't have time. We need to get to the castle at the top." He pointed way, way up. "We need to meet the bus back to the boat right over there." His jutted chin indicated a parking lot on the opposite side of the square.

Maria sighed with what could only be relief. "Good. Then I'll just sit here and have a coffee and wait for you."

The professor's eyes went as wide as an owl's. "But you'll miss the castle." Horror laced his words as if she were committing a sacrilege.

She flapped her hand, shooing him away. "I'm not climbing any more hills. I need coffee."

The hapless professor finally gave in. "We'll be about an hour."

Maria waved them away cheerily. "Then I can have a pastry as well."

"She's quite the character," Cathe noted.

And Jack added, "She and Agnes would get along extremely well."

Leaving Maria behind, they crossed the street to a steep set of narrow stairs. Once again, Cathe let the others climb ahead of them, slowing to eke out more time with Jack.

"You okay?" he asked, taking her hand.

"Stairs are the worst on my knees," she told him, instead of admitting how badly she wanted alone time with him.

His smile spread wide across his face. "I feel everything getting creaky," he said in solidarity.

But when she lay in Jack's arms, she didn't feel old at all.

Climbing leisurely, the stairs lead to a dirt switchback trail that was less steep. A part of her wondered how she'd go back to her life the way she'd planned. How would she forget the sweetness of his touch, the tenderness of his kiss, the beauty of his lovemaking, the gentleness of his soul?

But she couldn't hurt him. She *wouldn't* hurt him. The only way was to never see him again. The thought was an ache squeezing her heart into a tiny ball.

She'd have to get over it. She couldn't bear the weight of guilt that hurting him would lay on her.

"I'll be so ready for lunch," Jack said. "Maybe Maria had the right idea, stopping for coffee."

"But then we'd have missed the beautiful castle," she said too brightly, trying to hold her feelings inside.

They caught up with Declan, Rose, and the professor at a vista over the river. From there, the town square was plainly visible, and Rose pointed. "I honestly think that's Maria at that little café."

It probably was. Cathe wished they'd stopped too. At another café where she and Jack could sip coffee, eat pastries, hold hands, look into each other eyes.

And spend the last day together, just the two of them.

At the top, the castle wasn't open to inside tours, but they could go anywhere on the grounds, down through the tunnels, beneath the massive archways. Peering into dank, cramped prison cells, Cathe took pictures, then focused on the cannon placements used for the town's defenses.

Until finally the professor looked at his watch. "It's time for us to go back if you don't want to miss the bus."

Cathe laughingly said, "We're too hungry to miss the bus." After all the walking, she was dying for lunch.

And for some real alone time with Jack.

After picking up Maria at the coffee shop, the shuttle returned them to the ship where everyone else was already seated for lunch.

Celia claimed, "I'm all packed. Now it's your turn." There was that glow about her again, as if she'd done far more than pack in the four hours Cathe had been gone.

She was happy for her sister. And sad for herself, she had to admit, sad that Denny was gone, that Jack would soon be out of her life too. Sad this vacation was almost over. She hadn't truly wanted to come. Celia had made her. But now she wouldn't have missed this week for anything.

She'd have to give up Jack. But she'd never give up the memories.

21

"Y ou'll pack for the Rupster, won't you?" Agnes confirmed over lunch, with that delightful gleam in her eyes for Jack.

Declan asked, "Where the heck did you come up with the Rupster?"

Agnes daintily dabbed a napkin to her lips. "From hipsters. Since we were young in the sixties." Agnes would have been in her forties, but that would seem young to her now. She patted Dad's hand. "You don't mind, do you, my dear?"

His dad laughed heartily, a strong, deep sound Jack hadn't heard in years. Agnes was good for his father. "My dear, I adore being the Rupster for you."

The little lady added, "I didn't forget my question about packing the Rupster's luggage so we can go up on the sundeck." She tipped her chin up and patted her cheeks. "I've already put on my sunblock."

Jack didn't repeat that he'd told her at breakfast he would. "It will be my absolute pleasure."

She thanked him with handclaps and a resounding, "Thank you, thank you."

While his father added more sedately, "I appreciate it, son."

The moment they'd scraped the delicious flan from their bowls, Celia and Gray left the table. "We're heading out for the bike ride now."

Rising, Cathe said, "I better do my packing." She fluttered her fingers. "I'll see you all at dinner."

Then she looked at Jack.

He wondered if there was meaning in that look. After the brilliant morning hike—her hand in his, her scent mesmerizing him, her laughter reaching deep down inside him—he decided there absolutely was meaning in that look.

But for the sake of propriety, he let her go for now and headed to his stateroom.

He and Dad didn't need to be off the boat until nine the next morning, when they would board their bus for Prague. It was easy to gather up all their stuff. He'd turned in a bag of laundry yesterday, and the staff returned it, all neatly folded, while he was out. All he had to do was lay the garments in the case. Dad had grumbled about the expense, but Jack considered it money well spent since they hadn't needed to pack as many clothes. His father had always been a penny pincher, but Jack appreciated convenience.

How long it would take Cathe to pack? Certainly not the full afternoon. He snapped the two suitcases closed after changing into clean shorts and shirt and leaving out clothes for the next day.

Celia and Gray were out for the afternoon. His dad and Agnes were up on the sundeck with Rose, Declan, and Barbara. Five minutes later, he knocked at Cathe's cabin.

When she opened, he gathered her into his arms and kicked the door shut behind him.

THEIR GROUP MET FOR THEIR LAST DINNER ON THE BOAT, everyone enthusing about the day they'd spent in Passau. Jack, however, didn't tell anyone how he and Cathe had spent the afternoon. It was too beautiful to share.

Celia and Gray enjoyed the bike tour. "But there was this woman." Celia growled. "She was riding my butt. I finally had to stop and tell her to back off."

Gray smiled indulgently. "She complained you weren't riding fast enough."

Celia shot him a look, but despite her moaning, a deep fondness laced her gaze. "I just wanted a leisurely ride to enjoy the scenery. And she kept telling me how to ride a bike as if I didn't know. I have a bike at home, and I ride every once in a while."

Gray kissed her hand. "You are certainly better at it than me. Maybe I was the one who wasn't fast enough."

Celia leaned in to kiss Gray's cheek, despite all the onlookers.

Jack was happy for them.

"I wasn't holding back for you." Celia grinned. "I was mean and went a little slower every time she got on my tail."

Cathe puffed out the exasperation her sister obviously felt. "Why didn't she just pass you?"

Rolling her eyes, Celia thinned her lips. "I have no idea. But in the end, that's what I told her to do." She glanced around the dining room, probably searching for the unfortunate rider.

"Admit it," Gray said, a laugh in his voice. "You had fun giving her a bad time."

Celia offered him a sneaky, adoring smile. "Yes, I did." Then she leaned forward to look past Jack's father. "Agnes, tell us how your day went."

Agnes beamed at the attention, as if she'd been feeling left out, and grabbed Dad's hand. "The Rupster and I had the most marvelous time." She gestured in the air, her fingers waggling. "The bus ride took us everywhere we could possibly want to go. We saw cathedrals and bridges and churches and..." She paused then. "I can't understand why they have so many churches in Europe."

"It was a way for the church to bring in money and followers. Purely economic," Declan said.

It was a very pragmatic point of view. Their waiters arrived with the meals then, and with a flourish, Jahz set Agnes's steak and lobster in front of her. "My dear, do enjoy."

For the last night, one of the offerings was steak and lobster, which they'd all ordered. No one wanted to miss out on the celebratory event.

Agnes tittered at Jahz's courtliness, putting her hands to her mouth. "Oh my. I'll never eat all that."

Mihai added, "Tonight you may take a kitty box." When he was suddenly the center of all eyes, he tipped his head coyly and said, "I have a kitty at home who receives all my leftovers in a box."

Everyone laughed at the description as Mihai leaned between Gray and Celia to set down their plates. He said softly, almost suggestively, "If you cannot finish all of yours, dear lady, we shall pack it up for a late-night snack." Looking at Gray, he winked. "It's definitely good enough to share."

Putting Cathe's plate in front of her, Jahz said, "My dear, the same goes for you. We can accommodate anything." Jack was thankful he didn't wink.

Though they'd spent a passionate afternoon, Cathe was still hesitant. They'd walked most of the hike hand in hand, but she didn't feel at ease being as obvious as Gray and Celia.

Wistfully, Jack wished for the easy relationship those two had formed. But he also knew there was no attachment, at least not on Celia's side. Or so she claimed. He couldn't handle the casualness of that either.

As they all dug in, Jack asked, "Rose, what did you and Declan think of the hike?"

Rose moaned, whether it was for the steak and lobster or the hike, or even the afternoon she'd probably spent in the suite with Declan. "I loved it. So many hills to hike up and down. The slow walking can be a killer on my feet, so it was wonderful to stretch ourselves."

Agnes looked at her fondly. "You didn't need to hold back just for me, dear."

Rose rushed on as if she'd said the wrong thing. "I didn't mean that at all. There just wasn't any opportunity. We took so many tours. But this was the only one I would consider a hike. And I'm very glad you didn't miss us on the bus." Smiling at her pseudo-mother-in-law, it was clear she adored Agnes.

The little lady clapped her hands, the sound soft where her palms didn't actually meet. "I'm so glad you and Declan have had just as marvelous a time as we have." She reached over to squeeze the Rupster's hand.

The moniker would never fail to make him laugh, and Jack was so glad his father had found Agnes on this trip. Hopefully, the relationship would blossom. Did the chance for new love end at a certain age? Or could it go on for a lifetime?

His heart plummeted, knowing Cathe didn't see new love in her cards, though her husband had been gone for two years.

How was he supposed to compete with the ghost of a lost love?

Agnes clapped her hands, drawing Jack out of his thoughts, her smile lighting up the room like a hundred candles.

"I want to propose a toast." Agnes lifted the champagne glass Mihai had just refilled. "Your glasses."

No one dared not obey. "Here's to the most amazing trip of my life." She turned sharply to Declan and Rose, her mouth a round O. "Except for that wonderful trip to Ireland you took me on. That really was the best." She smiled widely. "Because that's when you two fell in love."

Rose blushed, but Declan raised her hand to his lips for a fervent kiss on her knuckles.

Agnes glowed once again. "But this trip isn't over yet. Because we'll meet again in Prague."

Jack's heart fell into a barely there rhythm. Cathe and Celia would not be in Prague. This was the end of the line.

Cathe spoke, her voice slightly dulled. "I'm sorry to say that Celia and I leave in the morning. Flying home."

Agnes set down her glass, Declan grabbing the stem before it toppled, and her hands flew to her mouth. "Oh. Can't you stay a few extra days and come to Prague?"

Celia looked at Cathe, as if she needed guidance, but Cathe's face remained resolute. "It's all arranged. It's too late to change things at this point." She ended the sentence with a what-can-we-do shrug.

Though he probably shouldn't, Jack reached for her hand, squeezing her fingers in his.

This was the last supper. He'd known it. And yet there'd been a part of him that for a single moment had hoped Agnes could change her mind.

By the set of Cathe's jaw, there wasn't a chance.

And yet the indomitable Agnes cried out with pleasure. "But that means we'll all have to see each other when we get back home. We must have parties and barbecues." She looked at the Rupster, and Jack was gratified his father smiled back. Perhaps the two elders in their party had already decided on this. The gleam in Agnes's eyes shouted that they had.

Yet Jack's heartbeat slowed to sludge. As much as his heart wanted to hope, his head told him Cathe wouldn't let herself be drawn into any barbecues or parties when they were home.

When she left this boat, when she flew home, when she walked in her front door and closed it behind her, she would be done with him forever.

After dessert and cappuccinos, they all rose, the meal over.

The men shook their waiters' hands, handing over envelopes with extra tips for all the hard work that Mihai and Jahz had done for them, for all the laughs, all the fun, all the good food, and all the flowing drinks. The women hugged and Cathe discreetly passed the two men an envelope from her and Celia.

When it was Agnes's turn, she held up her arms like a child and each of the gentlemen bent down to hug her gingerly, as if her bones might break in a too-tight hug. Jack would miss Agnes. He would miss them all. There was Prague and probably a couple of tours together, but without Cathe, everything would be different, darker, as if the skies had turned dull and gray.

Jack had lost his taste for the remainder of the trip. But for Agnes and his father, he'd put on a happy face.

Yet the night wasn't over, and he took Cathe's hand before she could run off. "Are coming up to the lounge? There'll be music and champagne flowing and everyone saying goodbye."

Hesitation glimmered in her gaze. But she glanced at Celia already heading up the stairs to the lounge, her hand in Gray's.

Something that Jack couldn't define shifted in her expression. Whether it was resolution or resignation, she got to her feet and curled her fingers around his.

Her touch sent shockwaves through every part of his

body. It wasn't about sex. It wasn't even about making love. Maybe it was just relief, or knowing that while her hand was in his, he could pretend this wasn't their last night.

In the lounge, the tables were filling up, and Blondie played the piano in a hyped-up version of *How Deep is Your Love* by the Bee Gees. Agnes laughed and clapped her hands and swayed her hips, until she had to grab hard to her walker's handles. The L-shaped sofa right near the dance floor was still empty, and they grabbed the seats before anyone else. A waiter arrived in moments, taking orders for champagne and Grasshoppers and Toasted Almond drinks. Celia and Gray nestled together in the sofa's corner, their hands entwined, shoulders bumping, heads together as they whispered about only God knew what.

As Blondie transitioned into a slow version of Elton John's *Tiny Dancer*, Jack held out his hand to Cathe. "Dance with me?"

Once again, hesitation clouded her eyes. As if one more dance, one more champagne, and one more night spelled doom.

Then, thank God, she let him pull her to her feet and into his arms.

The feel of her against him was glorious. She lightly sung the words in his ear, her soft voice beautiful. "I always loved this song. I loved all Elton John's songs." Her breath was a tantalizing whisper across his ear. "I even loved *Sympathy for the Devil* by The Rolling Stones." Her body vibrated with a giggle he felt from his chest to his toes. "And *Angie*. I listened to that song over and over."

He had to admit, though not aloud, that *Angie* was his least favorite by The Stones.

"And what about that song by..." She frowned. "I can't even remember his name. But there was that video with all the girls playing guitar wearing little black dresses and slicked-back hair and shiny red lips. That was awesome."

"*Addicted to Love* by Robert Palmer, and those girls were totally hot when I was a hormonal twenty-year-old."

She laughed, and it sounded so good, resonating inside him.

"One day, it was a long while after that video came out, but I'd been watching it for some reason," she confessed. "I slicked back my hair and put on red lipstick on and threw the door open when Denny got home."

She surprised him with her ability to laugh at the mention of her husband's name. But it was the fondness of the memory.

"I wore one of those little black dresses. And he started humming that song."

He wasn't sure whether her excitement and her laughter thrilled him or terrified him. But her story stopped there, though he had a feeling it wasn't the end.

She breezed right on through. "It wasn't really a great song. It was just a great video. But," she added, "the slicked-back look didn't suit me at all. I just did it one time for fun."

He thought about his own marriage, which had lacked anything even close to fun. Was it him? Or was it being married to the wrong woman? Or maybe he just hadn't been capable of laughter back then.

Blondie switched from *Tiny Dancer* to his rendition of *Hooked on a Feeling*.

Jack was hooked on Cathe, his body, his heart, his soul, and he held her tight as the words washed over them. It might have been his imagination, but he wanted to believe she hugged him tighter too.

Cathe and Celia were the first to break up the party, with their early rise to get their bags outside the door for the trip to the airport.

With hugs and waves, they left the little group. Then Agnes called it quits, and the night ended. Jack's heart wasn't in staying anyway, not without Cathe.

In their stateroom, Jack helped his father into his pajamas. When he tucked him in as if he were a child, his dad said, "You don't have to come back right away. I'll be fine on my own."

While the roles reversed and he'd become the parent and his father the child in many ways, there remained that piece of him wanting to keep his love life private.

All he said was, "I'll be here at two when you like to get up."

His father waved his hand, lying in his bed, a diminished version of himself, the covers pulled to his chin. "I'm good by myself."

Jack knew better. "If you had a fall on the last day on the boat, we couldn't get around Prague."

His father nodded, closed his eyes, and Jack left the stateroom when he heard the first soft snores.

Making his way down to Cathe's cabin, he was already anticipating where Celia would spend the night. And it wouldn't be in the twin bed next to Cathe's.

Tonight, Cathe would be all his.

SHE OPENED THE DOOR. SHE'D HOPED JACK WOULD COME even as she prayed he wouldn't. It would only make the parting harder. Yet she needed tonight with him, needed his arms around her and his kiss on her lips. It didn't matter that she'd made love with him this afternoon. She wanted more memories.

Jack didn't disappoint her. Pulling her close the moment the cabin door closed, he took her with a kiss so deep it stole her breath. Then, like a romantic movie hero, he swept her up in his arms and carried her to the bed.

Celia hadn't even come back to the cabin, and Cathe took a shower, rubbed in lotion, pulled down the bedclothes, and seduced herself with thoughts of the coming night before Jack even arrived. And now she was so wet and so ready.

But Jack toyed with her first. Peeling off her nightgown, he trailed kisses from her earlobe, along her jaw, and down her neck to her nipples. Pinching one, he took the other in his mouth, sucking hard and wringing the first cry of pleasure from her lips.

Tangling her fingers in his hair, she pushed him down. He went slowly, caressing her with kisses across her skin, dipping his tongue into her belly button, making her laugh, then parting her legs and falling between them. He opened her like she was a flower and he was a hummingbird tasting her nectar, as if he were filling himself up with memories too. As he slid first one, then two fingers inside her, she went over the edge, writhing beneath him on the bed, crying out softly.

The sensation went on and on, dragging her under, until he crawled up her body and she felt him inside her. Having quickly learned what she needed, he pounded against her, sending her into another orgasm. Until finally the overwhelming feelings subsided and she could breathe again.

Laughing, because she couldn't help herself, she opened her eyes to look at him above her, moonlight shining on him as it fell through the aquarium window. "Oh my God."

He grinned. "I guess that means it was good."

She stroked her fingers through the mess she'd made of his hair. "It was amazing."

Maybe it was menopause or the lack of sex for so long.

But certainly it was Jack.

Then he moved again inside her, slowly, his hands framing her face as he braced himself on his elbows. It was the slow ride that always did her in, his body inside her stroking that special spot. Every gentle glide made her quiver, pushed her up one more step on that stairway to heaven.

"Oh God," she whispered. "You're doing it again."

"I want to do it again. I want to feel you come around me."

He kissed her, his tongue in her mouth, his hand between them, on her breast, pinching her nipple, shooting shafts of pleasure straight down to her core. He drove her to madness with that slow, delicious rhythm. She wanted to buck and cry and scream and beg him to take her faster, harder. But she wouldn't. Because this was so good, too good, perfect.

Running his hand down her flank, he fitted his fingers between them, found her button, and pressed it like a detonator.

She cried out as sensation roared through her like the flash of fire from a rocket blasting into space. Then Jack slammed into her, taking her the way she craved, a perfection so intense, she almost passed out. Her body clamped down on him, and he groaned against her ear, his body throbbing deep inside her, the pulse of his climax filling her up. In that moment, she pushed her hand between their bodies and squeezed him in just the right spot. And he swore, a word she'd never heard from him. A word that told her how good it was. How good *she* was.

How good they were together.

22

C athe lay in his arms. Jack wondered if the bed was actually smaller than the twin bed of his youth. And yet there was more than enough room for them both with Cathe's body draped over his. The moonlight falling through the high window gleamed on her skin. The sweat of their lovemaking was drying, but the perfume of their sex scented the air.

She whirled a finger slowly in his chest hair. The light touch on his skin and the heat of her body somehow both lulled and stirred him at the same time. He didn't want to go back to the stateroom he shared with his father. He didn't want to let her out of his arms, out of his sight. There was something in him that was afraid she'd disappear like a puff of breath in a frozen landscape. He sensed that's how he'd feel when she was gone, as though he were trudging through a frozen tundra. That was why he couldn't get let go, thinking about the hours and days and months of his life left ahead of him, the loneliness without Cathe. He might have been fine if he'd never found her. He could have gone on telling himself he didn't need another partner, because all he'd known was his wife and failure. But Cathe showed him there was more. So much more.

And yet she didn't want it with him.

As the lassitude of amazing lovemaking stole over him, he couldn't help opening his mouth, couldn't help uttering the words he feared would do him in.

"I want to see you when we get back home." *I want, I need, I have to*. He didn't know which words would sway her, if any at all.

She tensed against him, just as he'd known she would.

And the sensation ripped him apart. So did the softness of her voice. If she'd been angry, he could do battle. It was her gentle tone that killed him.

"You know that's not possible, Jack." She used his name like she was a mother trying to make a little boy understand that his old dog was never coming back.

He argued, even knowing the uselessness of it. "Everything is possible." And he wanted everything with her.

She stopped the slow caress in his chest hair. "I'm hurting you. That was never my intention. But it's Denny," she whispered.

The name on her lips scorched his skin.

"I can't lie to you," she went on, each word slicing off another piece of his heart. "He was the love of my life. I can't let him go." She tipped her head to look at him, her eyes dark in the moonlight behind her. He was sure she must see the gleam of tears in his. "I'm so sorry. You're a wonderful man. And I know you'll find someone who can open her heart fully to you."

That woman would never be her. She'd buried her heart right alongside her husband.

JACK LEFT HER CABIN TO RETURN TO HIS FATHER, HIS footsteps slow, his back bowed, as if she'd dumped the weight of a thousand words on his shoulders.

She hated what she'd done to him. She should never have started this. They were fine just being friends. Kissing him had been a bad idea, making love with him worse, even as good as it had been. She'd committed unconscionable acts against him because she'd known all along that he wasn't Denny. That no one was Denny. Her husband would always be inextricably woven into her life, into her thoughts, into her feelings, into her heart. And that wasn't fair to any man. Especially not Jack. He was too kind, too sweet. He didn't deserve what she'd done.

But she had no other choice except to let him go. Continuing the affair after this trip would be worse.

No, it had been best to cut the tie in that single moment, after the sweetness of his arms, after the beautiful lovemaking.

She would always have this week to remember.

CATHE ARRIVED IN THE DINING ROOM A LITTLE AFTER SIX the next morning.

Jack was already seated.

She and Celia had set their bags outside the door for pickup, then come here for breakfast.

Celia dropped a kiss on Gray's lips. Of course he was waiting for her.

How it hurt to look from Jack to them, from Jack's beautiful, unsmiling face to their glow, Jack's hunched shoulders to Celia and Gray's secret looks that spoke of everything they'd done in the night. And everything they'd do again on romantic holidays.

Cathe could say nothing more than, "You didn't have to come in for breakfast. It's so early."

Jack's hand moved. She sensed his desire to touch her. But after he glanced at Celia and Gray, his hand dropped away. Perhaps that was the worst of all, that now they couldn't even touch each other. She wished more than anything he hadn't come into the dining room. Letting him go last night had been bad enough. She'd lain awake until the first rays of dawn sparkled through the aquarium window.

Celia had returned, rumpled and radiant. "You look like crap. Didn't you sleep?"

"Hopefully, I'll sleep on the plane," Cathe had mumbled.

Then she'd gotten up, and they were here.

Jahz and Mihai arrived with coffee, juice, and smiles. "It's so good to see you on your last day. Safe travels," they said as if they were one voice.

Gray smiled. "I'll have bacon and eggs," ordering off the menu rather than heading to the buffet.

"Since this is my last day of vacation—" Elbows on the table, Celia laced her fingers and propped her chin. "—and I'm dieting the moment I step off the plane." She gave them all a pretty smile that Cathe envied. "I'll have the bacon and eggs too."

Cathe thought her gorge would rise. Food was the last thing she wanted, but she'd regret it later if she didn't eat something now. "I'll go to the buffet."

Next to her, Jack said the same. "Just the buffet, thanks."

Celia laughed, shaking her head at them. "Party poopers. This might be your last really good meal, Cathe. Because plane food sucks, even if we did upgrade to premium economy."

Cathe tried to smile. "Maybe Jahz and Mihai will let me take a kitty box."

Her sister laughed, but Jack's lips didn't even twitch. They all rose to look over the buffet, Celia and Gray making themselves toast to go with their bacon and eggs.

Jack stood next to her, a plate in his hand. "I'm sorry if you didn't sleep well last night. I didn't either."

She feared he'd rehash everything he'd said last night, and she was quick to say, "I'll sleep on the plane. We have a stopover in London."

Moving down the buffet, she took minuscule spoonfuls of scrambled eggs and potatoes, a strip of bacon, a slice of salami. She'd loved the European breakfasts in the beginning, meats and cheeses, open-face sandwiches. But now she didn't feel like any of it.

Jack dropped equally meager portions on his plate. "I guess neither of us is terribly hungry."

Maybe he was hoping she'd change her mind. But she simply nodded and headed back to the table where she poured extra cream and sugar into her coffee, wanting the milky sweetness. Jack sat beside her while Celia and Gray still manned the toaster.

"I wish you were coming to Prague with us." Jack held his fork suspended over his plate but didn't eat.

She smiled warmly, even though she didn't feel it. "We had extra days in Budapest at the beginning." But she wished they'd added the Prague extension too and couldn't help adding, "Prague would have been nice, but it's too late now."

It was too late for anything, especially when she saw the desolation in Jack's eyes.

Gray and Celia returned with the toast right as their bacon and eggs arrived.

"Just the way I like them." Celia beamed a smile at Mihai. "Runny yolks, so I can soak it all up with my toast."

Thankfully, they all began eating, and Cathe didn't have to make conversation. It would have been impossible with Jack's enticing scent of aftershave and shampoo wafting over her.

His aroma had remained on her skin all night after he left. Maybe that was why she hadn't slept.

Then, all too soon, the meal was over and it was time to collect their carry-ons and purses from the cabin.

Cathe stood, just as Gray leaned in to kiss Celia, and said, "I'll see you out on the dock."

A horrifying need filled Jack's eyes as he gazed at Cathe, a terrifying sadness that tore a hole deep inside her.

But all she could say was, "Goodbye. It was a lovely trip. Tell your father he was a delight."

Then she turned, almost running away, before she could cry, before she could throw herself at him. Before she changed her mind and begged to see him when he got back from Prague.

JACK WATCHED HER GO AND SAW AN IMAGE OF HIS BODY lying prostrate on the floor, gutted like a fish.

Gray looked at him across the empty plates and coffee cups. "Don't let her go."

What the hell was he supposed to do about it? He turned all his wrath on Gray. "What about you and Celia? You're letting her go."

Gray smiled. It wasn't triumph or one-upmanship, or even happiness. It was a smile of pure understanding. "I'm not letting her go. She's given me an opening to see her again, and I'm barging right through."

Jack had seen them together, and their relationship was entirely different from his and Cathe's. Those two couldn't get enough of each other, and they didn't care who saw. Celia was divorced. She wasn't living with the ghost of love lost. She wasn't living with a memory that had damn near become a paragon in her mind.

No. Cathe would never let go.

But Gray seemed to see it all. "Everyone has demons. We just have to learn to fight them. And I'll show Celia that I'm the best thing that ever happened to her. Just like she's the best thing that ever happened to me."

"That's the crux of it," Jack admitted. "I'm not the best thing. Cathe had a good marriage. She adored her husband. And no one will ever replace him."

"But he's dead," Gray said brutally. "And she's not." Leaning an elbow on the table, he pointed a finger at Jack. "And neither are you." Then he stood. "They should be on their way to the dock. Why don't you come out with me and say goodbye?"

"Cathe already said her goodbyes."

Gray's silence lasted three beats. "But you didn't say your goodbyes. So get up off your ass and let's go."

He didn't need Gray to tell him. He'd intended to go all along, needing one last look at her, one last memory.

Luggage was still being loaded onto the bus, but the passengers destined for the airport were already boarding. Cathe and Celia pointed to their bags, making sure they got on board, and the driver hefted them into the hold.

Celia turned then, saw Gray, and the smile that spread across her face was like the sun that came out after forty days of rain. Maybe Gray had already won his fight, even if Celia didn't know it.

She almost flew to Gray across the concrete, throwing her arms around him, kissing him with a depth of passion that turned Jack inside out.

He'd felt that passion with Cathe in the solitude of her cabin, when she kissed him, caressed him, whispered his name as he filled her up. But now, when she turned to watch Celia and Gray, then finally saw him, the only thing he felt was the deep well of emptiness that stretched between them.

He couldn't let it end this way.

She stood alone by the side of the bus, a few steps away from the other passengers who were boarding or securing their luggage. Jack marched straight to her like a man on a mission. He didn't give her a chance to speak, just took her face in his hands.

And he kissed her. Everything he felt, everything he wanted to say, everything that lay buried deep in his heart, he pushed into that kiss. His heart leaped inside his chest when she opened to him, when her body pressed against him, her arms around him, her taste filling his mouth, his head, his heart.

Maybe this was the moment. Maybe this was the change of heart in a kiss that seemed to last forever, entering him, becoming part of him.

Yet it ended all too soon as Cathe stepped back, her hand on his cheek. "Thank you for such a wonderful time. I'll never forget this trip."

His heart stopped like her words were a death knell. There was no change of heart.

There was just goodbye.

23

Celia primped one last time in front of the ladies' room mirror. It had been three months since their cruise. And tonight was the culmination of all her hard work on the gala she'd spent so many hours organizing.

Stepping into the hotel ballroom, she entered the fairyland she'd created for her patrons. Barely a penny had come out of the charity's funds. She talked everyone from the hotel to the caterers to the DJ into donating their goods or services.

She'd festooned the ballroom in silver and gold, with tinsel and fairy lights all around, silver and gold balloons dancing across the ceiling. Gold tablecloths draped the round tables, accented by silver napkins and silver slipcovers over the chairs, gold bows tying them down. The dinnerware was porcelain, the wine goblets crystal, and the cutlery silver-plated. She'd donated the Christmas tree herself, and her volunteers, including Cathe, spent an entire morning decorating the eight-foot tree and hanging the tinsel.

And the cost for each patron was a whopping two hundred and fifty dollars a plate.

Then there was the auction. She and Cathe had combed the Bay Area for donations, everything from weekends at high-priced hotels in San Francisco to a day at the zoo to a dinner cruise around the bay. People had donated jewelry and cloisonné vases and hand-carved wooden bowls. Many of the items on the auction tables were made by local artisans who saw this not only as a donation but as promotion, just like the hotel and caterer did.

This was her night, and Celia smiled to herself. After working so hard, she would have her reward next month, a ten-day Caribbean cruise with Gray. Ten amazing days and nights during which she hoped she never saw the outside of their veranda stateroom. The ship had room service.

As the caterers busily filled water jugs and the bartenders set up their bottles and glasses, Celia felt an arm slip around her. Cathe murmured close to her ear, "This is absolutely amazing."

Celia kissed her sister's cheek. "You helped do most of it."

And this, the elegant tables, the fairy lights crisscrossing the room, the tinsel winking in the light, was the culmination of all their work.

"You've outdone yourself." Cathe tipped her head and raised her eyebrows in a "wow" gesture. "And you look amazing."

Beaming at the compliment, Celia truly felt amazing. She'd chosen a floor-length silver-and-gold dress to match the décor and topped her elegant chignon with a silver tiara. Around her neck, a heart of gold lay warmly against her skin.

"And you look absolutely stunning." Celia stepped back, holding Cathe's arms out as she appraised the floor-length blue velvet gown. The garnet and moldavite necklace Cathe had purchased in Český Krumlov circled her throat, and her wedding band and engagement ring circled her ring finger.

They were fixtures, never to come off, as if they were bonded to her skin.

And she saw the sadness in Cathe's eyes reflected in the glitter of fairy lights, as hard as she tried to hide it. Though she'd put on a good show helping Celia with the gala over the last couple of months, there was a new air of melancholy about her. Her despondency had slowly dissipated over the two years since Denny's death. But now it was back in full force, her shoulders slumped, her eyes clouded with misery, her smiles forced, as if she were acting in a play.

Cathe hadn't contacted Jack since they'd returned. Not that Celia knew because she'd asked Cathe, oh no, but because she'd seen Declan and Rose, and invited them to the gala. She'd even been so bold as to ask for a donation to the auction. Agnes contributed a collection of her favorite classic movies on Blu-ray, the most important being *The Quiet Man* with John Wayne and Maureen O'Hara. She even gave up a movie poster of *The Quiet Man* that she'd purchased on her trip to Ireland.

When Celia asked how she could bear to part with the collection, Agnes waved her hands like a magician. "I have duplicates of everything, my dear."

That visit was how she knew that Agnes and Rupert had been seeing each other since the cruise.

She'd invited them all to the gala, and Declan had sprung for the tickets.

But the best was the surprise she'd created just for Cathe.

She could only hope her sister didn't freak out and refuse to speak to her ever again.

CELIA HAD DONE A BRILLIANT JOB WITH THE DECORATIONS. The ballroom was like something out of a fairytale. Cathe had helped, of course, even worked on donations for the auction. But her sister was the driving force, securing donations for the venue, the food, and the alcohol. With the number of ticket sales, the gala would be a smashing success.

Celia was an awe-inspiring event planner. She could make this a career. But Cathe knew Celia didn't want to be tied down to a job. With the brilliant divorce settlement from Bart, it was her time to enjoy life.

Cathe pasted on an enthusiastic smile she didn't feel, but the patrons were arriving and she had to put on a good show. She refused to let anyone know how hard the last three months had been, not even telling Celia. Every time Celia started to ask how she was doing, Cathe steered her in another direction.

She didn't want to talk about Jack. It was bad enough that she couldn't stop thinking about him or reliving those romantic nights in his arms. That she couldn't stop remembering the exquisite sensation of his fingers caressing her skin or his lips tasting hers. She'd thought the memories would fade as the days of September waned, especially since the moment they returned Celia began working manically on the gala. Cathe had offered to help all she could, thinking it would take her mind off the trip, that Jack would fade if she kept herself busy.

But standing here tonight in the beautiful glow of the string lights crisscrossing the ceiling and the candles flickering on each table, the memories were stronger than ever, the ache like a stranglehold on her throat.

Denny had been gone two years. Over that time, she'd eventually stopped crying in her lonely bed at night, stopped standing for hours at a time staring at the wall of family pictures on the landing. The pain had lessened to a quiet numbness.

Until Jack.

After Jack, the agony of her losses became acute again. Her need for him overwhelmed her, along with the loneliness that welled up since the last night with him. Since that last kiss.

That's why she couldn't be with Jack. Because there would always be this pain and anguish. The moments of happiness with him would rise up to smash her down, reminding her of what she'd lost. She couldn't do that to Jack. These last three months had shown her that. It wouldn't be fair to make him witness her desolation.

And it wasn't fair to ruin Celia's night of triumph either. So Cathe shook off the maudlin thoughts, flexed her fingers, and joined her sister at the door to greet the guests. There were dignitaries from the small municipalities around Silicon Valley and the press to whom Celia had handed out tickets for gratis to gain coverage for the event, hoping the attention would be even bigger next year.

The ladies were gowned in full-length extravaganzas that appeared to be made by exclusive designers, their husbands festooned in tux and tails. Cathe stood beside Celia as she smiled and glad-handed. Many of the patrons were cream of the crop, made of money and power. But quite a few were like her, people who believed in what Celia was doing and wanted to help by paying the steep price. For all her help, Celia had offered Cathe a free ticket, but she turned it down. Like her sister, she wanted to support the charity. And she knew that even after all the work she'd done, Celia had purchased her own ticket.

The room filled up with handsome couples and gorgeous dresses and laughter and voices and clinking glasses and the pop of champagne corks. Celia leaned close to say, "You don't have to stay here with me. Go get yourself a glass of champagne."

"I'll only go if you let me bring one for you."

Her beautiful sister smiled. "Deal."

The line was already five deep in front of the two bartenders, and when it was her turn, she ordered two glasses. Flutes in hand, she wended through guests clustered around the tall café tables Celia had the caterers set up on the dance floor. They would be removed later for dancing.

Breaking through with a clear path to the front entrance, she ground to a stop, almost losing precious drops of champagne.

Rose and Declan were each giving Celia hugs, then Agnes rolled forward, lifting her arms for Celia to bend down to her. And Rupert was at her side.

Cathe's heart skipped so many beats she thought it had stopped.

And there Jack was, dressed in a tailored tux that fit him like he'd been born in an English manor house.

Her heart tripped all over itself then, making up for all the lost beats, sending her blood rushing over her eardrums and making them pound.

He was so beautiful. She'd seen Jack wear T-shirts and shorts, polo shirts and long pants at dinner, but in a tux, he was magnificent.

She couldn't breathe. She wanted so badly to rush to him, to throw her arms around him, to tell him she'd been wrong, that she'd made a mistake.

But she couldn't. She wouldn't. It was just a momentary lapse. She couldn't give him false hope just because the sight of him stunned her.

As Celia went up on her toes to hug him, she whispered something in his ear that made him smile. And his gaze roamed the room.

Cathe knew he was looking for her. But nothing would be different when he found her.

Ducking quickly behind a nearby group, Cathe took a

moment to compose herself. She slugged down a gulp of champagne, not tasting a drop, and felt it flutter in her veins. Liquid courage? She certainly needed it.

Peeking through the crowd, she found Celia was now greeting another couple. Jack headed to the bar. Glancing left and right, he was obviously looking for her.

Cathe dashed back to her dastardly sister.

At a break in the receiving line, most of the guests having arrived, she shoved Celia's glass at her. Her sister laughed. "You've already downed half of yours." She pointed at Cathe's flute.

Cathe lit into her. "You invited him without telling me." She stabbed an accusing finger in Celia's face. "What have you got to say for yourself?"

Her dastardly darling sister smiled. "How was I supposed to invite Declan, Rose, Agnes, and Rupert without inviting Jack?" Then she leaned close to whisper, "I tell you, Rupert and Agnes are totally an item. They're over at each other's houses all the time, despite the distance between San Jose and Oakland. It's crazy." Her smile transformed her features into a twenty-year-old girl again. "I think they're in love."

A couple of late arrivals distracted Celia for a moment, and she gave her practiced meet and greet, finishing the introductions with, "Help yourself at the bar."

The two of them once more alone by the door, Cathe wasn't about to let her sister off the hook. "You should have at least warned me."

Celia shot her a disgusted look. "If I'd warned you, you wouldn't have come."

"Just tell me you are not matchmaking," Cathe demanded, her nostrils flaring.

"I told you. I couldn't invite Rupert without inviting his son."

But Cathe recognized that glint in her sister's eyes. She was definitely matchmaking.

Another couple headed toward them, and Celia flapped her hand. "Go over and talk to them. It'll get worse if you put it off. They all asked about you, and Agnes is dying to see you."

As Celia turned away, Cathe admitted to herself that she was acting like a teenager. Like a girl who had a crush on the team captain and knew that if he took one look at her, he'd see everything written in her eyes.

But she was fifty-seven years old. With her champagne glass like a talisman in her hand, she held her spine stiff and headed to the cruise group.

With their walkers, Agnes and Rupert were not equipped for standing at café tables. They'd already found seats at the front table near the dais where the speeches would take place.

The same table where Cathe was supposed to sit with Celia.

She would have to murder her sister.

Rose and Declan wheeled the walkers to the side of the room while Jack helped Agnes and Rupert settle into their chairs.

When he stood tall again, he saw her.

A shiver ran through her. It could have been desire or terror. Her heart, which had only just calmed, raced again. There was nothing to do but go to him.

He seemed to follow her every step, his gaze on her hair, her blue velvet dress. Then finally meeting her eyes.

And suddenly she was right in front of him.

She hadn't rehearsed what she'd say to him, and her voice came out in a horrible croak. "It's so good to see you all here supporting Celia. And the charity too."

His eyes spoke the words he didn't say. He hadn't come for Celia or the charity. He'd come for Cathe.

Agnes saved her, bless the little woman's heart. She raised her arms, crying out, "I need a hug, dear."

After a hug and a kiss on the cheek, then a shake of Rupert's hand and another hug—because really, Cathe had to hug the delightful man—Agnes was spouting again. "My dear, we've talked a million times about our trip. It was so enchanting. I'm trying to get Declan to plan another one. We must have another go, don't you think?"

Cathe nodded. "Of course. It was such a marvelous week." That was the thing about the elderly. They could forget what they had for breakfast or what happened yesterday or names of new people. But when something truly important happened, it was ingrained on their brain. Especially if they talked about it incessantly, which Agnes obviously had.

When Declan and Rose returned, there were more hugs, more cheek kisses, and a waiter passed by with canapés that Agnes and Rupert couldn't resist.

Agnes pointed at Rose. "And don't say I'll spoil my dinner with appetizers. Tonight, I get to eat as much as I want." Everyone laughed because Agnes always made people laugh.

Smiling, Rose agreed. "You can eat whatever you want. Besides, you eat like a bird. So go ahead, have as many as you'd like."

Agnes ate like a bird, tiny bites of bruschetta, then a shrimp puff. And that was it. The tiny lady patted her stomach. "My goodness. I'm already full."

The guests began taking their seats at the dinner tables as Celia worked her way through the crowd, laughing, smiling, directing.

Noticing the waiters lining up with bread baskets and salad plates, Cathe said, "I'm sure they'll serve dinner soon."

Since Jack would naturally sit next to his father, Cathe skirted the table to take a seat opposite Rupert.

But Jack followed her.

He pulled out her chair, leaning close to whisper, "Don't think you're getting away from me." And he sat next to her.

There was no way out.

Especially not after the tantalizing whisper of his warm breath across her ear.

The chairs were close enough that she couldn't help cataloguing every delicious part of him. She breathed in the subtle scent of aftershave laced with his pheromones, relished the warmth of his skin and the deep blue of his eyes flecked with a tiny emerald light.

Everything brought her body to life the way it hadn't been since that final, devastating kiss on the dock in Passau.

She could admit these things. It was impossible not to, not when she breathed him in with every rise and fall of her chest.

But it made no difference. Eventually, all that would fade. They'd had only a week compared to a life with Denny spanning more than thirty years.

Then Celia was climbing the steps of the dais. The sightline forced Cathe to turn toward Jack, and their knees touched in the small space beneath the table. Even through the velvet dress, his heat suffused her body.

To match the height of the sexy high heels she wore, Celia pulled up the microphone. "Bay Area Women's Shelters has so much to thank you for, most especially the marvelous donation of your time and your ticket price. We'll do so many good works with this money, from building new shelters to offering counseling and interview training. And even providing legal help." She raised her hands after a moment to quiet the deafening applause. "Let me tell you how tonight will go." She flourished a hand to encompass the ballroom. "First, we have dinner." She signaled the waitstaff to serve the salads, and the whitecoats moved from back to front. "After that, we'll have a few speeches, nothing too long, I promise, but there are a few dignitaries with us tonight who would like to say a word. And then we'll have our auction." She swept her arms to indicate the tables on both sides of the room. "For those of you who haven't put in a bid, please take the time to look at all the amazing items we have for you tonight. Lastly, if you look at your program, you'll see a list of our donors, and we want to thank every one of them, especially the hotel for donating the space, our caterers for donating all the food and alcohol, and to our DJ for choosing all your favorite songs." She smiled at the crowd. "And then we'll dance the night away." After the brief speech, Celia received another enormous round of applause.

But before she could step down from the dais, her gaze seemed snagged by something on the far side of the ballroom. She stood still, her lips slightly parted, which made almost everyone in the room crane to look at the entrance.

The latecomer was decked out in a formfitting gray tux that complemented his silver hair. He was the epitome of a silver fox.

Gray stood a long moment, his gaze laser-focused on Celia. A look blossomed in Celia's eyes that Cathe didn't think she'd ever seen before. Celia put her hand to her chest as if she'd lost her breath, and a hot flame of desire flickered in her eyes. Only those at the front table could see it, all their cruise mates who realized Gray's arrival was a complete surprise.

Finally, Celia gathered herself and raised her hands once again. "I want all of you to enjoy every moment of the evening." Then she rushed off the stage, stopping as her feet hit the floor, her gaze flicking from Gray at the door to the table full of her friends.

Cathe saw the deep breath her sister took. But instead of running to Gray, she made graceful steps to the seat beside Jack.

But there was one more empty seat at the table.

Agnes swiveled around. "What? What's going on?"

Of course, Agnes couldn't see over the heads surrounding her. It was Rose who leaned close and said, "Gray is here. And we weren't expecting him."

Agnes's hands flew to her mouth. "Oh my goodness. Why aren't you running into his arms, my dear?" She blinked owlishly at Celia. She might not remember Gray's name, but she knew what this meant.

But Celia merely smiled. Cathe felt honor bound to come to her sister's rescue. "Celia and Gray will have their moment," she told Agnes. "But maybe they need a little privacy. Let's allow them to take it at their own pace." It wasn't an admonishment, just a reason.

Agnes clapped her hands. "Oh, how exciting. I can't wait." Then she looked at Celia. "You take all the time you need, dear. I'll zip my lips." And she zipped her lips with a finger gesture.

They all knew Agnes's silence couldn't last.

Then Gray was there, his hand on the back of Celia's chair. "Thank you for saving a seat for me." He didn't touch her as he sat. He just looked, his eyes roaming her face as if he had to memorize her features all over again.

Celia played it cool. "I'm so surprised you came, but I'm very glad. And thank you for your donation for the dinner ticket." Which meant Celia hadn't known about his ticket.

Mental telepathy seemed to flow between them. Cathe just didn't know exactly what it said, only what she hoped, that Celia had finally found her forever man.

The waitstaff reached their table, setting down salads and bowls of dressing. After they'd dressed their mixed greens, Jack leaned close. "I loved all your photos. You're an amazing photographer. Didn't I tell you that?"

Cathe almost dropped her fork, saying the words before she thought better of them. "How did you see all my photos?"

He smiled, a hint of wickedness in it. "You shared all your photos with your sister. And she shared them with Rose, Declan, and Agnes." He paused before adding, "And my father."

She chanced a quick look at Rupert, who stared adoringly at Agnes.

Jack went on. "Dad let me see everything. But my favorite is still the one of the Parliament Building the night we sailed." Laying his hand over hers, his touch wiped any words right out of her head. "It's amazing," he praised her softly. "I'm glad you donated a framed copy of it for the auction."

She had to say immediately, "I never even thought of it. But Celia pushed me." She wouldn't have been able to stop herself from asking, even if she was in a torture chamber, "Do you really think it's that good?"

Jack let his gaze trace every contour of her face. "It's that good. It deserves to hang in someone's home or even in a gallery. I told you what a fantastic eye you have."

She whispered, "Thank you," overcome by his praise. Then she had to know. "What did you think of the one with the woman feeding the birds along the waterfront in Passau?"

It had been her favorite. She would have donated that photo except there might have been legal issues with permission from the woman. But she'd blown it up and hung it on the wall with all the family portraits.

"You captured it perfectly, down to the birds' wings and the seed in the air."

She wanted to cry, realizing in that moment how badly she'd wanted Jack to see all her pictures. She'd longed to tell him he'd been so right, that she loved photography. She wanted to tell him all about her drives to regional parks, to the zoo, the city, even to the train station to take her photos.

"I've signed up for a February class to learn how to use all the camera functions, about framing photos, contextual stuff."

He took her hand again, his touch warm. "You have a good eye, so learning the technical end will only improve what you see. I'm happy for you."

"You have a good eye too. Many of the pictures I really liked were of things you pointed out to me."

He paused a single beat before saying, "Maybe you'll take me on one of your photography field trips."

Her world stopped. She wanted nothing more in the world that to have Jack by her side.

But she couldn't.

And yet a tiny voice deep inside cried out. *You can do whatever you want.*

✦ 24 ✦

C elia still hadn't caught her breath, and her words came out strangled. "What are you doing here?" She spoke softly, not wanting to catch Agnes's attention. The dear lady would probably burst out with something totally embarrassing.

Gray's deep voice dripped like melted caramel over her nerve endings. "You told me about the gala. I looked it up on the website. A fabulous website, by the way, in case you were the one who designed it."

"I didn't do the work. But I was very good at describing what I wanted."

He smiled devilishly. "Oh, I know how very good you are at describing exactly what you want." The words and his deep voice sent a shiver of desire straight to her center.

She absolutely could not wait for their Caribbean cruise in January. "I'm happy you approve. Thank you for buying a ticket to support the charity."

Under the table, he took her hand. "You couldn't have kept me away. Even if you told me not to come." He waved his hand over the ballroom's decor. "It's fabulous. You're amazing. I bet you didn't take a single dime from the charity. You probably even paid for your own ticket tonight."

She couldn't help but laugh. "Yes, I paid for it. I wanted to give my ticket to Cathe, but she refused. She said if I was paying, then she was paying. The whole cruise group came out to support us." She looked fondly at her shipmates, then clasped Gray's hand on her lap, her heart hammering, her breath quickened. "I'm so glad you came. I've missed you."

"Even though we talk every weekend?"

She'd wanted to call him every day, just to hear the deep timbre of his voice and let it melt everything inside her. But every day was too much. She didn't want to ruin the good thing they had. But this was absolutely perfect. "Even though we talk every week—" She dropped her voice. "—I don't get to kiss you over the phone."

Was it terrible that they had phone sex? She hadn't even told Cathe. But it was so good, though nothing like the touch of his lips on hers. "Did you book a hotel?" Her words came out in a rush.

"I've got a room here at the hotel."

Her heart wanted to tumble all over itself. "Did you get a king-size bed?"

He laughed wickedly. "It's a suite." He leaned in to whisper in her ear. "And it has a two-person tub. Didn't you have a fantasy about a bathtub?"

That had been one of their phone sex fantasies, the two of them in a bubbling tub. "I'd invite you to stay at my place, but I love the sound of your suite."

The salad plates were whisked away and their meals set down. She had the steak while Gray had the salmon. They traded forkfuls, and both were delicious.

Her body tingled, her mind a whirl. Suddenly, she wanted nothing more than for this gala to be over so she could drag Gray up to his suite.

Maybe once a quarter or even once a month wouldn't be enough.

She wanted once a week.

And possibly more.

With dessert and coffee served, it was her turn at the microphone again, though it was ridiculously hard to tear herself away from Gray.

Up on the dais, she introduced the mayor, a woman who gave an amazingly short speech, then the foundation's director, who went on a little too long, and finally the CEO of a major corporate contributor.

Just before she went back up on stage to introduce the silent auction, Agnes waved her hand furiously, so hard Celia was afraid she'd tumble right out of her chair.

"Might I have the microphone for just a few moments up on your beautiful stage?" the little lady said in a loud whisper that everyone at the table heard.

The request didn't fit with Celia's carefully choreographed schedule for the evening. But this was Agnes, and Celia felt magnanimous since Gray had appeared. She leaned down to murmur, "Of course. But I only have five minutes to spare. Is that long enough?"

Agnes beamed at her, her face a swathe of glorious wrinkles attesting to life and laughter and love. "Five minutes, I promise. Thank you so much, dear."

Celia could only smile. "Then let's go."

Miraculously, Agnes's walker appeared at her side, and Declan helped her. While Celia climbed the dais steps and pulled the microphone off its stand, Declan helped Agnes roll up the ramp. Though none of her speakers had needed it tonight, Celia was glad for it now.

When Agnes was firmly on the dais, she reached up to hug Declan, whispering something in his ear. He smiled, nodded, then jogged down the ramp once more.

Celia made the introduction. "We have a very special guest tonight. I haven't a clue what she'd like to say to you, but I know it will be remarkable. Please welcome Agnes Hathaway."

Celia handed Agnes the microphone, the lady staring at it a moment in bewilderment. Then she said, "Is it on?" Her words boomed across the ballroom, followed by feedback.

Covering the microphone with her hand, Celia said, "You don't need to hold it right against your lips." And she moved the device to the correct spacing.

Agnes beamed at her once more, and Celia's heart soared. If she made it to Agnes's age, she wanted to be just like this little woman.

"Thank you so much, dear." Then Agnes made a shooing motion, and Celia smiled as she walked gracefully down the steps. Seated beside Gray once more, he took her hand, holding it in his lap.

Agnes began to speak, the audience riveted by this unexpected turn. "It's so marvelous to see all of you. I don't know a single one except for the people I'm sitting with at this table, but I know you're all doing good works." She smiled as everybody clapped. When the room became silent once more, she began again. "I'm eighty-seven years old, and I lost my dear departed husband just a few years ago. I have to say I've only been in love twice in my lifetime. My first love died in the war." No one had to wonder which war.

There were soft murmurs of sympathy for her losses, but Agnes kept on smiling. "There's that old saying that it's better to have loved and lost than never to have loved at all. I don't know who said that," she added with a flip of her hand. "But maybe you young people out there—" She punctuated with a finger pointed at the crowd. "—don't believe that. But I have to tell you with ancient authority that it's true. I miss both my loves terribly, and I wish they were here. But I would never give up that love to spare myself the pain of loss. I want you to know that I would do it all again for the right man." A raucous round of applause followed, which she quieted with a wave. "And I want to tell you that love is always possible, no matter your age. It can hit you like a lightning bolt or it can sneak up on you on soft kitty-cat feet."

The gathering was silent, listening to her with rapt attention.

It amazed Celia that the woman remembered everything she wanted to say. She couldn't remember names, and she might repeat a story several times without realizing she'd already told you. But up there on that dais, all her faculties shone through.

"I'm not sure what happened this time." Agnes smiled as brightly as the star on top of the Christmas tree. "I don't know whether it hit me over the head or it snuck up on me. I just know that love has come again, and I'm not about to ignore its call." She swished out a hand, and finally, her gaze rested on Rupert. "Darling man, would you join me up here?"

Jack rose then, helping his father take hold of the walker Declan had surreptitiously brought from the wings. Staying with Rupert until his dad was safely on the stage, Jack backed out of the spotlight that was now shining on the elderly couple.

As they faced each other, Agnes said into the breathless silence, "I would let go of my walker to take your hand, but I'm afraid I'd lose my balance." Laughter rippled through the ballroom. "So instead, I'll just say this. I've found love a third time, my darling Rupster." All the people who loved the old lady snickered, but at least Agnes remembered the name she'd made up. "I've found love again for the last time in my life, and I welcome it with open arms. My darling, will you marry me?"

A roar rose from the spectators to the accompaniment of

thunderous clapping. With Agnes's words and the angelic smile on her face, there was hope for them all.

Celia wondered if there could be hope for her.

Rupert laid his hand over Agnes's on her walker. "My darling Agnes, I would go down on my knees to accept your proposal, but I'd have to ask my son to help me back up. So I'll just say, from the bottom of my heart, I love you and I want to marry you, the sooner the better. We don't have any time to waste."

As they kissed primly on the lips, the crowd erupted, getting to their feet and clapping loud enough to pop a few balloons drifting across the ceiling.

AMID THE RAUCOUS APPLAUSE, CATHE LEANED CLOSE. "DID you know anything about this?"

Jack shook his head, his heart bursting. If there was hope for Agnes and his father, there was hope for him. And for Cathe.

He wanted nothing more than to tell her what was in his heart. But he bided his time, helping his father off the dais, hugging the tiny Agnes with a huge heart. After he'd helped Dad back into his chair, he cupped his father's face in his hands. "I'm happier than I can say."

While everyone swamped Agnes with congratulations and hugs and kisses, his dad said softly, "I don't know how we'll arrange this. I certainly don't want to make life difficult for you. But I do love dear Agnes, and I want to be with her. Do you think your mother will mind?" His voice shook on the question.

Jack wanted to gather his dad into his arms, as if he were the father and Rupert the son. "Mom is looking down now and wishing you all the happiness in the world." When he hugged his father again, his gaze caught Cathe's over his father's shoulder.

The mistiness in the depths of her blue eyes could have been for the happy couple. Or she might have heard the words and taken them to heart.

He could only pray.

On stage, Celia clapped her hands, and her patrons subsided into their seats.

With one hand to her chest, emotion rippled through her voice. "I certainly can't follow that with anything better. I hope it's one of the happiest moments you've witnessed in many a long year." She raised her hands like a ringmaster. "But we have results for the silent auction. I want to thank every one of you for putting in a bid. We haven't tallied the proceeds yet, but I must say this feels like the most successful night we've seen in a long, long time." She looked from Dad to Agnes, then back to her audience, and opening her tablet, she began reading. "First, we have a pair of vintage Japanese Satsuma vases going for two thousand dollars."

The clapping was deafening, but not equal to that of Agnes's proposal and Dad's acceptance.

As Celia continued listing the auctioned items, Jack kept a running tally in his head. The proceeds for the charity would be extraordinary. He couldn't help picking up Cathe's hand to kiss her knuckles. Then he toasted. "To your sister's success. This is amazing."

Cathe clinked her glass with his. The longer he sat with her, the calmer she became, the more accepting of his presence. Her shock had worn off. He hoped that boded well too.

"Then we have *Budapest by Night*, an amazing piece of artwork by my sister Cathe Girard." Celia, smiling widely, looked at her sister. Jack clasped his hand around Cathe's fingers. "The winning bid by an anonymous donor is one thousand dollars."

A cheer rose from their table, then traveled around the room.

Tears streamed down Cathe's cheeks as she held her hand to her mouth, and the wild beating of Jack's heart drowned out everything but the happiness on her face.

Celia added, "It was a very close race. This was one of our most popular offerings."

Squeezing Cathe's hand, Jack said softly, "I told you your photographs were amazing. And your sister is amazing. The auction has brought in fifty thousand dollars on top of the amount raised through tickets."

She stared at him with eyes blurred by tears.

It took several minutes for Celia to make her way back to the table, glad-handing, cheek-kissing, and a heartfelt hug from the foundation's director.

"Your sister has a new career, if she wants it," Jack said.

Gray, standing next to Celia, added proudly, "She's a hell of a woman." Then he held onto her as if she might float away like one of the balloons if he didn't ground her.

"I don't think she wants a job." Cathe kept her voice soft, her eyes on Gray and the happiness brimming in her sister's eyes. "She just wants to do it for charity when the fancy strikes her. Making it a career would take all the fun out of it."

"I get it," Jack agreed. "Suddenly there's all that pressure. You aren't your own boss anymore. And it becomes work instead of love."

"That's it exactly."

The same was true for Cathe. She'd probably never show her photographs at a gallery or studio. Though he could help her add them to stock photo sites where the pressure wouldn't exist.

Hand held high, Celia made a signal, and the music began. While no one was paying attention, the dance floor had been cleared of all the café tables and was now open for anyone who wanted to take a turn around the floor.

"Thank God the music isn't terribly loud." Cathe leaned in close to his ear. "Sometimes you can't even hear yourself talk at these things, let alone think."

With the soft whisper of her breath across his ear, he rose, holding out his hand. "Dance with me?"

The tunes were old favorites, just as Blondie had played on the boat, some slow, some with a beat to get your heart pumping.

But this was Nat King Cole singing *Stardust*.

Cathe didn't hesitate, and he led her onto the floor just as Celia and Gray slid into their seats, sharing a tender kiss.

Then Jack forgot everything but Cathe in his arms. God, how he'd missed the feel of her against him, the scent of her hair, the taste of her lips. And the ache around his heart began to melt as he swung her around the dance floor.

The time was never better. "I missed you."

Her lips parted, and he waited for her to say she'd missed him too. But she closed her mouth on the words.

Still, he dove into the deep end headfirst. "I know you'll always love your husband. He'll always be your first love. I don't care if that means I'm second best. I don't even care if I'm his stand-in for you." As Nat King Cole sang of stardust memories and lost love, Jack told her what was in his heart. "I don't care about any of that as long as I'm with you. I don't want to be alone for the rest of my life. I don't want you to be alone either. I love you. I will always love you."

As they danced around the floor, mistiness rose in her eyes, and he pushed his case. "If Agnes and my dad can take a chance at their age, then you and I can take a chance now. Agnes was right. We never lose the ability to love. It doesn't mean we don't love those we've lost. It just means we can love again."

She swallowed, the hardness of it seeming to trickle down her throat. "I'm so afraid."

At least his arms were around her. At least she was talking to him. At least she wasn't running. "What are you afraid of?"

She licked her lips, breathed in, out, and finally said, "I'm afraid of losing again. I'm afraid of the pain that will come. I don't know if I can do it all again. It was so hard."

But she wasn't telling him she had no capacity to love him or that he could never fill her husband's shoes. This was all about the two of them.

He whispered his fears. "I'm afraid of the pain if I let you walk away now. And I promise that I'll make these the most wonderful years of your life. It has to make up for the pain either of us will eventually feel when we finally have to let go of each other." They weren't a young couple just starting out. They didn't have a whole lifetime. But he wanted her for all the years he had left. "This is through thick and thin." Turning slowly on the dance floor, he had to ask, "Are you willing to be alone for the next thirty years because you're afraid of losing? You're stronger than that. And I'm willing to take a chance."

He stopped right there, amid all the couples whirling around them. Taking her face in his hands, he kissed her, an endless kiss, the most beautiful kiss he'd ever known. It wasn't even passionate. It was simply love in all its forms.

She melted against him the way he had always hoped and prayed she would.

HIS LIPS WERE LIKE AMBROSIA, AND HIS BODY SOLID, A ROCK she could always lean on. Maybe they had only a year. Or maybe they'd have thirty. If Denny had lived, she would have had this wonder with him. But he was gone. And if she didn't take this chance with Jack, she would never know the wonder of love again. All she had to do was let go of the fear, let go of the memory of that day someone, she couldn't even remember who, had called her from Denny's office and told her he was dead. She never wanted to feel that pain again.

But then she would never feel the beauty of love again either.

She broke the kiss, her body still pressed against his, and looked into his eyes. "I've been miserable these past three months. And if I let you go now, it'll hurt just as badly as letting you go years from now. But the difference is that I'll miss all the years we'll have in between." She swallowed, and it was hard and her skin burned and fear rumbled in her belly. But she forced herself to say, "I loved my husband with all my heart. I always will. But I know he'd want me to love again. And Agnes and Rupert have shown me that there's always more room for love in a person's heart. That it's possible to love more than one person with all your heart." She needed only one breath to finish telling him. "I won't let fear stop me. I love you. And I want to love you for the rest of our lives, no matter how long that is."

Jack gathered her tight in his arms, swinging her around the dance floor, showing her how much he loved her, how badly he needed her.

And he held her as if he'd never let her go.

They lay together in the hot bubbling waters of his suite's tub. Everything Gray claimed about the room was correct, luxurious, with a thick eiderdown on which he'd made love to her, and the tub that more than fit the two of them.

"The evening was a great success, don't you think?" Celia shouldn't need reassurance. She should know in her gut it had gone well, even stupendous. But she still wanted to hear it from Gray.

"Your charity is dying to get you on the payroll to handle all their fundraising events."

She smiled, feeling giddy. "It was good. It was a lot of work." She tipped her head back to look at him. "But I really enjoyed it, and I want to do more. I just don't want to be tied down by an actual job. I can do this for other charities as well." The world was her oyster, and Gray was the pearl in the center. "Wasn't Agnes adorable up on stage?"

With her head on his chest, his chin brushed her hair as he nodded. "The little lady is incredible. I'm thrilled for her and Rupert."

"I hope they both have years and years left."

"Just like Cathe and Jack," he added.

She twirled a finger in his chest hair. "I knew it the moment they walked hand in hand off the dance floor. There was that glow about her. And Jack looked like he was floating six feet off the ground." Celia had been sure even as Cathe yelled at her for inviting Jack to the gala. She'd done the right thing.

She'd wanted to dance with Gray but had stayed in her seat, watching Cathe and Jack make their way back to their seats. Cathe had said immediately, "Jack and I have decided to start dating."

She hadn't said they were in love or that they'd move in together, but Celia had known the meaning behind those words. Cathe was finally ready to let Denny go. She'd taken Agnes's sentiments to heart. She'd loved and lost, but she didn't have to remain lost forever. Especially not when a man like Jack Kelly absolutely adored her.

Agnes had clapped her hands, a delighted smile creasing her beautifully aged face. "I'm so happy. I just knew it would happen." She beamed like the sun shone right out of her. "Now we can double date."

A look of terror had passed over Jack's features, but Rupert smiled. "Whatever my darling Agnes wants."

Agnes was a hoot. "It was wonderful." Celia snuggled against his chest in the hot water.

"I'm happy for them all. They've learned there's always another chance for love. If you're open to it." A familiar sensation rumbled in her belly as Gray put his finger beneath her chin. He tipped her head back, forcing her to look at him when he murmured, "Just like there's another chance for both of us."

She was afraid she'd strangle on the words. But she pasted a smile on her lips and said, "Of course there's a chance for us. That's why we're getting together every month instead of every quarter." She hoped that would appease him.

He trailed his fingers through her hair, around her ear, down to the slope of her throat. "I don't believe once a month will be enough."

She pretended she hadn't heard, even if she felt the same way. "We don't have to take a cruise every month. We can just visit each other on opposite coasts. And once in a while we can fly somewhere fun, like Hawaii. Or Barcelona. Or Rome. We'll have fabulous vacations together."

Candlelight flickered in his eyes. It was so Gray, so romantic. He'd lit candles all around the tub and scented the water with lavender. But the glitter in his eyes terrified her. "A week's vacation, or even a ten-day cruise, won't cut it."

"Of course it will. We both have responsibilities. I've got my event planning. You've got your clients. With all the flying back and forth, once a month is all we can handle."

"If we live together, we won't have to fly back and forth."

Her body stilled against his, her hand flattened on his chest, and her heart took a nosedive. "That means one of us would have to move."

"I'm willing to cross a continent for the woman I love."

God. He'd said it. The *love* word. It changed everything. A rush of panic galvanized her limbs.

She pushed herself out of the tub, water streaming down her naked body. Suddenly she was self-conscious about all that bare skin, about the bulge of her belly, the crepey skin of her arms, the lines on her face. Grabbing a fluffy bath towel, she wrapped herself in it like a security blanket. "I really can't move, Gray. You know that."

"I said I'll move. I love you, Celia. I want to be with you in any way I can."

She held up a hand. "But what about all your clients? You can't desert them for a woman."

He laughed, the bubbles covering his beautiful body. He was perfect. She wasn't. Men remained perfect far longer than women did. Later, he'd figure that out, and he would stop wanting her.

"I won't desert anyone. Especially not you." He pointed a finger at her. "I can work from anywhere. This is the age of video chats, email, texting, and online research sites. There's nothing holding me in Florida."

"Except the weather. Back there, you can golf all year round." She was stretching, but she didn't care. Any excuse would do.

"Then we can spend winters in Florida and summers in California."

She turned, saw herself in the mirror, and even as she didn't want to see, she forced herself to look. "I'm almost sixty years old."

He rose from the tub, water glistening on his skin and his taut body. Grabbing a towel, he slung it around his waist. "Agnes is almost ninety, but she's not afraid."

Hot and cold chills ran the length of her body. "Agnes is Agnes. And Rupert is in exactly the same shape as she is. They don't have to compare their infirmities."

He came to her, and hands on her shoulders, he turned her to look at him. "You're perfect. You're beautiful. You're amazing in bed." He pulled her hand down to touch him. "Feel what you do to me," he whispered. "Even now, after we've already made love, I want you again. I love you. And you're the only woman for me."

She closed her eyes against his earnest gaze. "But how long will it last?" Her words echoed in the room, surrounding her, hounding her. "You're in the prime of life. And pretty soon, some gorgeous creature thirty years younger than you will catch your eye."

He gripped her chin, insistent but not painful. "Don't do

that. Don't demean me by saying I'm only after a pretty face. I want the whole woman. And you're the woman I want. I won't suddenly have a midlife crisis and start looking at women young enough to be my daughter."

"All right." Her gaze darted over his handsome face. "What about someone forty-nine who hasn't hit menopause yet?"

He closed his mouth, his teeth grinding. "I'm not your ex-husband. I'll never get tired of you, and I'll love you for the rest of our lives. Even as our bodies age, even when we fall into decrepitude, I won't stop loving you. And I won't stop wanting you."

Tears picked her eyes. "The day we got married, my husband vowed to love me for the rest of our lives. It didn't last."

He slid his hands to her shoulders, held her close to his chest, his thumbs under her chin, tipping her head back to look into her eyes. "That's because he's an asshole and an idiot. But I'm neither of those things." He paused, letting that sink in. "I watched my wife cheat on me and degrade me. I've been through a catastrophic divorce without ever having children. And now it's too late."

"It's not too late if you're with a younger woman." It ripped her insides out to say the words.

But he shook his head in a sharp movement. "It's too late for me. I've lost that desire. Now all I want is you and your children and the grandchildren they'll eventually have. All of you will be my family. I've been through enough to have learned what I want. I'm not like your ex-husband, who learned nothing."

She winced at his harsh tone.

He trailed his hands down her arms, back up, held her shoulders. "This is what you have to ask yourself. Are you old enough to overcome your fear of never being wanted again? Of becoming undesirable? Of having love walk out on you?"

She closed her eyes so she couldn't see into his, yet tears leaked out between her lashes. "I'm not afraid. It's just reality."

"It isn't reality. Look at me." He shook her lightly until she opened her eyes to meet his beautiful brown gaze, flecks of hazel in the iris. "Reality is only what you believe. If you think I'll walk out on you in a year or two, then that's what will happen. If you're sure I'll lose my desire for you and fall for a younger woman, then it'll happen. Like a self-fulfilling prophecy." He looked at her for a long moment, touched a tear on her cheek. "But you can will our love into reality. You can make it last. You just have to believe." His words ended on a groan of pleading. "Please don't leave me."

GRAY'S GREATEST FEAR WAS THAT HE COULD NEVER CHANGE Celia's mind, that even if she said yes in this moment, she'd wait for the day he stopped wanting her.

An ache in his belly said he should walk away, avoid the pain and degradation of begging her. He'd never even begged his wife. He'd simply shut his mouth and his eyes.

But with his whole being, he wanted Celia. He wanted what Agnes and Rupert had found. He wanted the relationship that Jack and Cathe were destined to have. Never having had it with his wife, he craved it now.

And he needed it with Celia. Without her, he would wither and die. Or he'd become a grumpy old man playing away his days on a golf course in the hot Florida sun.

"Save me, Celia. Say you love me, you want me, and there's no fear big enough in this universe to stop you from being with me."

"But—"

He pulled her close, closing her mouth over the word, kissing her with all the passion he would feel for her forever. Then he murmured against her mouth, "Does that feel like it's going to end? Does it feel like I'm lusting after younger women? Or does it feel like you're the only woman I want for the rest of my life?"

She turned from him, stared in the mirror, and he knew she was seeing all the lifelines on her face, all the laugh lines, all the misery lines.

"You're not judging yourself," he told her. "You're judging me."

She shook her head, still transfixed by her reflection. "I know you mean every word you say. But no one can tell how they'll feel in ten years."

His heart shriveled. He'd lost. She'd been hurt, ignored, and finally discarded. What her ex-husband had done tainted her for the rest of her life. The rest of *his* life.

He couldn't take the sight of his failure, leaving her for the bedroom and the bedclothes still scented with their sex and their desire and their love. His clothes lay in a crumpled heap on the floor while she'd been neater, draping her beautiful gold-and-silver dress over a chair. He was tempted to pull on his boxers and tug on his pants. Because there was no hope. Her heart was closed.

But then he reached behind, holding out his hand, and he called to her, "Come here."

He only knew she'd done what he asked when he felt her warmth beside him. "Look at that bed. Look at the sheets." He turned her. "I want you to breathe deeply."

She swallowed. Then she breathed in the scent of his desire.

"If I want you this much now, when you're in menopause and you have the beautiful lifelines of a fifty-nine-year-old woman and the body of a mother who bore three children, why would I suddenly start wanting someone thirty years younger?"

He could toss her on the bed, make love to her once more, and try proving that his desire would never end. But it wouldn't work.

"Believe in me," he murmured. "Trust me." It was his last plea, his only play.

And finally, softly, with barely more than a movement of her lips, she asked, "Do you want to make love to me now?"

He pulled her close. "With every cell in my body."

"And tomorrow?" she whispered.

"Tomorrow, the day after, the month after, the year after. And my next lifetime too."

"Maybe I can try." She drew in a trembling breath. "Because I love you. And I'm more afraid of letting you walk away now than I am of having you walk away weeks or months or years from now."

He took her face in his hands. "I love you with all my heart. I'm never walking away. And I know that you love me. We'll always be together if you let us."

"I love you too." She sniffled. "I'll let us be together. Will you make love to me?"

"Always and forever."

Hours later, as she lay in his arms, she whispered, "I will always love you."

He kissed her hair. "I'll always love you. And I'll always want you."

EPILOGUE

Rupert Kelly and Agnes Hathaway were married in a civil ceremony the second week of January. They'd chosen that week so everyone could board the Caribbean cruise Gray and Celia had already planned. They'd all crowded into the judge's chambers for the ceremony, Rose and Declan, Jack and Cathe, and Dad's precious granddaughters. With the room full, Gray, Celia, and Barbara stood just outside to witness their vows.

Then the nine cruise veterans boarded a plane Declan had chartered to fly them to Fort Lauderdale for their sunny Caribbean cruise.

The charter had been cheaper than buying first-class tickets for all. Declan insisted that Agnes's honeymoon had to be first class all the way.

When Jack offered to help pay, Declan had waved him aside. "The bride's family pays for the wedding. And since this wedding cost nothing, I'm taking care of the honeymoon."

And, as close as they'd been to the departure date with

empty staterooms on the boat, Declan had secured an excellent deal.

But it was still a fabulous gift to all of them.

He and Cathe were now seated in lounge chairs on the aft deck as the ship steamed along, the Caribbean sun leaching the cold from their bones after a rainy winter in the Bay Area.

Bringing her hand to his lips, Jack kissed her knuckles. He'd never been more grateful for anyone in his life. "When I get back, I'll start moving over all Dad's stuff."

Declan had purchased a bungalow one door down from the massive Victorian he and Rose lived in. For years, Agnes had occupied an apartment on the first floor. Declan had even installed a ramp for her walker. But the apartment had only one bedroom, and though Agnes and his father were now married, they still needed help. The bungalow was a two-bedroom, one for the newlyweds and one for Barbara, who would continue to live in.

Jack felt guilty about the money the man was spending for his father's benefit, but Declan had explained away his concerns. "It's an investment property since I'll own the bungalow. I'm just not charging rent. But I didn't charge Agnes rent before. I actually come out ahead with the equity in the house and the ability to rent out Agnes's old apartment."

"At least let me pay for Barbara," Jack insisted. Declan, however, hadn't conceded. He probably felt guilty for foisting the decision on Jack, when Agnes could very well have moved into the Oakland Hills home, Barbara too.

Jack had resigned himself.

And Dad's move freed him up for another decision. "I've been thinking it's time we stopped commuting between Belmont and Oakland."

He felt the stillness of Cathe's body all the way down to

her hand. And finally, she said. "Would you want to live in Oakland? Or Belmont?"

He tipped her chin, making her look at him. "Belmont would be a lot better, not so far from Dad now that he'll be in San Jose. Or from your sister."

Her breath of relief wafted over him. "That would be good."

He was pushing her; it had only been a few weeks. But he knew what he wanted and needed. "I also think we should make it official. You and me. Together. For the rest of our lives."

Her hand trembled in his. They hadn't talked about marriage. But he couldn't stop himself under the enticing Caribbean sun.

"There's so much to think about." The tremor in her hand had moved to her voice.

"Is it about your daughter? About what she'd think of you abandoning her father for another man?"

She chuckled softly, though without an ounce of humor. "Sarah knows I'm not abandoning her father's memory. She thinks you're awesome. I just..." Her voice trailed off.

They'd hosted a dinner, introducing their kids. Her daughter Sarah had gotten along well with Fiona and Hailey. But they were still two separate families, and this beautiful thing between them was so very new.

"You just don't want her to think I'm marrying you for your money." Humor laced his voice.

She laughed out loud. "You're the one with all the money, Mr. Big CEO."

He liked it when she cupped him in her hand and told him she'd never made love with a bigwig executive. "And I do mean big," she added.

He sobered enough to say, "I don't care about the money. I just want you to be mine for the rest of our lives. And I don't want to have to figure out whether I call you my lady friend or my girlfriend or my significant other. I just want to say you're my wife."

Her eyes misted over.

And he prayed he'd won.

SHE WAS ABSOLUTELY GOING TO CRY. WHEN DENNY DIED, she knew she'd never fall in love again, never marry again. She was absolutely sure she'd never have another lover.

Jack changed all that. She'd learned her heart was big enough to give her love to both men. And she wanted to be with Jack for the rest of her life. But getting married at their age was a whole different thing than marriage at twenty-five. Now there was a ticking clock. What if he had a heart attack?

Jack said the words she couldn't get out. "I love you. I want to be with you forever. Didn't we already agree we'd live like we had another thirty years together?"

Thirty years. As long as her marriage to Denny. Somehow it both entranced and terrified her.

"I love you too," she told him.

She'd overcome her guilt and grief, committed herself to Jack, and squashed the fear that Denny—or Sarah—would think she was disloyal by falling in love with another man. But even as she'd tried, she hadn't squashed the fear of losing him like she'd lost Denny.

"I think about Agnes and Rupert," she said. "What will happen when one of them goes?" Tears gathered in her eyes.

He shook his head. "They're not thinking about that. They're living for the moment. We need to as well."

Her heart pounded as she swiped at her wet cheeks. "I love you so much."

"I love you with everything in me, body and soul." His

words wrapped around her like a warm embrace. "And I want to be your husband. I want to make love to you, fall asleep with you in my arms, and wake up beside you every morning. Marry me and live in the moment with me."

She hadn't lived in the moment since Denny died. Maybe she'd never lived in the moment. Even these last wonderful weeks with Jack, she'd pretended they were young and carefree with no worries for the future. But marriage was forever. Marriage was total commitment without reservations. Marriage was the true test of her ability to live fearlessly, the true test of her love for Jack.

What if she couldn't do it? What if she failed him by trying to keep one foot in and one foot out of their love affair?

Did the questions really matter? She couldn't lose him. And that meant she wouldn't fail him. There was only one answer. "I love you. And I'll marry you. We'll have the most perfect life together." Then she smiled. "With how long people seem to live these days, we might even have forty years."

He hauled her onto his lap, kissing her with a passion she'd never believed old people could feel when she was just thirty.

She whispered against his lips, "I will love you for the rest of my life."

Jack answered with all his heart. "I will love you every hour of every day of every year for the rest of time."

"WELL, SOMETHING IS CERTAINLY GOING ON OVER THERE." Celia's sunglasses masked her eyes.

Gray gazed across the sparkling pool at Cathe and Jack, who alternated between laughing, smiling, and kissing.

He knew exactly what that "something" was. He and Jack had talked about it beforehand. And it was his turn to step up to the plate.

Today was a sea day, cruising through the Caribbean. Passengers sat poolside enjoying the sun, and others, like Rupert and Agnes, played games in the lounge. And, of course, there were the newlyweds, which he still considered Declan and Rose to be. They'd disappeared after lunch, presumably for a nap. They hadn't even bothered to say it was jet lag.

And that's right where he wanted Celia. Making love in their veranda suite where he could once again assure her that he'd want her for the rest of his life.

He thought she'd come to believe it, because there was no more discussion of living on separate coasts or once-a-month visitations.

"It looks like a proposal to me." He smiled heartily at Celia. "And it looks like she said yes."

From the side, he saw the crinkle of Celia's eyes behind her sunglasses.

"You're happy for them?" he asked.

She turned to him, her lips curved in the softest, sweetest smile. "It's more than I could ever hope for. Cathe was born to be married. And she'll love being Jack's wife." She waved a hand toward them. "It's obvious they adore each other."

"Do you think we deserve a happy marriage?"

She looked at him for a too-long moment, and he felt a prickle of anxiety.

"Aren't we fine the way we are?" she countered.

He could stammer or stall, but he would never get the answer he wanted if he refused to ask the question she didn't want to hear. "We're great. But we should be married. That's what I want."

She swallowed, then swallowed again, as if her throat were parched. "You know—"

He cut her off. "I know we've decided to spend a few months at your house and a few months at mine, following the seasons. That's all great."

She looked at him, saying nothing. And he forced himself to go on. "But that's not enough. I want to be married to you so I can spend my life showing you how much I need you, want you, desire you, and love you."

She tipped her head. "But do we need marriage for that?"

It was her ultimate barrier, and he needed to crash through it. "Yes, we need it. Marry me. I love you."

WAS THAT FEAR RUMBLING IN HER STOMACH? YES, CELIA thought, definitely.

But what was she afraid of? That he'd stop wanting her and leave her, that he would ignore her the way Bart had?

She loved him. She knew he loved her.

Maybe she was just afraid of the future.

She'd turn sixty next month. Gray was sixty-five. They had a lot of years ahead of them, years they would spend together. She knew it in her heart.

And if that was true, did she want to feel this nagging sense of inadequacy for the rest of her life?

She opened her mouth, closed it again, afraid of the words that would come out. But she had to say them. "I still don't like looking too closely in the mirror. I still look at you when you're sleeping and think you can't possibly want me forever. I'm still afraid. I'll always be afraid." Even as his features tightened, she breathed deeply and, on the exhale, she went on. "But I hope that someday you can teach me how to just be who I am without tormenting myself." She smiled, feeling the slightest tremble on her lips and in her heart. "And I'll marry you. Because I love you so much more than I can ever say."

Gray flew off his lounge chair, grabbed her up and danced her around the deck, calling out, "She said yes. She said yes."

Then he hauled her into his arms, ran for the pool, and did a cannonball into the deep end. They broke the water's surface, arms around each other, lips locked, the sound of whoops and cheers all around them.

She knew she'd made the right choice, the only choice, and she whispered against his lips, "I love you."

And everything in her knew he felt exactly the same.

THE SHIP'S CAPTAIN STOOD ON THE STAGE OF THE BIG theater and intoned in a sonorous voice that carried over the boat's concert hall, "I now pronounce you men and wives."

He sealed the marriages of Celia to Gray and Jack to Cathe amid a thunderous ovation.

In the audience, Rupert said, "I hope their kids aren't upset that they're not here to attend the weddings."

Agnes waved an airy hand at him. "Oh, piffle. They're all as tickled pink as we are." She clapped her hands once more, then looked at him wide-eyed. "I just thought of it. I'm finally a grandmother. I've never been a grandmother before."

Rupert chuckled. "You will always make me laugh, my dear."

Agnes replied, with that special twinkle in her eye, "And you will only always make me tremble with desire, my dear Rupster."

Declan and Rose looked on with smiles as the elderly couple pushed themselves up on their walkers. Agnes and

Rupert rolled their way to the stage to give and receive hugs from the happy newlyweds.

"She'll always be a character," Rose said, having heard every word of the exchange.

"Tremble with desire?" Declan shuddered. "I think I'm a little horrified."

Rose pecked him on the lips. "I'm absolutely sure I'll still desire you when I'm eighty-seven years old."

He stroked a finger down her cheek. "I'll never stop desiring you. And I hope nobody *ever* says that's horrifying."

Then he kissed her. Passionately. Both of them knowing that later, in their stateroom, they'd show each other just how long desire will last.

The *Once Again* series, where love always gets a second chance.

Book 10 **Margaritas in Mexico**. He thought he had all he needed in his life. Until the holiday of a lifetime... when he found her. A sizzling mature romance!

Once Again
Dreaming of Provence | Wishing in Rome
Dancing in Ireland | Under the Northern Lights
Stargazing on the Orient Express
Memories of Santorini | Siesta in Spain
Top Down to California
Cruising the Danube

Get 3 free books just by joining the newsletter for Jennifer and Jasmine! Plus updates on sales and exclusive subscriber contests. Sign up at **http://bit.ly/SkullyNews**

ABOUT THE AUTHOR

NY Times and USA Today bestselling author Jennifer Skully is a lover of contemporary romance, bringing you poignant tales peopled with characters that will make you laugh and make you cry. Look for *The Maverick Billionaires* written with Bella Andre, starting with *Breathless in Love*, along with Jennifer's new later-in-life holiday romance series, *Once Again*, where readers can travel with her to fabulous faraway locales. Up first is a trip to Provence in *Dreaming of Provence*. Writing as Jasmine Haynes, Jennifer authors classy, sensual romance tales about real issues such as growing older, facing divorce, starting over. Her books have passion and heart and humor and happy endings, even if they aren't always traditional. She also writes gritty, paranormal mysteries in the Max Starr series. Having penned stories since the moment she learned to write, Jennifer now lives in the Redwoods of Northern California with her husband and their adorable nuisance of a cat who totally runs the household.

Learn more about Jennifer/Jasmine and join her newsletter for free books, exclusive contests and excerpts, plus updates on sales and new releases at **http://bit.ly/SkullyNews**

ALSO BY JENNIFER SKULLY/JASMINE HAYNES

Books by Jennifer Skully

The Maverick Billionaires by Jennifer Skully & Bella Andre

Breathless in Love | Reckless in Love

Fearless in Love | Irresistible in Love

Wild In Love | Captivating In Love

Unforgettable in Love

Once Again

Dreaming of Provence | Wishing in Rome

Dancing in Ireland | Under the Northern Lights

Stargazing on the Orient Express

Memories of Santorini | Siesta in Spain

Top Down to California | Cruising the Danube

Mystery of Love

Drop Dead Gorgeous | Sheer Dynamite

It Must be Magic | One Crazy Kiss

You Make Me Crazy | One Crazy Fling

Crazy for Baby

Return to Love

She's Gotta Be Mine | Fool's Gold | Can't Forget You

Return to Love: 3-Book Bundle

Love After Hours

Desire Actually | Love Affair To Remember

Pretty In Pink Slip

Stand-alone

Baby, I'll Find You | Twisted by Love

Be My Other Valentine

Books by Jasmine Haynes

Naughty After Hours

Revenge | Submitting to the Boss

The Boss's Daughter

The Only One for Her | Pleasing Mr. Sutton

Any Way She Wants It

More than a Night

A Very Naughty Christmas

Show Me How to Leave You

Show Me How to Love You

Show Me How to Tempt You

The Max Starr Series

Dead to the Max | Evil to the Max

Desperate to the Max

Power to the Max | Vengeance to the Max

Courtesans Tales

The Girlfriend Experience | Payback | Triple Play

Three's a Crowd | The Stand In | Surrender to Me

The Only Way Out | The Wrong Kind of Man

No Second Chances

The Jackson Brothers

Somebody's Lover | Somebody's Ex

Somebody's Wife

The Jackson Brothers: 3-Book Bundle

Castle Inc

The Fortune Hunter | Show and Tell

Fair Game

Open Invitation

Invitation to Seduction | Invitation to Pleasure

Invitation to Passion

Open Invitation: 3-Book Bundle

Wives & Neighbors

Wives & Neighbors: The Complete Story

Prescott Twins

Double the Pleasure | Skin Deep

Prescott Twins Complete Set

Lessons After Hours

Past Midnight | What Happens After Dark

The Principal's Office | The Naughty Corner

The Lesson Plan

Stand-alone

Take Your Pleasure | Take Your Pick

Take Your Pleasure Take Your Pick Duo

Anthology: Beauty or the Bitch & Free Fall

Printed in Great Britain
by Amazon